TRAGEDY OF ERRORS

Three Americans . . . two men and one woman . . . all of them seemingly innocent . . . one of them as dangerous as a bomb about to go off . . .

It was Mr. Moto's job to unmask the fiendishly clever mastermind of evil who was spinning so violent a web of deception and destruction. Already Moto had made one mistake—and there was a corpse to show for it. Now he knew that he could not fail again—for his next mistake would be his last . . .

RIGHT YOU ARE, MR. MOTO

by John P. Marquand

(Original Title: STOPOVER, TOKYO)

POPULAR LIBRARY • NEW YORK

Published by Popular Library, CBS Publications,
CBS Consumer Publishing, a Division of CBS Inc., by
arrangement with Little, Brown and Company, Inc.

December, 1977

Copyright © 1956, 1957 by The Curtis Publishing Company

ISBN: 0-445-04125-0

(Original Title: STOPOVER: TOKYO)

The author wishes to thank Music Publishers Holding Corporation
for permission to quote from the following songs: "Every Day
is Ladies' Day With Me" (Copyright 1906 by M. Witmark & Sons.
Copyright renewed); "The Streets of New York" (Copyright 1906
by M. Witmark & Sons. Copyright renewed); "Because You're You"
(Copyright 1906 by M. Witmark & Sons. Copyright renewed).

To
TIM and LONNY
*Who may grasp the significance of this book
more readily than that of some of my others*

I

Jack Rhyce had not expected to see the Russians in San Francisco. The word in Washington had been that Mr. Molotov and his delegation would have left the city, several hours before Rhyce's arrival; but no one could have notified Jack Rhyce of the change of plans without creating undue attention. It had also been a mistake to make a reservation at the Mark Hopkins Hotel, but they had said categorically in Washington that the celebration of the tenth anniversary of the United Nations would be over. Instead, the Russians were just leaving the Mark Hopkins when Jack Rhyce arrived by taxi from the airport. There was hardly time for him to get his bags out before the driver was shooed away by a police escort, and there was nothing left for him to do but stand in the small crowd that was gathering.

"What's going on?" he asked the bellboy. The question was unnecessary because at the moment he asked he saw the limousines and the faces of the drivers.

"It's the Russians," the bellboy said.

"What?" Jack Rhyce asked. "The Russians aren't staying here, are they?"

"No, sir," the bellboy said, "but Mr. Molotov has been having a cocktail with Secretary Dulles."

"Well," Jack Rhyce said, "good for Mr. Molotov."

It would have looked conspicuous if he had moved backwards. It was better, in his opinion, to stand quietly and watch. The guards were coming out and grouping themselves around the leading limousine. At first glance the men seemed interchangeable with any of the people who protected top-flight Russians—heavy, stocky men with potatolike faces, and not a beauty in the bunch; but then they were not selected for show. Russian features were hard to classify, and he had been out of touch with the problem for quite a while, but he was sure two of them were officers high up in the NKVD. He could only hope that the recognition was not mutual; not that there would have been any great harm in it. After all, nothing could have been more natural than that he should be in San Francisco at this particular time. Still, he would have felt easier if he had not encountered the Russians just when he was on the point of flying to Japan. He knew that one should never underrate them, not even when they were being jolly good fellows in front of the Mark Hopkins Hotel.

"The one with the glasses is Mr. Molotov," the bellboy said.

Jack Rhyce had not seen Mr. Molotov for quite a while, but he was not likely to forget him, with or without glasses, since they had met twice on social occasions and had once exchanged amenities over caviar and vodka, at the end of the war, when Jack Rhyce had been traveling with one of the American missions. Mr. Molotov was in no hurry. He smiled happily as he walked toward the limousine. His expression was exactly the same as it had been in Moscow when he had slapped Jack Rhyce on the shoulder.

"Young man," Mr. Molotov had said, "let us touch glasses in token of a lasting friendship between our two countries."

"This is a great honor, sir," Jack Rhyce had answered.

"No, no," Mr. Molotov said. "You and I both are men."

"Yes, Excellency," Jack Rhyce said, "and all men are brothers."

He was younger in those days, with a lot to learn. He had made his last speech in Russian, when the Foreign Minister had been speaking in English, and Russian had not been necessary.

"Young man," Mr. Molotov had said, "you speak Russian not badly."

Jack Rhyce instantly realized that by showing off his Russian, simply because he was proud of being top of a language class, he had called attention to himself. His chief had spoken to him very roughly about it afterward, and the Chief had been absolutely right.

"Just get it through your head," the Chief had said, "that boys like you aren't supposed to be heard at all, and that you don't wear striped pants all the time. Never try to be conspicuous. Never."

It was good advice, and Jack Rhyce seldom needed to be told things twice.

There was no way for him to discover whether any of the Russian party recognized him now or not. He could only tell himself again that, even if they did, it should make no particular difference. Mr. Molotov, still beaming, waved to the crowd. Then the car door closed. The Russian party was gone as completely as though it had never been there. They had his dossier, of course, but they had him connected with Washington and Berlin. There was no reason whatsoever for them to believe that he was going to the Orient. Still, he wished that he had not seen the Russians.

Jack Rhyce had been a guest in so many hotels that he could instantly catch the atmosphere of any place in which he stopped and could immediately fit into its background. For God's sake, as the Chief had once told him, never chaffer too long at a hotel reception desk, and as rapidly as possible get up to your room, and never be seen hanging aimlessly around the lobby. Experience had taught Jack Rhyce that the Chief nearly always was absolutely right. Twice during the war he had been to the Mark Hopkins Hotel, but only to ascend in the elevator to that popular cocktail room known as the Top of the Mark. He had been with the paratroopers in those days, and he had never dreamed that anyone would select him for what he was now doing, but even then his memory had been excellent. Consequently, he had the general layout of the hotel straight, almost the instant he was inside the door.

"Would you please hand me my briefcase, son?" he asked the bellboy.

The way you handled a briefcase could make you look like a traveling salesman or a corporation lawyer. It was better at the moment, Jack Rhyce thought, to be placed as a corporation lawyer. He printed his name carefully in block letters on the registration card.

"The name is Rhyce," he said. "John O. Rhyce, from Washington, D.C. I don't suppose you have any letters waiting for me? Or telegrams or messages?" He spoke in a gentle, cultivated voice with an accent difficult to identify.

"No messages, Mr. Rhyce," the clerk said, "but we do have your reservation. It's lucky you didn't come a day earlier, what with all the goings on. I hope you saw Mr. Molotov. He must have been leaving just when you came in."

"Oh, yes," Jack Rhyce said. "He was pointed out to me."

"Front," the clerk said—"Room 515."

If Jack's guess was right, he would be in the middle of the corridor, and he always slept more soundly there than at either end. It was a pleasant, airy room which looked toward the Bay.

"Well, thanks, son." Jack Rhyce said. "That extra quarter is for showing me Mr. Molotov."

Until the bellboy left, he stood gazing admiringly at the view, but as soon as the door was closed he started on a tour of inspection which was as routine as a plane checkup. No transom; the door lock sound, and in good order; no balconies or closely adjoining windows; no air shaft in the bathroom. It was five o'clock in the afternoon, ample time in which to make a final appraisal of all his personal effects before he went to dinner.

First he examined his passport. Unlike several others that he had carried, it told his true history except for his occupation—height five feet eleven, hair light brown, eyes blue, no distinguishing marks or features. His place of birth was Lincoln, Nebraska, where as a matter of fact his mother and his elder sister still lived. His date of birth was January 13th, 1920. His occupation was educator. A good deal of thought had been given to his photograph, and the general result was useful, in that it only vaguely resembled him. There was no disguising his high broad forehead, or the arch of his eyebrows, or the firmness of his jaw, but if he changed his expression he could repudiate the whole document, if necessary.

8

Next, he turned to his briefcase. He had been taught and he understood the great importance of cover. The proper odds and ends and letters in a briefcase could be of the utmost value, and one of the rules of the game was that one never could be too careful with cover details.

The latest advices were that Japan was getting hot again and with a tensing in the Pacific area, there was bound to be increased interest in any strange American in one of several quarters. Thus he expected and hoped that someone would go through his personal effects, either during his stopover in Hawaii or directly after his arrival in Tokyo, and the sooner this happened the better, as far as he was concerned. The main point was to demonstrate as early in the game as possible that he was harmless, with absolutely nothing to conceal.

He put his briefcase on the writing table and drew out its contents, placing the items in a neat row. He was satisfied with the way everything looked. The letters had obviously been well handled, and the odds and ends beside the letters were the sort of things that would get into a briefcase by accident, and each added its bit to the owner's background. There was, for instance, a small box of deodorant powder which confirmed his new personality, since affable people who wished to please dreaded perspiration. The New Testament which was also in the briefcase he had felt was too obvious by itself, and he had compromised by adding a small volume of the sayings of Buddha, published by the Oxford University Press. Both these volumes were also well worn, with many cogent passages marked in his own writing. The letters indicating his family background gave him particular pleasure. He could not forget the work which had gone into the one from Omaha, Nebraska. Not only the words but the handwriting accurately revealed the writer's character.

DEAR, DARLING BUNNY:

I am so pleased and so proud that this wonderful chance has come to you after so many years of working so hard for other people. I know you don't know much about the Japanese, any more than I do. But we both know their hearts are in the right place. And your personality that inspires trust in everyone will get through to them, I know, in spite of all the barriers of race and creed. I would be worried about the Oriental women that you are going to meet over there if I did not have a mother's knowledge of a devoted son. I know you will be thinking of me as much as I of you. Send me a postcard every day, and happy landings.

MUMSIE

Although Jack Rhyce admitted that the letter might seem exaggerated, at the same time people who skimmed through briefcases often required definite leads, and the Oedipus complex was universal. After all, there could be little sinister about a mother's boy.

The second letter was written in a girlish hand on the stationery of the Department of Sociology of Goucher College.

DEAR JACKIE:

I'm going to miss you terribly. But seriously, sweetie, I think it's a grand thing that you are going away to new countries for a while, to study how other people live—not that I want you to get interested in any girls there, or anything like that. But seriously, sweetie, although I don't like to be a "bore," I do think the time has come for you to make up your mind. In fact, the time has come for both of us. This doesn't mean that I don't love you dearly, sweetie, but a girl can't stay waiting all the time for any man, can she? And this has been going on ever since we met at your Senior Prom—remember? I know your mother is a darling, but honestly, I don't feel that she need interfere with a happy marriage. I've been reading a lot about these problems lately, and all the authorities say that they can resolve themselves, but we all have to do our part. I simply can't do everything. And so as you wing your way over the ocean, I hope . . .

Jack Rhyce did not read the rest of it, because he was familiar with the contents. The letter had been composed, though not handwritten, by an elderly spinster who specialized in cover work, and who had no sense of humor. She was not even amused by the signature, "Loads of love, your HELENA."

"Why do you think that's funny?" she asked him. "That's exactly the sort of girl who would want to marry you if you had a mother like that."

Both letters showed signs of constant reading. For the past two weeks he had spent a half hour perusing them before going to sleep, and his fingerprints proved it.

Then there were the more formal letters of introduction to representatives of a completely genuine institution known as the Asia Friendship League in Japan, and all other countries where the League had branches. The beauty of it all was that there was nothing wrong with any of this part of the cover. The organization had been honestly conceived by public-spirited citizens, and, at least in its Washington headquarters, had no employees with subversive records.

Connecting him with the Asia Friendship League had been the Chief's idea. It happened that the Chief had known the man who had given the money to form the Asia Friendship League. He was a Texas oil millionaire named Gus Tremaine who had established a charitable trust for tax purposes, and in fact had not known that the Asia Friendship League existed until the Chief had informed him of it personally. The trust money, Mr. Tremaine had explained, was handled by a board, the meetings of which he seldom attended; but he was most co-operative after the Chief had talked to him, and he had called and written the chairman of the Asia Friendship League personally.

Jack Rhyce now had the letter written to him, as a result, on the League's letterhead:

ASIA FRIENDSHIP LEAGUE
NATIONAL HEADQUARTERS
WASHINGTON, D.C.

DEAR MR. RHYCE:

It is a real delight to hear from Mr. Gus Tremaine that he has commissioned you, on his behalf, to make a survey of our work in the Orient, and to write a

11

general report for him. This is just the sort of thing we like, and we like it all the better when it shows Mr. Tremaine's interest. You must not be prejudiced by any idle gossip regarding the Institute of Pacific Relations, or anything like that. You will find that in our show we have all the cards on the table and nothing up our sleeves. The main ideal behind our organization, endorsed by all the fine people whose names you see on the left margin of this letter, is in one word—good will. In fact, we have only one ax to grind, if you call it an ax, and that is that a lot of people out in the Pacific area need a lot of help, but not handouts that smack of colonialism. Our concept is simply to help folks to help themselves.

However, I am, as it were, talking out of school. You'll understand our aims better after we have lunch and spend an afternoon together on any day you name next week. And on your travels, you'll find out, too, what a swell, alert team of truly dedicated folks we have in Tokyo, Seoul, Hong Kong, Saigon and Thailand.

Well, anticipating a word from you, and looking forward to being of any help to you in any way I can, in what I honestly predict will be for you a real eye-opening adventure—

Cordially yours,

CHAS. K. HARRINGTON

This letter also showed signs of repeated reading. It had interested Jack Rhyce from the beginning.

II

As soon as he had received the Harrington letter, Jack Rhyce had asked to see the Chief, who listened carefully while Jack read the letter aloud.

"Well," the Chief said, "what's so funny about it?"

"I didn't say it sounded funny," Jack Rhyce said. "I said I thought it sounded phony."

"I wish you wouldn't bother me about these details, Buster," the Chief said. "The whole department is working on this cover for you. We're giving it everything we've got, and then when we come up with something you merely say it's phony."

"I only mean," Jack Rhyce said, "I sort of get the idea that this whole Friendship League setup sounds a little too good to be true."

There was an appreciable pause, and it seemed to Jack that perhaps the Chief was reviewing the bidding. It was the Chief's open mind that had finally put him where he was, in spite of competition.

"Have you read their literature yet?" the Chief asked.

"No, sir," Jack Rhyce said.

"Well, read it," the Chief said, "before you make any snap judgments. Of course it sounds like a front organization, but as far as we can see, this one is harmless, although Bill Gibson has not reported on it yet. Anyway, Chas. K. Harrington is harmless, and everyone else in his executive suite. They ought to be. They are drawing higher salaries than you or me, and they have expense accounts besides. Frankly, I never thought of this outfit to cover you until I saw that the Tremaine Foundation had set it up. Gus and I were in the war together. He's a Texan. Do you like Texans?"

"Not always," Jack Rhyce said.

"Well, I think maybe you ought to meet him," the Chief said, and looked hard at Jack again and smiled in a frigid way.

"You see, Gus is like you, Buster. He just doesn't believe that the world is full of people who want to do good by spending other peoples' money. But you're going to understand it. You'd better start learning, because we're going to turn you into one of those people."

"Maybe I'm not the right type, sir," Jack Rhyce said.

"You're going to be," the Chief said. "You're going to be a mother's boy, and have a sweetheart. I think we'll have her in the sociology department at Goucher College. You'll only have about two weeks before you start, so throw yourself into it, Buster."

Naturally, he was most anxious to throw himself into it. He had only been told until then that Gibson, in Tokyo, had requested help, and that he had been selected, but he still did not know what his mission was, and he had been careful not to ask. Now, however, as he sat in the Chief's office, listening to the humming of the air-conditioner, and the sounds of the Washington traffic, he understood that the plans had solidified, and that his briefing was about to start.

"Do you know what I found out the other day?" the Chief asked him. "I discovered that the boys and girls in the office call me Dick Tracy. Why do you suppose they do that?"

"Well," Jack answered, "I'd say it was mainly out of affection, and not because they think you're a figure of fun, or a comic, or anything like that."

The Chief turned on another of his icy smiles.

"Right," he said, "comics aren't comics any more. When I was a kid I was supposed to laugh at the Hall-Room Boys and Mutt and Jeff and the Katzenjammer Kids, but that's all over now. Nothing is really funny any more, not even a good pratfall, because it may have international significance. Right?"

"If you say so," Jack Rhyce said, "but I don't follow you."

"Now don't get fresh, Buster," the Chief told him. "I admit that I am circuitous this morning. I'm sorry to harp on the remark you made about this Asia Friendship

League letter. You said you thought it might be phony, but I'm afraid you think it's funny too. Please don't think it is, because I'd like to have you come back alive from Tokyo."

He paused, and a silence fell between them.

"Let's skip that last remark," the Chief said. "All I'm trying to say is that these people like this Chas. K. Harrington aren't funny. Often they're not even stupid. Please don't underrate them, Buster. Oh, sure, a lot of them are grotesque. Most of them are ignorant in many sectors, because they're usually narrow and dogmatic—but don't forget they can be dangerous. They do have a certain idealism, and a kind of selflessness. They have what Tennyson called 'an all-increasing purpose' even if it's fuzzy-minded. Never underestimate the do-gooders, Buster. As a class, they've made us a hell of a lot of trouble in the last thirty years. Please never think of them as being funny."

When the Chief got started, he had an orator's ability to begin in a slow, haphazard manner, and then with no appreciable effort to pull everything together.

"Incidentally," he said, "I wonder if you have ever read *Heaven's My Destination* by Thornton Wilder. I don't suppose so, because it was written when you were in short pants, except that of course they weren't wearing them when you were a boy, were they? I wish you would read it before you go to sleep tonight, because his central character is a do-gooder. Some people thought he was funny, but he wasn't. You're giving me your full attention, aren't you? You see, your cover is a do-gooder and you've got to understand the species."

He stopped and gazed at Jack Rhyce, but of course Jack was giving him his full attention.

"The thing to keep clearly in mind is that this individual you're going to represent, whom I call a do-gooder for want of a better word, is a distinctly modern type. There was nothing like him in the days of the Roman Empire, and he can only survive today in a country rich enough to afford him. There have been plenty of philanthropists before, and socialists and revolutionists—Tom Paines, and John Donnes, and Karl Marxes, and Arnold von Winkelrieds, and Wilhelm Tell, and Spartacus, and lots of other

15

active characters whose hearts have bled for the common man, but not the same way our modern hearts bleed. Do-goodism in its purest form is new in the world. Maybe it's our greatest hope, but it's also our biggest danger—seriously."

"You mean certain people and ideologies take advantage of it?" Jack asked.

"You're smart today, Buster," the Chief said. "The trouble is, we're an incorrigibly romantic nation who believe, like Little Orphan Annie, that Daddy Warbucks will always be just around the corner. Do-gooders are unrealistic and their older models weren't, basically. The older models thought things through, but we don't think. We feel. The same used to be true of you, but I trust you're getting over it."

"How do you mean—it used to be true with me?" Jack asked.

"Do you remember," the Chief asked, "that damn-fool remark you made to Molotov just before we yanked you out of the paratroopers, about all men being brothers? That's what I mean—it was do-goodism. I damn near sent you back to the army after that."

Jack Rhyce was startled. The truth was you never could tell what the Chief would remember.

"I agree with you, sir," he answered. "I hope I'm better now."

"But I don't want you to be better *now*," the Chief said. "I want you to be a do-gooder. I want you to throw yourself into it. Now you've shown me your letter. Here's another for you, Buster, and after you read it maybe you won't feel that Chas. K. Harrington's Asia Friendship one is so phony. Don't hurry with it. Take your time."

He opened the top drawer of his desk and pulled out a photostat of a letter dated a week before from Amarillo, Texas.

DEAR MR. HARRINGTON (he read):

Due to my business commitments here and there I've been kind of out of touch with your project, the Asia Friendship League, but I've heard a lot about the fine things you're doing out there, and I feel right gratified, to use a Texas phrase.

Now just in order to keep myself up to date, I am commissioning a young friend of mine, for whom I can vouch in every way, because we've rode the range together, and eaten brains at the same barbecue, to make a survey for me of everything you're doing, so I can have the whole picture straight, right here at El Rancho Chico.

The name is Jack Rhyce—a good real American, by the way, though I'm not anti-foreign or anti-anything, partner. Take him right in and shoot the works to him, and send him around the world to all those places which I hope to see myself someday, where they ride in sampans and leave their shirttails out.

You're going to like Jack, so just feel free to tell him anything, because, honestly, he's a prince. And here are a few facts. Jack graduated from Oberlin College in 1941. He has a fine religious background, but is at the same time a real he-man. For example, he played right tackle for Oberlin on the team that almost got to the Sugar Bowl or someplace, and also commenced interesting himself in civic and welfare projects. For instance, during summer vacations, he was counselor for the Y.M.C.A. boy's camp at Lincoln, Nebraska; and helped out in various recreational projects, including the organization of the Tiny Tim Football League, which proved very popular.

He tells me he thinks he would have gone into settlement work if it had not been for the war, but he was just as quick as a Texan to heed his country's call, serving in the paratroopers until wounded. After this he did desk work for various services in Washington, and since then has stayed in Government, not wearing striped pants, but traveling the world for projects like Point Four and things like that. Jack's got a lot of swell ideas, and you two are going to have a lot in common. He's at loose ends now, and I don't know anyone who will understand and appreciate what you're up to better than Jack.

Why is he at loose ends? Well, frankly, because I've been lucky enough to shanghai him out of

Washington with the eventual plan of having him as a sort of leg-man for me out here at Amarillo. How was I able to shanghai him? Well, frankly, don't kid Jack about it, but Cupid has entered into the picture in the shape of a very lovely little trick who is working in the department of sociology at Goucher College, whose name is Helena Jacoby. What with his lovely mother, whom he's never let down since he was five, and this Cupid deal, Jack needs a little more dough. Well, that's the story, Harrington. You'll hear from him, and give him the red carpet treatment all the way to everywhere, and so, *hasta mañana*.

GUS TREMAINE

The strength of the letter was that its main facts were provable by investigation. He had been to Oberlin. He had played right tackle. He had been a Y.M.C.A. camp director, and his parents did entertain strong religious convictions. He had been a paratrooper until the Chief had run into him at Walter Reed hospital. Since the war he had served in Washington.

"How do you like it?" the Chief asked. "It ought to be good, because I spent two nights over it, personally."

Jack Rhyce handed back the copy. It was amazing how intricately the Chief's mind could work.

"It looks pretty good, sir," he said, "but it might help if you were to tell me just why you've selected me for this spot, and what I'm supposed to do when I get there—in Japan."

For a moment the Chief looked annoyed, but finally he nodded.

"Maybe you've got a point there, Buster," he said. "You know I never play fun and games with anyone intentionally, don't you? I think it's early to give you the breakdown, but maybe you've got a point."

He paused and tapped his desk with his pencil.

"All right," he said. "Question Number One: You're going out to the East because you're not known there. Europeans, and especially Americans, stand out like sore thumbs in the East. Everybody knows your income and your girl friend in the Orient. Even the rickshaw pullers

18

know whether you are a spy or not. Orientals are experts about people, as you'll find out, and that's why we are working so hard on your cover, but it won't help indefinitely. They find out everything eventually."

"What about Sorge?" Jack Rhyce asked. "He lasted quite a while."

He was speaking of one of the greatest men in the profession—the German Sorge who, in the guise of a newspaper correspondent, ran the Russian spy ring, and for years had given Moscow accurate intelligence regarding all Japanese intentions. He had been a foreigner, alone in a highly suspicious country, who had been watched by a highly organized secret police, and yet it had been a long while before the Japanese caught up with him.

"Sorge," the Chief said. "Exactly. Sorge had a good cover. But the Japs got him in the end, and made him sing. He must have forgotten his pillbox. I want you to keep yours handy, Buster."

They were both silent for a few seconds. They were professionals, and there was no need to underline anything.

"All right," the Chief said. "Question Number Two: You're going out to assist Gibson. You'll be under his orders." And then he lowered his voice. "Gibson's got the wind up, and he doesn't scare easy. He thinks the Commies are planning a political assassination, and anti-American demonstrations in Tokyo. This is serious when you consider the total political picture." The Chief pushed back his desk chair and stood up. You never realized how tall he was until he was on his feet. He selected another chair and drew it close to Jack.

"Gibson's vague. But you know as well as I do that he's damned intuitive. He says a new personality is running things." The Chief's voice dropped to a still lower note. "An American personality, Gibson thinks. He asked for you particularly."

"Did he say what the personality is doing?" Jack Rhyce asked.

It was never a good idea to ask the Chief direct questions, and he was not surprised that the Chief was annoyed.

"Damn it," the Chief said, "Gibson was necessarily

vague. That's the trouble with this cold war. It's all vague. It isn't a question of stealing the secret plans. It's organization and propaganda and sudden ugly incidents; and our side hasn't learned yet to organize or to understand what people want. All we know is what they ought to want, but maybe we're learning slowly."

The Chief described a circle in the air with his right hand.

"All we can do is to sketch this character," he said. "He's an organizer, a new mind in the apparatus. There's been a sudden marked change in Japan, according to Gibson's estimate. The neutralist intelligentsia are getting more neutralist. There's more anti-Americanism, more pro-Communism. The Communist choral groups are getting better. There's more and better Red literature in the bookshops. There are new ideas. For instance, there's a new labor union that sells clothes at 40 per cent below the retail price. It's the bread and circus idea, but somehow it's done on subtler lines. It's Gibson's notion that all this is only the prelude to large-scale disturbances. You'll have to see him to get it straight, or maybe you'll even have to see the character."

This piece of exposition impressed Jack Rhyce because it lacked the Chief's usual balance.

"Maybe I haven't quite followed you," Jack Rhyce said. "It seems to me everything you say sounds like the usual Moscow technique."

Certainly he and everyone else had seen enough of it. The undeviating quality of the Moscow manufactured procedure was its greatest strength, because there came a saturation point when simple-minded men accepted boredom. The Chief nodded slowly.

"I'm sorry if I gave you that impression," he said. "Actually yours was my own initial reaction, until I examined the orders to organizers and all that sort of thing. It's all gayer. It doesn't taste so much like castor oil. You'll find you almost enjoy it. When was the last time you were in Tokyo?"

"Eight years ago," Jack said, "and only for two days. Tokyo looked pretty well bombed out then."

"Well," the Chief said, "I was there six months ago, and really you wouldn't know the place now. The Japs have that resilience, or national will to live, or whatever you may call it. The whole town's built up and it's bigger, better, busier. And any fool can observe that its atmosphere is predominantly American. It used to be Germany before the war, but now in Japan the fashion is the U.S.A. Even the shop signs are in English in districts no American ever visits. Maybe they think America is good because we won the war. I wouldn't know. I wouldn't care. Of course Japanese culture never will be American, but oh, boy, they have the superficialities! You hardly see a kimono in Tokyo any more. You don't hear the sound of a geta on the sidewalk. Go to a ball game—and you might think you were back at home from the sounds the crowd makes. The girls all wear American dresses and the men are in business suits. Do you think I'm getting away from my point?"

"I know you couldn't do that, sir." Jack Rhyce said, and he was quite right, because in the next few words the Chief pulled everything together.

"They like everything American. That's the point," the Chief said. "They don't fall for anything Russian. And this new propaganda has an American touch. It has jazz and neon lights in it. It's damn clever. And I think Gibson's right—it's dangerous. Communist-made Americanism always is, because it can form the background of serious disturbances. Frankly, I wouldn't say that Japan is very firmly in the camp of the freedom-loving nations. Why should it be? Well, we lost China, and God help us if Japan goes Communist. We'll be in the grinders then; and frankly, Gibson thinks there's a hell of a better chance of its happening than there was six months ago. Something new has been added from America and things are accelerating."

Jack Rhyce knew that the Chief had not given all the details yet. Certainly the Bureau's organization in Japan was not so ineffective that it had not turned up a few concrete facts.

"I hope you're going to tell me what's been dug up," Jack Rhyce said. "After all, I have personal reasons for being curious."

"Oh, yes," the Chief said, and he sat down behind the desk again. "I've made a few mental notes. Of course we have our contacts in the left-wing organizations, but as far as we can make out, none of our people has seen this individual. However, there is reason to believe that he has been to Japan several times. We think we know his cover name. It's Ben Bushman. There's a lot of talk about a Ben in all the recent intercepts. The man who is really masterminding things out there is a Russian named Skirov who comes over to Tokyo to meet Ben. Gibson thinks there's a meeting due pretty soon. I don't need to ask you if you know about this Skirov, do I?"

"I know who he is all right, sir," Jack Rhyce answered.

The Chief smiled faintly, indicating that they both understood that the question had been a joke. Skirov had been on the Moscow first team for a long while, and the latest evaluations had placed him close to the first ten in Moscow.

"Yes," the Chief said. "He's been improving in the last few years like rare old wine, and he's slippery as an eel, always behind the scenes. Am I right in remembering that you've seen Skirov once?"

Jack Rhyce shook his head.

"No," he answered, "I'm sorry, sir, I missed him if he was at any of those parties in Moscow, but I have him clear in my mind, just as everyone else around here has. I examined his photographs only last week."

"You mean in relation to the new Politburo setup?" the Chief asked.

"Yes, sir," Jack Rhyce said, "in that connection, and I can give you his description verbatim."

The Chief sighed and tapped his pencil on the desk.

"I suppose it's too much to think you'll run into Skirov over there," the Chief said, "but if you should you know what the orders are regarding Skirov, don't you?"

"Yes, sir," Jack Rhyce answered.

The Chief had stopped tapping his desk. The pencil was motionless.

"No matter what it costs," he said, "don't forget the sky's the limit if you contact Skirov. There's just a hope that this new one—this Big Ben—may lead you to him, but I doubt it. Skirov never sticks his neck out. That's why your main mission is this Big Ben. I want him located and taped."

"There's no personal description of him yet, is there?" Jack Rhyce asked.

"Nothing that is definite," the Chief said. "He may be big, because he's referred to occasionally as Big Ben. Once the phrase, 'the Honorable Pale-eyed' was found in words contiguous to Ben's. I wish the Japanese were as clever at giving nicknames to foreigners as the Chinese. . . . But I'm getting off the point. All we have about our boy are theories. It looks as though he were energetic, and therefore young. If he's young, he must have some sort of war record. I'd say he was college-educated. He must have been in the East for a while at one point, because our bet is that he has a smattering of Japanese and a little Chinese. This might put him in the preacher class, but I doubt it. He must have a vigorous, engaging personality, be quite a ball of fire in fact; but he isn't in our files. There's one thing more that I'm pretty sure of. It looks to me like a safe bet that Big Ben has been in show business."

"What makes you go for that one, sir?" Jack Rhyce asked.

"The Communist drama groups in Japan," the Chief said. "You know how the Communists have always used folk drama to make their little points. I saw a lot of their plays before the war, in China. Now, according to Gibson, these productions, which used to be excruciatingly dull, have been jazzed up. Pretty girls are singing blues, there's soft-shoe and tap dancing, and American-type strippers."

"He sounds like someone in the Hollywood crowd," Jack Rhyce said.

"It could be," the Chief answered. "Naturally we've given some thought along that line, but Hollywood is more of a generic term than a place. For my money, Ben has been around the live stage, specifically musical comedy. I rather think, since we haven't dug him up, that he was in some Little Theater group. Or maybe he was in one of those road companies that are always traveling around the country doing revivals of Sigmund Romberg or Victor Herbert. Well, there's your picture. We want to know who Ben is, and you're going to help Gibson find out."

"What do we do if we find him?" Jack asked.

The Chief laughed, one of his rare laughs.

"You know my motto," he said. "Always do it with velvet gloves—when possible. I wouldn't want to hurt this Big Ben for the world, if it isn't necessary, but we don't want political assassination or anti-American demonstrations either. Anyway, Bill Gibson will give you the line to take. Of course, if you run into Skirov, that will change the picture, and Bill's got his orders, too, about Skirov. Also, if you stir things up, it may be that the whole Skirov apparatus will get ugly. Don't forget that one. Now, there's one thing more." The Chief looked at his watch again.

"What's that, sir?" Jack Rhyce asked.

"Beginning tomorrow I want you to take two weeks off to study that material, and I want you to go up to the Farm to do it, and every afternoon you're to have a workout with George and the boys. Right through the whole curriculum—everything."

"It isn't necessary," Jack said. "I know those things."

"It won't hurt to have a refresher course," the Chief said. "From now on you're a do-gooder. And do-gooders don't carry rods. I want you to be good if you have to rough it up with people. Really, Jack, I'm most anxious for you to come back to me alive."

III

One of the troubles with working in the office was that you could have no real life of your own because you knew too much, and because the off moment might arise when you forgot what was classified or what was not. The only people with whom you could be at ease were those of a selected group from the office, and even with them you could not wholly relax. Nevertheless, you always had to appear to be normal, because in no respect could you seem peculiar or conspicuous. It was no wonder that Jack Rhyce sometimes laughed sourly when he read the advertisements in *True Detective* magazine; no wonder that most members of the group went on drunken sprees when they returned from various assignments. The Chief was always lenient about these lapses, as long as they were done at the Farm. The worst of it was, that sometimes you hardly knew who you were, after months in foreign parts, and yet you finally adjusted to anything.

The Chief had once told Jack Rhyce that he had only one handicap: he was too good-looking, too athletic and well-set-up to avoid attracting attention. But for once his athletic build, his guileless face, and his irrepressible interest in everything around him were all helpful to his cover. As he sat in his bedroom in the Mark Hopkins, Jack Rhyce had almost forgotten who he was. His mind, in the solitude of the Farm, had absorbed all the facts and details, both about himself and Big Ben. He had almost developed a genuine enthusiasm for the self-improving opportunity that this trip to the Far East would give him, and he had been able to communicate this enthusiasm to Mr. Chas. K. Harrington, in several of his interviews.

Of course he had still harbored the suspicion, after that

25

talk with the Chief, that there must be something wrong about the Friendship League, and the Chief was amused when he heard about it.

"I don't think so, although we haven't got a final check," he said. "The thing that saves them is that they're too damned obvious. After the Institute of Pacific Relations investigations, any sensible Comrade would think that this is a trap; but give them a good looking-over, Buster."

He had not forgotten what the Chief had told him. As he sat in his locked hotel room there in San Francisco, checking over for the last time the contents of his briefcase, he had an unworldly feeling. None of his precautions seemed correct for anyone who was going to write a favorable report about a fine organization, and who was so fortunate as to have his expenses paid to a wonderful part of the world. He examined the last papers in the briefcase, down to the final odds and ends that had seemingly fallen there by mistake—those bits that gave more veracity than any letters could, and all revealed character: the paper of matches from an inexpensive hotel, and a very respectable one, in midtown New York; the theater-ticket stubs to the matinee of a play which had only one week left to run; the memorandum of telephone numbers—all of persons to whom Chas. K. Harrington had referred him, in case anyone should want to confirm. There was one thing that bothered him slightly in his final summing-up. The net result of that briefcase, he suddenly feared, was too neat, too virtuous, lacking any sign of human weakness, and most people did have frailties. Perhaps, although it had been carefully discussed in Washington, it had too many earmarks of obviousness and exaggeration. He sat for a moment thinking carefully of possible remedies, and suddenly he had it. He would go to a drugstore that very evening and get a paper-bound copy of the Kinsey Report of the sex life of the American Female, and put a plain paper cover over it. It would take several hours to get the book authentically dog-eared, but the trouble might be worth it. No one who searched that briefcase would ever doubt his character again—not with the New Testament, Buddha and Kinsey all together. He was still congratulating himself on the idea when his room telephone rang.

There was no reason, as he thought it over later, why the jangling of the bell should have run through his nerves like an electric shock. It must have been that sight of the Russians that made him start at the sound, and also, as far as he could tell, the fact that no one knew that he was in San Francisco. He watched the telephone for a considerable time without lifting it, but the bell continued ringing. Whoever was calling the room must have been very sure that he was there. He finally picked up the instrument.

"Hello," he said, and he spoke in the mellifluous, accentless voice that he had spent such a long time cultivating.

He was startled when a girl's voice answered.

"Hello"—the voice had a slightly husky quality, and sounded very young, and at the same time seductive. "Is this Mr. John Rhyce?"

"Yes," he answered, and he timed the pause very carefully. "Yes, this is Mr. Rhyce."

The voice changed immediately into confidential happiness. The words tumbled over each other in what seemed to him a Midwestern manner.

"Gosh, I'm glad I contacted you, Mr. Rhyce. I was afraid you might have left your room, or something. This is Ruth—Ruth Bogart."

"Oh," he said. "Oh, yes"—and he tried to cudgel his brains. Having been in the profession for a considerable period, he was naturally good with names and faces; but he could not place any Ruth Bogart.

"Don't you know who I am?" she asked.

"Why, no," he said, and he laughed. "I don't, to be quite frank; but then perhaps I'm not the Mr. Rhyce you're looking for either. Rhyce is a common name, but mine is spelled with a *y*."

"Of course it's spelled with a *y*," she said. "Oh, dear, didn't Mr. Harrington tell you? I'm one of the Asia League girls, and we're going on the same plane tomorrow."

"Why, no," he said, "Mr. Harrington didn't tell me."

27

"Oh, dear," she said. "He promised he was going to. Have you inquired for wires and everything?"

"There wasn't any wire," he answered.

"Oh, dear," she said. "Charlie gets so absent-minded sometimes. Well, just the same, I'm Ruth Bogart."

There was a slight pause while his mind moved rapidly, since there were a number of possibilities in that call, and the most important one was that it might have originated with the Russians.

"Well, it's very kind of you to give me a ring," he said, "especially when you must have many acquaintances in the city, Miss Bogart."

"No," she said, "I haven't, and it's awfully lonely in a strange city, isn't it?" If it weren't for her American voice, and the implacable self-confidence of American women, he would have thought the approach was crude. "I'm stopping here at the Mark, too, and—maybe I'm butting in, but Charles—I mean Mr. Harrington—did suggest I call you. I was hoping if you weren't too busy or something, we might have dinner. There's a place here called Fisherman's Wharf, I understand, where they have divine sea food. My room is 312."

"Why, that sounds swell," Jack Rhyce said. "I could certainly do with some sea food. I'll be knocking on 312 in just a jiffy."

It was much better to see what was going on than not, and he especially liked the word "jiffy," for it had a suggestive Friendship League sound. He looked in the mirror above the bureau and straightened his coat. Then he bent down and tested the laces of his brown crepe-soled shoes. Finally he gave a parting glance at his briefcase. It was the oldest game in the world, to lure someone away so that his room could be searched, and a girl was conventionally the shill. He very much hoped he was correct in this suspicion, because the sooner he was placed the better. The only doubt he harbored was how dumb he ought to be. Should he put his briefcase in the upper drawer of the bureau, or should he simply leave it on the writing table? He compromised by tossing it carelessly on the bed, closed the room door noisily behind him, and walked down the corridor eagerly and merrily, just in case anyone should be watching. There was an old saying in the

28

business that a lot of men had saved their lives by giving the impression that they were easily beguiled by women. There had been a girl in Istanbul once, and a very pretty one, too, but that was another story, and he had been sorry when he heard later that she had fallen from a hotel window and died of a broken neck.

One of the oldest tricks was also the ambush, the alluring call on the telephone, the welcoming inward opening of the door, and the blow on the base of the skull. He was still whistling when he stepped out of the elevator and walked down the corridor to Room 312. A great deal of thought had been given at the Farm to the right and wrong way of entering a strange room. He rose to the balls of his feet, rapped briskly on the door of Room 312 with his left hand, his right low at his side, shoulders forward, knees bent, but only slightly.

"Oh," a voice said. "Just a moment, please."

His memory of the Russians made him very careful. He moved closer to the door and touched the knob with his left hand in order to be fully prepared when it turned. As the door opened inward, Jack Rhyce moved with it, almost touching the panel with his left shoulder, knees still bent, right hand still slightly down. There was bound to come a moment when the situation would reveal itself, and when you had your opportunity to advance or retreat, as long as you were moving with the door. Jack Rhyce entered the room almost on tiptoe, knees still bent. It was a duplicate of his own, and the bathroom door was closed. A glance at the bed showed that someone must have been resting on it at almost the moment he had knocked. He also had a glimpse of two matched suitcases of canvas airplane luggage. Of course he saw all those things at the very same instant he saw the girl who stood by the door.

She was very pretty, which did not surprise him. He would have estimated her age at not over twenty-five, until a glance at her hands made him doubtful. Her height was five feet six, hair dark brown, eyes gray green. Her face was longish with a mouth that showed character, although you could not tell much about a woman's mouth when touched with lipstick. She wore a green dress of

29

heavy silk with a thin yellow stripe in it, and she held a red leather handbag.

"Why, Mr. Rhyce," she smiled, "I didn't know you'd come rushing down quite so rapidly."

He smiled back in the overcordial manner that anyone might use when meeting an attractive girl. She was using very little make-up. The color in her cheeks was natural, and she had only a touch of lipstick. He had grown adept, long ago, in spotting persons engaged in his line of work. There was something indescribable about them that could awaken his intuition—an overalertness, perhaps, or a general impression of strain—but her personality baffled him, and he could not reach an immediate conclusion.

"I guess I hurried down faster than was polite," he said, "because it was such a surprise, and a real pleasure too, to hear a friendly voice in 'Frisco. I hope I didn't sound rude, or anything like that, when you called me, because that was my last intention. I'm terribly sorry that Charlie didn't say anything about you, and a little surprised, too, because without wanting to be forward or anything, I don't see how anyone like you could possibly skip anyone's mind."

He could not help being pleased with the general tone of his speech, all of which reflected his new character.

"Why, Mr. Rhyce," she said, "what cute things you say."

Her looks, and then the word cute, were like a tag in the museum case, although the possibility remained that she, too, had a cover.

"Well, I can only say it is a real pleasure, making your acquaintance, Miss Bogart," Jack Rhyce said, "and it will be fun exploring San Francisco with you. I'm especially glad you mentioned Fisherman's Wharf, and after that we might visit Chinatown. I believe it is the largest Chinese district anywhere in the United States."

There was no doubt that his weeks of work were paying off, and Mr. Wilder's novel had been of great assistance.

"I think dinner would be lovely," she said, "but I'm afraid I'll have to beg off on Chinatown, although it sounds awfully romantic and all that; and anyway, you and I are going to see a lot of these Oriental people pretty

30

quickly, aren't we? I'm a little woozy, because I've just flown in from Chicago, and we have an early start tomorrow."

There was no doubt that she was very pretty, and of course, like all American girls, she obviously knew it. In the elevator she opened her red leather bag and took out a gold compact—genuine, not an ordinary plated job. She looked at herself critically in the little mirror, standing with her back to the elevator boy. Jack Rhyce could not avoid a sympathetic interest because it was the correct technique for examining the elevator operator.

"Oh, I forgot to powder my nose," she said.

Her nose looked straight and determined. It did not need powder, and he told her so.

"Well, anyway," she said, "this is a very exciting hotel. Do you know who was here this afternoon? Mr. Molotov himself, who was calling on Mr. Dulles. I had the good fortune to have a glimpse of him just as he was getting into his car."

"Did you?" Jack Rhyce said heartily, "I had that good fortune, myself. I was just getting in from the airport."

They were by the front door then and the doorman was whistling for a taxi.

"I know," she said, and gave him a playful smile. "I saw you, and I did hope you would be you."

It disturbed him that he had not seen her.

"You were so busy looking at those Russians," she said, "that I thought you almost wanted to speak to them."

"Well," he said, "I guess I forgot to look for pretty girls, or anything, being to close to Molotov. He was quite a character, wasn't he?"

"I thought he was cute," she said. "I was surprised. I thought he was just an old Teddy bear, didn't you?"

"Well," Jack Rhyce said, "not exactly a Teddy bear."

He kept wishing he could place her, so that he could be more at ease. The business with the compact mirror still disturbed him.

As he sat down beside her in the taxi, she took out her compact again, and Jack Rhyce's shoulders stiffened slightly because there was really no valid reason for doing so a second time. Then she snapped her bag shut, and put

31

her hand over his, where it rested on the seat beside him. Jack Rhyce was startled because her gesture did not fit correctly with the picture at the moment.

"It is so romantic, isn't it," she said, "to see the sun setting over the Golden Gate? I never thought I'd have the opportunity."

"Yes," Jack Rhyce said, "I agree with you. It is going to be a lovely sunset."

But he was no longer listening to his words or hers. Her fingers were pressing on the back of his hand, first long, and then short, the Continental Code.

"Being followed," he read: *"Orange-and-black taxi."*

He was not disturbed by the news that she had given him, but on the contrary, rather relieved. What did disturb him was his inability to place the girl.

"Okay," he signaled back. *"So what?"*

"Have message from Chief," she signaled back.

There was a happy smile on his face, and he drew his hand away. There were plenty of people in the outfit whom he did not know, since the cardinal principle in conducting such an operation was to have an individual know as few others as possible. What bothered him was that he still could not be sure of her.

"Driver," he asked, "what is the best place for sea food at Fisherman's Wharf?"

"I will never recommend one over another," the driver said, "but a lot of newcomers here sort of go for Fisherman's Grotto, maybe on account of the name."

Jack Rhyce studied the back of the driver's head carefully, thinking that he had talked more than was necessary, but then taxi drivers were apt to be verbose. He turned to the girl beside him.

"That's quite a name—the Fisherman's Grotto," he said. "Do you think we'd better try it?"

"Why, yes," she said. "I think it would be lovely," She sounded very happy, just the way a girl should who is being taken to dine at a place like the Fisherman's Grotto. "I always love to dine in new places, don't you? And we have so much to talk about, so many notes to compare."

"Yes," Jack Rhyce said, "and I can't tell you how pleased I am that we will be traveling together."

32

"That's why they hurried things up back East—just so we could," she said. "Mr. Tremaine said that so long as you were going, I might as well go with you, since you've traveled so much and this is all a new experience for me. He's a lovely old man, isn't he? I mean Mr. Tremaine—just a regular old Teddy bear."

"I never thought of him in that category, exactly," Jack Rhyce answered.

"It seems to me," she said, "that you don't seem to think of anybody as Teddy bears."

"Well, frankly, no, I haven't—not for a good many years," Jack Rhyce said. "And maybe it's just as well."

"Oh, dear," she said, "I hope you're not going to be a dim-view artist. I didn't think you would be, from what I heard of you at Goucher."

"Where?" he asked.

"Why, Goucher College, of course," she said. "Helena and I are both in the Department of Sociology, and we room together. In fact, frequently we're mistaken for each other."

"Now that you mention it," Jack Rhyce said, "I can see you look like Helena."

"I've heard so much about you," she said, "that I almost called you Jackie. What's the latest news of your mother?"

There was no time to answer because the taxi had stopped at the Fisherman's Wharf. Jack Rhyce was out and beside the driver as quickly as he could manage it. An orange-and-black cab had stopped behind them, and a slender man in his sixties got out of it. It was a calm, still day, and close to sunset, but there was plenty of light. He noticed that the Fisherman's Wharf was well equipped with artificial illumination. It was not the sort of place to finger anyone. The elderly man from the orange-and-black cab lingered outside the Fisherman's Grotto, examining some abalone shells. Jack Rhyce pulled his thoughts together abruptly. Granted there was no immediate danger, he would have felt safer if he had not met the Russians. There still remained the possibility that he had been spotted standing in the crowd, and the present reaction still might be more than a routine checkup.

"Helena says you always call your mother 'Mumsie',"
the girl beside him said.

"Oh, yes," he said, and he laughed in an embarrassed
way, "but it's only a holdover from childhood."

Her last few words filled him with relief because it
would have been difficult, at least in his judgment, for
anyone outside of the office to have strung so many facts
so consistently together. He was reasonably sure by now
that she was the girl at Goucher College who had handwritten the "Dear Jackie" letter. For a second his mind
moved from immediate necessities long enough for him to
wonder how the Chief had ever found her, but it was
none of his business, and the Chief would never tell. Still,
he needed to make a further check before he finally accepted her.

"Well," he said, "so here we are at the Fisherman's
Grotto," and he smiled and nodded to the headwaiter.
There was still a choice of tables because the hour was
early.

"I believe it's the season for Dungeness crabs," he said
to her, "and if you've never tried one, they are a most re-
warding experience."

Her smile was exaggeratedly gay and provocative, and
he was naturally quick about playing by ear. She was telling him, as clearly as though she were speaking, that they
both should be absorbed in each other's words and
glances, and oblivious to what went on around them.

"Why, I never heard of them, Jackie," she said.
"That's what Helena calls you, isn't it? Jackie?"

"Let's not go on any more about Helena," he said.
"She's quite a distance away—already."

"Oh, dear," she said, and her smile grew reproachful.
"I'm afraid you're mad at Helena because of what she
said about your mother. You can't blame her for being a
little tiny bit jealous, can you?"

"Well, it does get me a little miffed," he said, "and after all, as I repeat, Helena isn't here."

"Well, I think you're being rather naughty, Jackie," she
said. "Do you think I'd make a better mother substitute
than Helena?"

"I have an idea you'll be much better," he said. "In

fact, I'll be glad to experiment. And may I call you Ruth?"

"Why, yes," she said, "only I hope you don't think I'm being forward, or susceptible, or anything like that, because that isn't really the case at all. I just believe in being myself, Jack. Don't you?"

It was one of the worst conversations in which he had indulged since he was sixteen, but as he threw himself into the make-believe, the thing assumed a quality that was almost genuine, particularly in the boy-meets-girl scene. The bored look of the waiter as he handed the menu proved, at any rate, that the audience believed.

"I think this occasion calls for a Martini or something like that, don't you?" he asked.

"I don't know that I care for a Martini," she said, "and I don't know that it would be any too good for you, either, now that I'm a mother substitute." Their glances met, and they both smiled fatuously at her little joke. "But I would like a nice bottle of that lovely California wine that is made by those priests, or something."

He was somewhat embarrassed that she had been smarter than he. Admittedly, it was conceivable that you might not know what went into a cocktail, but he wanted to tell her that you could also doctor a bottle of wine just as easily. In the end it might not have looked well if neither of them had taken a drink.

"We'll have both Martinis and the wine," he said, in a big-brotherly, reproving voice.

The most harmless thing in the world, the Chief was accustomed to say in one of his best lectures on cover, was a young couple falling in love. It was clear from the way she looked at him that she, too, could have heard that lecture of the Chief's. If things went right, he decided, no one would be surprised, if, after dinner, they stood for a while gazing across the bay at the lights of Alcatraz and if he put his arm around her and whispered in her ear, or if she whispered back.

It was a problem to appear completely engrossed in her, and at the same time to examine the man two tables behind. He looked like a bank clerk about to reach retirement age, and he made no apparent effort to hear what

they were saying, showing that his job, obviously, wa
only to keep them both in sight.

"You can't blame me for being surprised when yo
called," Rhyce said. "No one gave me the least inklin,
that you'd be coming along, too."

"I know," she said. "It was Mr. Tremaine. He's impul
sive, the way, I suppose, all rich people are."

Jack Rhyce laughed in an embarrassed way.

"I hope this doesn't mean they're losing faith in me, o
anything like that," he said.

"Oh, no," she answered quickly, "it was only that i
suddenly occurred to Mr. Tremaine that your job migh
be bigger than he thought, and that you might need som
help. A girl with a typewriter, and things like that, yo
know."

"Are you good with a typewriter?" he asked.

"Yes," she said, and she laughed. "Any sort o
typewriter."

"I hope we'll only have to use a standard brand," h
said.

They looked at each other exactly as though they wer
falling in love.

"I didn't know the job was getting bigger," he said
"I'm very glad you're coming."

"So am I," she said, "because I love to travel. Yo
know, just after I graduated from secretarial school
worked for a while for a man named Mr. Jackson, i
Washington. He used to joke and say I had an itchin,
foot, and it's awfully hard for a girl to travel alone."

"Well, where did you go to after you worked for M
Jackson, if you had an itching foot?"

"Oh, I went to Europe as soon as I could," she said. "
had a divine time traveling around there, seeing monu
ments and things like that, but I was with an insuranc
firm in London, mostly."

"Who was your boss in London?" Jack Rhyce asked.

"His name was Mr. Billings. It was a pretty big com
pany in London," she said, "and it was a group of lovel
people. I love London, don't you?"

"Yes," he said, "the few glimpses I've had of it. Fron
my point of view, London is a man's town."

"But a girl can have a good time in a man's town
36

sometimes," she said. "I love everything about London. I always feel at home when I can hear Big Ben."

Jack raised his wineglass carefully. It reflected the old man eating two tables behind him. He was not listening, but it was still better to go on with the double talk.

"I wonder how Big Ben's striking these days?" he said. "It seemed to me his timing was erratic the last time I was in London. You know, I've been told you can hear Big Ben right in Tokyo, over the BBC—that is, when Radio Moscow doesn't interfere. I wonder if we'll hear Big Ben when we get to Tokyo?"

"I think we will," she said, "almost right away."

"Well," he said, "we'll have to remember to tune in."

She had told him almost everything, but she was still talking brightly, as though she were completely unconscious of it.

"I love to be in strange places and see strange people, don't you?" she asked.

"Yes," he answered. "Strange faces always fascinate me, too. I often play a little game with myself wondering who people are, and what they're thinking about; but maybe it's a bad habit and a waste of time."

"You can't ever tell though, can you?" she said. "Now there's a little old man, all sort of worn and threadbare just directly behind you, two tables away, and he keeps looking at us now and then, as if he were lonely. I wonder what he's been doing all his life."

Jack Rhyce laughed as though she had said something highly amusing.

"Whatever he'd done, he's kept alive," he said.

"They say, don't they," she said, "that San Francisco is the gateway to the Orient? And it's true, isn't it? Because I see there's an Oriental here. I can't tell whether he's Chinese or Japanese. Can you?"

"Where?" Jack Rhyce asked, and without intending it, his voice had an edge to it.

"Over there near that case with the queer fish on ice," she said.

A young Japanese, whom he had not noticed, had entered the Fisherman's Grotto.

"Oh," he said, "yes. I'd put him down for Japanese,

37

and Nisei from his build. It's funny. I didn't see him come in."

She laughed again as though he said something highly amusing.

"Well," she said, "maybe we'd better go back to the hotel before we get into any trouble, because I didn't see him come in either."

"The only trouble we'll have here is to get the attention of the waiter," Jack Rhyce said. It was safe, in his opinion, to discount the Japanese.

The old man behind them must have paid his check already, because he rose when Jack Rhyce signaled to the waiter, sauntered slowly out of the restaurant—pausing, just as he passed their table, to light a thin black cigar, and to glance down at his wrist watch. The waiter arrived with the check just as the stranger went out the door. Jack Rhyce had a bill ready.

"Thanks," he said, "and keep the change."

He pushed back his chair. Miss Bogart raised her eyebrows. The lights were on outside and there was still daylight in the sky. Their shadow called a taxicab. The tension that had built up inside Jack Rhyce subsided slowly.

"He was a dear old man, wasn't he?" Ruth Bogart said. "I wonder where he's going now?"

"Home," Jack Rhyce said. "He's finished work, I think," and he linked his arm through hers affectionately, partly for relief, and partly because of cover. "The whole thing was only a check on our baggage," he told her softly.

This could be the only possible explanation of the shadow's actions. His glance at the watch and the lighting of the cigar confirmed the theory. They were only to be watched for a definite time, so that a warning could be given, in case they returned too soon—and now the time was up. He could light a cigar now.

"I think there's light enough," he said, "if you should care to look at Alcatraz through the telescope."

"That would be lovely," she said—and then she giggled—"as long as we don't get any nearer."

"That's one place where we probably won't end up," he said. Then, when he put a coin in the slot of the telescope, he added in a lower voice, "We can talk at the hotel. I think we're in the clear now."

"Why, it's fascinating," she said. "Hurry and take a look, before we have to spend another dime."

He had been careless, because he thought they were in the clear. Otherwise, he would not have kept his attention so long on Alcatraz. Consequently, when he heard a step behind him, he almost whirled around in a guilty way, instead of turning slowly.

"Sir," a voice said before he saw the speaker, "I beg your pardon, but would you like to see Chinatown?"

It was the young Japanese from the restaurant, the one whom he had thought might be American.

"No, thanks," Jack Rhyce said, "not tonight."

The Japanese, he saw, was at most in his early twenties. His neat, dark suit, his shirt open at the neck, and his hair done in a crew cut, gave him the appearance of a college student.

"There are many interesting things to see in Chinatown," the boy said. He was not persistent, but he was still there.

"I know," Jack Rhyce said, "but not tonight, thanks."

He had not seriously thought until then that there might be something wrong with the picture. The young man's hands were at his sides. There was no indication of a forward motion, and nothing in the face, or eyes, or shoulders, or in the set of the feet indicated trouble. Nevertheless, the Japanese had not moved.

"Excuse me, sir?" he said. "Would you mind if I ask you another question?"

"Why no, not at all," Jack Rhyce answered heartily. "Go ahead and ask it, son."

After all, he was a liberal-minded educator who liked kids. He smiled encouragingly at the Japanese.

"I was so near enough your table at the Fisherman's Grotto, sir," the young man said, "that I overheard some words you said to the young lady." He smiled back at Jack Rhyce. His face looked thin, sensitive, and handsome. "It was only accident—I did not mean to be intrusive."

Jack Rhyce laughed like a good-natured schoolteacher.

After all, he had nothing to conceal, but, even so, he felt a slight tingling at the base of his skull.

"Why, that's all right son," he said, "perfectly all right. There's nothing I should mind having you overhear at all. The lady and I are strangers from the East, eating a fish dinner. What was it that we said that interested you?"

Jack Rhyce watched the young man move his fingers slowly across his palms before he spoke.

"Well, you see, I'm Japanese, sir," he said.

"Why, of course you are," Jack Rhyce said heartily, "and I can see that you're American, too. My guess is you were born right here in California. A lovely state, California."

"That is so, sir," the boy answered. "I was born here, and I'm a graduate of Cal. Tech."

"Well, well," Jack Rhyce said, "congratulations. That's a great school, isn't it Ruth—Cal. Tech.?"

"Yes, indeed it is," Ruth Bogart said. "One of my classmates at Goucher married a very cute boy from Cal. Tech. who majored in physics. I can't remember his name right now, but it will come to me in a minute."

"I was interested in what you were saying at the table," the boy said, "because I have relatives in Japan. May I introduce myself? My name is Nichi Naguchi. They called me Nick at college."

"Well, well," Jack Rhyce said. "This is a real pleasure, Nick. My name's Jack Rhyce, and this is Miss Bogart."

"I do wish we had time for you to show us Chinatown," Ruth Bogart said.

It was hard to tell whether or not the meeting was off-beat. After all, people were more breezy and friendly on the West Coast than the East.

"Well, don't hold back on us, Nick," Jack Rhyce said. "What was it you heard us say that caught your attention? Come on and tell us."

"Well, sir," the young Japanese said, "might I ask if you and Miss Bogart are going to Japan? You were saying you hoped to hear Big Ben strike in Tokyo, over the BBC."

The tingling at the base of his skull grew more pronounced. Now that Big Ben had been mentioned, he could not disregard the coincidence.

"Why certainly you can ask," Jack Rhyce said. "We haven't any secrets, Nick. Why sure, we're flying out that way tomorrow morning. Miss Bogart and I happen to be working for an organization in which we both take great pride—the Asia Friendship League—and I certainly hope that some of the things we're going to do may be of some assistance to your relatives there in Tokyo."

He watched for some revealing sign, however small, but the boy only looked reassured, and began to speak more eagerly.

"Since you have been so kind as to tell me," the boy said, "may I ask if you will not need a guide when you get to Tokyo? The Japanese language is difficult for Americans sometimes." He was overeager and laughed nervously. It was the first time that his Cal. Tech. veneer was gone. "I know a very good guide. He is my uncle. His English is very good. He is also fond of Americans, is very educated, knows all about Japan, all sights—everything. He can answer all questions, because he knows everything about Japan."

Jack Rhyce listened, balancing every word, but he could catch no undertone.

"Well, that's quite a recommendation, that he knows everything," he said, and he laughed before he finished. "Do you suppose he knows Big Ben?"

It was dangerous, but now and then you had to play a card. There was nothing he could see in the boy's face, except uncomprehension.

"Big Ben?" the boy repeated.

Jack Rhyce laughed again, very heartily indeed.

"Didn't you get it, Nick?" he said. "The clock that you heard us talking about, you know, the one that strikes."

He still could read nothing in the boy's face.

"Oh, yes," the boy said, "I forgot. I am very sorry. If you would like, I can give you my uncle's address. I can write it on a card."

"Why, sure, Nick," Jack Rhyce said. "Jot it down and I'll look him up if I should ever need a guide."

"Thank you," the Japanese boy said. "Thank you very much."

"Not at all, Nick," Jack Rhyce said. "The pleasure is

41

all ours, and I'll certainly give your uncle a buzz if I need him. Well, thanks, and so long."

"Good-by, sir," the boy said, "and good-by, Miss Bogart, and good luck, and a very happy trip."

They were alone, with their backs to Alcatraz. The wharf was more crowded now. No one among the parked cars or in the arcade seemed to take any interest in them, but it was safer to register an impression, in case there was anybody there who cared, and still to be very happy about what they were beginning to discover in each other.

"Well," he said, "that was quite a little human experience, wasn't it?" He put the card carefully in his wallet. "Everybody has always told me that San Francisco is a friendly city."

"Nichi Naguchi," she said. "They have funny names, don't they? But he was sort of shy and sweet. It was cute of him, wasn't it—thinking of his uncle? We should have asked him his address, so we could send him a picture card when we get to Tokyo. Oh, dear, that was stupid of me, not to think of it."

"It's all right," he told her. "I was just about to ask him myself, when I saw he had written his uncle's name on one of his own cards. His address is there, and everything."

"That was sweet and sort of sensitive of him, I think. Don't you?" she said. "Well, I'm glad we didn't ask him, because it might have looked too inquisitive. I don't like inquisitive people, do you?"

"No," he said. "They rub me the wrong way, somehow. This has been a lovely experience, getting to know you, Ruth."

"The same is true on my side, too," she said. "The more I know you, the better I think I'm going to like you, Jack. Let's stroll around and look at the fishing boats and things, before we go back to the hotel. Always get as much as you can out of any place you go to, has always been a motto of mine."

Undoubtedly she was as anxious to get back to the hotel as he, but it was never wise to hurry.

The elevator boy who took them to the third floor only looked bored when Jack got out with her.

42

"I'll just see you to your door," he said, "and see you're not locked out or anything."

"It isn't really necessary, Jack," she said, "but it's sweet of you to think of it."

When she took her room key from her handbag, he snatched it from her playfully, and there was even a merry, gentle little scuffle in the corridor, just in case anyone might be interested.

"Now really, Jack." she said, "now please try to behave."

When he turned the key in the door he was still laughing softly, and he approved of the way she covered him and watched the hall, and she kept the correct distance behind him when he entered the darkened room. The second the door was closed behind them he pointed to the closed bathroom door. She nodded, opened it, turned on the light, and pulled open the closet door afterwards.

"Okay," she whispered. "My God, I'm tired of being a Major Barbara!"

"Just a minute," he said gently, "just a minute before you get so frank." He took a pencil from his pocket and offered it to her. "Would you mind writing a few words on the back of this envelope?"

"Oh, so that's it?" she said.

"Yes, that's it," he answered, and his hand closed over her wrist. "I'll take your handbag while you're writing. It might get in your way."

They eyed each other for a moment.

"You don't miss any tricks, do you?" she said.

"I try not to," he answered. "Hurry, please."

"What do you want me to write?" she asked.

"Anything, as long as you write it," he told her. "Write 'I'll do my best to be a good co-operative girl if I go with you on this trip.' "

There was no hesitation when she wrote, but she did not write the words that he suggested. Instead, when she handed him back the envelope he read: *I don't like people who have to be so careful, and as I said, it has been a boring evening.*

Her writing was the same as the Helena letter in his briefcase.

"I'm sorry," he said, "if you think I'm disagreeable, but

43

I had to make up my mind about you. Let's check on the luggage now."

He pointed to her matched suitcases. They were lying one on top of the other, with a small envelope briefcase on top. She unzipped the briefcase while he sat on the edge of the bed watching her, aware for the first time that he was feeling tired. All of her gaucheness was gone. Even before she looked up and nodded, he knew that the baggage had been searched.

"Good job?" he whispered.

She nodded back, smiling, and held up both her thumbs.

"It must have been a woman or a ribbon clerk," she whispered. "They folded the nylons back beautifully."

"Briefcase contents?" he whispered.

"All through everything," she whispered. "They had it out all over the writing table."

"Careless of them," he said.

"Clever of me," she whispered, "for being dainty and using lots of dusting powder. See where they brushed it off?"

He looked over her shoulder at the glass top of the writing table.

"Gloves," he said. "They dusted with them before they put them on."

"Smart as a whip, aren't you, Buster?" she said.

"You bet," he said, "right on the ball. What makes you call me Buster?"

"The Chief," she said. "He calls you that."

"Right," he said. "Now—what's the word?"

"Gibson asked for both of us. Big Ben's coming over. It's definite, he's from the States."

They both stopped and listened. Another guest was walking down the corridor with jaunty, heavy footsteps, and just as the steps passed, they heard a man's voice singing softly:

> For every day is ladies' day with me.
> I'm quite at their disposal all the while!

The song was from *The Red Mill*—an old song, and slightly incongruous for that reason, but then the comedy
44

had been revived recently. They were both silent until the steps and the voice died away.

"Any identification?" he asked.

She shook her head.

"Nothing new. The Chief still likes show business."

"Well," he whispered, "things don't look too bad for us, now they've gone through the bags."

"Yes," she said, "I know, but what about that Jap?"

"I know," he said. "I'd like to get a check on him, but I think it wiser not to signal Washington. Don't you?"

They looked at each other, and nodded. From now on, any communication with the Bureau might ruin everything.

"Well," he said, "I guess that's that. I wish I'd met you earlier before I took on this cover. I hate to be such a pratfall all day long."

"Oh, well," she said, "it won't be as bad as all that. Breakfast downstairs at 7:30, what? Good night, Buster."

"Good night," he said, and he put his hands on her shoulders. "Don't worry. We'll get through all right."

"Hell," she said, "I've given up worrying long ago. Haven't you noticed that?"

IV

By the time he left Honolulu for Tokyo, Jack Rhyce was positive that he and Ruth Bogart were in the clear. It was inevitable, after a number of years' experience, that one should develop intuition. There was a sense of malaise—similar, he sometimes thought, to what phychiatrists called 'free guilt'—when you were being watched. You could not put your finger on any one thing, but finally you could learn to depend implicitly upon that feeling of imbalance. There had been none of that feeling in the airport at San Francisco, and none in Honolulu. When he showed Ruth Bogart the feather cloaks in the Bishop Museum, and the old mission house that had been transported in sections in ships around Cape Horn, he felt that he was exactly what he was supposed to be.

When the pictures of the early missionaries gazed at him sternly, he was able to gaze right back, and the question hardly crossed his mind as to what the Chief would have said about the missionaries. He was exactly what he should have been, and so was Ruth Bogart. He could even forget that they were boringly obvious. He was even able to take a surfboard out at Waikiki, in a perfectly carefree manner. He had learned a little of the trick of it while he had been stationed at Honolulu, during the last war, and it all served as part of the cover. He could be as expert as possible because he was a muscular do-gooder, full of good will toward the world. He was beginning to experience that wonderful feeling of complete creative success that came with perfect cover. There was confidence in such a feeling, but never overconfidence, only a thorough understanding of the cover itself, and a conviction that it had finally blended with his own personality.

On the afternoon when they boarded the plane for

Tokyo, and began flying into the setting sun, nothing changed his mood, and he had always been highly sensitive to airports. The passengers on the plane were interesting, but not outstanding; a Hawaiian-Japanese couple, a Dutch businessman, two British businessmen, and then thirty members of a world tour group, all of whom could only have been exactly what they were. The project, as he learned from the world cruise director in the course of the trip, had been started by a travel agency which had founded an organization named the World Wide Club. Members of this organization, it seemed, paid their dues into a general account for several years, until at last the total sum had become large enough to pay a liberal down deposit on a round-the-world trip—and that was not all, either. During the years (as the director, who was a retired chemistry professor, told Jack Rhyce) in which the fund had been building up, there had been bi-weekly study groups, so that everybody by now knew quite a lot about the places to which they were going. Jack fell into the spirit of their trip at once, and told the cruise director that it was one of the greatest ideas he had ever heard of, and one that ought to spread to every city of the country.

"You know," he said, "the thought has just occurred to me, that we might incorporate this very travel idea into the organization which I happen to represent—the Asia Friendship League. One of our basic problems is to stimulate an interchange of travelers. Don't you think it is a great idea, Ruth?"

Of course she thought it was a great idea, and except for the Dutchman and the Englishmen, they all became a congenial group, flying across the Pacific at nineteen thousand feet. There were very few cocktails served, except to the Dutchman and the Englishmen, but still they began singing songs, and Jack Rhyce threw himself into the spirit of it, and he did have a good baritone. As far as he could remember later, they broke away from cover only once; it was Ruth Bogart's fault, not his. When it had grown dark, and dinner was over, and the merriment had died down, he took the sayings of Buddha from his briefcase.

"This fellow Buddha," he said, "has quite a lot to say. Some of it's a little difficult, due to his antiquity and his

47

foreign way of life, but a lot of it fits right in with today. Would you like me to read you a little of it, Ruth?"

"Oh, shut up," she said, "and let me go to sleep."

"Why, of course," he said. "it was very thoughtless of me, chatting along this way, but I've been stimulated by this travel group and everything. Shall I ring to get you a pillow, Ruth? I know it is a tiring trip, with all this change of time and the plane vibration."

"Oh, shut up," she said again, and on the whole he could not blame her. They were silent for half an hour.

"Jack," she said. "I'm sorry."

"Oh, that's all right," he told her. "Everybody gets tired sometimes."

"Damn it, I'm not tired," she said. "It isn't weariness, it's schizophrenia. When we set down at Wake, can't we get away for twenty minutes and be ourselves?"

"Why yes," he said. "I think that would be a wonderful idea, but it will be dark at Wake—just before dawn."

"All right," she said, "in the dark then. In fact, it would look better if we did. We're supposed to be in love, aren't we? At least the idea is for us to give that impression."

"Yes," he said, "and you've been wonderful about it."

"Oh, shut up," she said, "and let me go to sleep."

She was still asleep hours later when the plane was letting down. He put his hand on her arm to awaken her, and she gave a start and looked around her for a moment, as though she did not know where she was or who she was. He knew exactly how she felt, because he had experienced the same confusion more than once himself. And this was dangerous, particularly on the beginning of a trip.

"Wake," he said, "in about thirty minutes."

"All right," she said. "I've got it now. I was having a bad dream, and I thought you were someone else."

"Just take it easy," he told her. "There's no reason for any bad dreams."

His guess about the time of arrival at Wake was approximately correct, because the announcement came over the loud speaker a few minutes later.

They would be on the ground at Wake Island in half

an hour. It would still be dark. There would be a change of crew, and an hour to two hours on the ground. Transportation would be furnished, so that passengers could go to the resthouse, which was only a short distance from the field, for early morning refreshment. He had not touched at Wake when he had been to Japan eight years ago, but had been on other islands like it—atolls that were pinpoints on lonely seas. Even in the dark, when he stepped out of the plane, he could almost swear that he had been on Wake before. The lights on the field, the activity around the hangars were exactly the same as on other islands, and there was also the same warm humidity, and the sticky smell of salt in the air. They had been given a leaflet describing Wake, and even a map of the island, but he really did not need it. There was the field with the familiar cluster of buildings around it, the tarred streets, the Nissen huts, the army shacks, and then the lagoon. There was no check-up on the passengers, and there was no reason at all why he and Ruth Bogart should not walk to the resthouse or anywhere on that small island.

"God," she said, "it's lonely."

"Yes," he said, "it's lonely all right." But he was surprised that she should be impressed by it, because nothing was more lonely than the existence of anyone who was in the business, and she must have guessed what he was thinking.

"I mean, this is a different sort of loneliness," she said. "I'm used to being lonely in the middle of everything, but this is being lonely in the middle of nowhere."

Except for the field, the personnel at Wake was still asleep. They walked alone up a road, illuminated only by dim electric lights, with ugly shadows of buildings on either side.

"We may as well take a look at the lagoon," he said. "It's later than I thought. It's getting light." It was true that the outlines of the buildings were growing more distinct. There was no reason why they could not be themselves for a moment.

"That crowd in the plane," he said—"did you think any of them seemed offbeat?"

"No," she said. "I had some ideas about the thin Englishman, but I'll clear him now."

"He'll do," he said. "I think we're still in the clear."

"Yes," she said. "I think so. You're still not worried about that Jap in San Francisco?"

"No," he said. "Not seriously, not after Honolulu."

"You don't think he was trying to tell us something, do you?"

"I've thought of that," he said, "but it doesn't seem to hold water. Let's forget him temporarily."

"I wish I could forget him and everything else. Do you ever feel that way?"

"Oh, yes," he answered, "lots of times."

"The hell of it is," she said, "that after a while you don't know what's what. You don't know what you are, because you can't be anything."

"Yes," he said, "I know what you mean. Maybe chameleons feel that way—not the kind you buy at circuses, but really good chameleons."

"We might have a nice time together, mightn't we," she said, "if we weren't all mixed up in this?"

"We might," he said, "but I'm not sure I would know how. I'm too much of a chameleon now. I might turn green and yellow and not know I was doing it."

"How long have you been in?" she asked.

"Long enough to forget what it's like outside," he said. "About ten years."

"Well," she said, "you don't act it altogether. Of course, I'm newer than that."

"Yes," he said, "of course. What were you doing outside?"

"College," she said, "majoring in Romance Languages. I met the Chief at a cocktail party in New York. Let's skip it, shall we?"

"Yes," he said, "let's skip it, but I hope your name isn't Ruth."

"Well, it is," she said, "and it's too bad you don't like it, and now let's both sign off. You're right. It's getting lighter."

"Yes, he said. "The lagoon's over there, I think. The Chief gave you a briefing, didn't he, about Big Ben?"

"Yes, I've got the whole story," she told him.

50

They walked for a while without speaking, through the moist hot dark. He could see the outlines of a dilapidated portable house, on the right, quite clear against the lightening sky; but ahead there seemed to be nothing, and of course there would be nothing except white coral sand and water. In a few minutes now, there would be a glow of sunrise, and there would be a few magic minutes that always came to atolls, when the colors of sand and sea would be unbelievably beautiful.

"It seems queer to me," he said, "that they haven't picked him out by now, if he is a big man, once connected with show business. I never know anyone in show business who doesn't try to push into the front row, and I never knew one who could keep his mouth shut for long."

"Why, what's the matter?" she asked him. "Don't you like the theater?"

"I used to," he answered, "but I get nervous when I go now. The actors are all so obviously what they are. That's what I mean about our boy. He ought to be obvious, too."

He was glad they had gone for a walk. The sky in the east was growing brighter, and in a few minutes it would be sunrise. He felt almost happy, walking with his partner. In the distance he could hear the explosion of a motor warming up, and the noise of the island generating plant, and then he heard another sound, nearer, but some distance away. She must have heard it too, because she put her hand on his arm, and they both stood still, listening.

"Someone singing," she said.

"Yes," he answered, "over by that house, I think."

"San Francisco," she said. "You remember, don't you?"

Of course he remembered. She was referring to the footsteps outside the hotel door in San Francisco, and that snatch of outmoded song, and now in the dark a man was singing another song from *The Red Mill*. The singer's voice was excellent. It sounded carefree and happy, and full of the joy of living.

". . . *In old New York!*" The words came carelessly and incongruously through the darkness. *"The peach-crop's always fine!"*

They stood motionless on the road, listening. Of course, it was only the time and place, he was thinking,

51

that emphasized the coincidence, but nevertheless it was the sort of thing that could not have happened once in a thousand times. It was the kind of long shot that might possibly have a meaning, and you never could tell exactly how things were balanced. He could tell himself it was only Wake Island, but still there was the coincidence.

"It comes from over by the lagoon," he told the girl beside him. "Let's move over that way." The song was coming from ahead and slightly to the right of them, and it continued as they walked.

> They're sweet and fair and on the square!
> The maids of Manhattan for mine!

Then the song was gone, but it had been just ahead of them, and there was light enough to see the lagoon, by now.

"From *The Red Mill*," Jack Rhyce said, in a loud and hearty voice. "It sounds like home, doesn't it? Do you remember the rest of it, Ruth dear?"

"Why, no, Jack," she said, "of course I don't. Not that old song. Do you?"

"Why, Ruth dear, you can't fool me on old songs. It goes like this: *You cannot see in gay Paree, in London or in Cork! The queens you'll meet on any street in old New York.*"

He had not sung it badly, and it was not a bad idea—in fact, it was the exact thing he might have done, considering. It seemed very natural when he heard a voice call back.

"Hey, let's do it again, whoever you are. *In old New York! In old New York! ...*"

The east was growing pink, but it was still not full day, so that shapes did not have the same definition that they would a few minutes later. A man in khaki swimming trunks was walking toward them. His yellow hair was dripping sea-water, and he had a towel over his right shoulder. At first, Jack Rhyce thought that the early light gave an extra illusion of size, but a second later he saw that the man was very large—two inches taller than he, he guessed, and a good twenty pounds heavier. He was

52

beautifully built, too, tall and blond, heavy sandy eyebrows, greenish eyes, and a large mobile mouth.

There was occasionally a time when you could be sure of something, beyond any reasonable doubt. You never could tell when or how the sureness would strike, but such a moment of utter conviction was with him now. He felt his heart beat with a quick, savage triumph that extended to his fingertips. It was one of those moments that made all drudgery worthwhile. He knew that he must be right. He knew that he could not be wrong. It was just as though someone were whispering in his ear, "There he is, there he is." It could not be anybody else. He knew as sure as fate that he was looking at Big Ben.

Nevertheless, even in that moment of revelation, he contrived to keep his balance because his training had been good. He knew that the one thing that would save the picture was to maintain the mood of the moment, which was one of joy of life and friendliness. Cover was the main thing, his common sense was saying, always cover. He found himself joining in the song without a quaver, just gay, always gay, and he put his arm around Ruth Bogart to emphasize this genial spirit.

The peach-crop's always fine!

He was singing. "Come on, Ruth . . ."

They're sweet and fair and on the square!
The maids of Manhattan for mine!

He paused to catch his breath, and the big man in the khaki swimming trunks raised his hand like an orchestra leader.

"Now we're hitting it," he said. "Come on, let's give it the works. Let's go. You take the lead, I'll follow. You know I'd pretty well forgotten those last two lines."

"Well, it's nice to meet another Red Miller," Jack Rhyce answered, "especially on a rock like this. All right, here we go. Come on and join in with us, Ruth. . . ."

You cannot see in gay Paree, in London or in Cork!
The queens you'll meet on any street in old New York.

53

If you had to be a damn fool, it was usually advisable to be one all the way down the line, and it required no intuition to tell him that it was important to be a damn fool now. He knew as sure as fate that he was talking to Big Ben, although he still had to prove it, and his main hope was that Big Ben did not have intuition, too—at least not so early in the morning. In the waxing light the man's size was more impressive than it had been before. In spite of all Jack Rhyce had learned at the Farm, he was not sure how things would come out if they reached a showdown in the next few seconds—but of course there was not going to be a showdown.

"Say, that was good," the big man said. And as far as Jack Rhyce could see, his smile was friendly, and his eyes showed no glint of suspicion. "You're not joining this flying installation here, are you?"

"No," Jack Rhyce said, and he laughed. "If you'll excuse my insulting such a lovely piece of real estate— Thank goodness, no. We're just passengers from the resthouse, only out for a stroll, and heading west in about an hour."

The big man draped his towel more carefully around his shoulders.

"Oh," he said, "you mean Flight Five-zero-one."

"Yes, I think that's the number," Jack Rhyce said. "It's sort of confusing, all this air travel. We were just saying, a few minutes ago, we didn't really know where we were. We *are* on Flight Five-oh-one, aren't we, Ruth?"

"Yes," Ruth said. "Don't be so vague, Jack. Of course it's Five Hundred and One."

Even the clumsy use of numerals could help with cover. They were just tourists indulging in a happy wayside adventure. The big man shook his head slowly.

"That's too bad," he said. "I'd hoped you were on some crew, or something, so we could think up some more old songs. You've got to think up something when you lay off on this rock. Let's see. There's a world tour group, isn't there, on this Flight Five-zero-one? There was something about it, seems to me, at Operations."

His voice was gentle and lazy, with a drawl that might have belonged either to the Tidewater country, or to the Southwest. Jack Rhyce did not attribute it to Texas, as he listened, and he was interested in more than the voice. Big Ben in trying to place them had overstepped, because it was doubtful whether a world tour group would be mentioned in Operations.

"That's right," Jack said, "there is a world tour group aboard, but we don't happen to be in the party. Miss Bogart and I are being employed by the Asia Friendship League, not that I suppose you would hear of it if you're working on an airline."

The big man shook his head vaguely in a way that expressed genuine regret.

"Well, it's too bad you're not staying on," he said, "because you both look like nice folks to get to know, and we might have gone swimming and fishing. We airline folk get lonely even though we move around. And now, as it is, we're just ships that pass in the night."

"That's a very nice way of putting it," Jack Rhyce said, "but it's a pleasure even to have made such a short acquaintance. I suppose we really ought to be getting back to that resthouse."

"Maybe so," the big man said, "but it's been a treat for me, too. Well, so long folks, and don't let those Japs give you wooden nickels."

"Well, so long," Jack Rhyce said, "and many happy landings."

They turned and walked back toward the airstrip. For a while he felt that the big man was watching them, but only for a very short time.

"Turn and wave to him," he said to Ruth Bogart.

"He's gone," she said. "He must be living in one of the huts back there."

"Well," he said, "that's that, at least for the moment."

"Do you think what I think?" she asked.

"I'm glad great minds think alike," he said. "It's lovely that we have so much in common."

"Oh, shut up," she said. "Do you think he is the same man that was singing in the hall?"

"Yes," he said, "I think so."

"Do you think he knew that we were in that room?"

Jack Rhyce sighed. You couldn't think of everything.

"That's a sixty-four-dollar question," he said, "but I shouldn't be surprised if we knew the answer someday."

No matter how you met a given situation, it was impossible to do everything right. There were other things he might have done at Wake Island, but he did his best to follow the maxims of the business, one of which was to disturb nothing unless it was absolutely necessary. Besides, he was only acting on a hunch. He had no way of proving it; yet if his hunch was right, they had him. Even if it had been wise, there was no necessity to ask questions at the moment. The man was obviously an airline employee. Now that he had appeared at Wake Island, he was as safe as a book in the reference library. Only a few discreet inquiries would be necessary to obtain his full life history, and all his life connections. The main question was how the inquiries should be made. As he said to Ruth Bogart, there was only one sixty-four-dollar question. *Did their man know who they were?* If so it would be best to break out of cover at once and communicate with Washington. Although hindsight was always clearer than foresight, Jack Rhyce could never convince himself that he had not moved properly at Wake. After all, he was under Gibson's orders, and he was only ten hours to Tokyo, but doubts still plagued him even after the plane had taken off.

"I might go up forward and have a chat with the crew," he said, "in a purely social way."

"I wouldn't, if I were you, Jack," she told him. "It could get back to Wake that you were asking."

Of course she was perfectly right, and besides, there had been no sign of recognition at that meeting, no uneasiness or tenseness that he had been able to detect.

"I didn't notice anything, either," she said, "except that I didn't quite believe that drawl."

"Yes," he said, "but I'm not sure."

"Did you notice his hands?" she asked.

It was an unnecessary question because he had not taken his eyes off them for more than a few seconds. There was nothing harder to disguise, or more revealing, than hands.

"The way he kept his fingers half-closed—they frightened me," she said.

He did not want to tell her that he had been thinking

56

several times what he could possibly do if Big Ben were once to get him by the throat.

"He looks very able," he said, "very first-class."

He was not thinking of the hands when he made that estimate, but of the wide forehead, the greenish eyes, the careless-looking good-natured mouth, and the general ease of motion which showed that mind and body moved contentedly together.

"Well," he said, and he took the sayings of Buddha from his briefcase, "let's wait until we see Gibson." All they could very well do was to wait.

V

The first time Jack Rhyce had seen the islands of Japan from the air was when he had flown over Tokyo as an Intelligence observer on a B-29 bombing mission. They had come in from the sea on that occasion, on much the same line of approach that they were making now.

"We are now approaching the coast of Japan," the steward said over the loud speaker. "The sacred mountain of Fujiyama is visible off the left wing."

No one could say that the Japanese were not realists. Their representations of Fujiyama on block-print textiles and on porcelains were exactly like that cinder-coned volcano. All the beauties and the difficulties of Japan were starkly obvious as one approached the coast by air. The sharp folds of the mountains showed why only a fifth of the land was suitable for agriculture. He could see the bright green of the rice paddies, now that the plane was letting down, and he could also distinguish the lighter green of bamboo and the darker shades of giant fir trees. The fishing boats off the coast added a last touch to the broad picture of the Japanese struggle for existence. You could understand a great deal about Japanese character the moment you saw the coast, especially its elements of persistence and tenacity.

Japan's army was gone, and its navy, but not, as the Chief had said back in Washington, its national will to live. In Jack Rhyce's second visit to Japan, his brief trip during the Occupation, the Japanese in defeat had seemed more bewildering to him than they ever had before. They displayed a disturbing absence of rancor, a good-natured acceptance of reality, almost a polite regret for any inconveniences they might have caused. There was a relief from tension which he could understand, but much of the new attitude was so far removed from other behavior patterns he had known as to be unsusceptible of analysis. It was all very well to quote, as Intelligence officers did in those days, the old Japanese motto about the supple bamboo bending with the typhoon and never breaking. He was sure that this was an oversimplification. He had kept looking for something inscrutable in Japanese behavior, but he could find very little that answered the definition. They had been picking up the Tokyo wreckage as though nothing devastating had happened, smiling cheerfully in the depth of their misfortunes. After all, there had been too many earthquakes, too many tidal waves, not to have had a deep influence on the national point of view.

On this, his third arrival, he was not surprised to find that the new air terminal, shining with glass and plastic, was much handsomer than any in New York. The immigration official hardly glanced at him as he stamped the passport, and the customs examination was only a formality.

"Well," Rhyce said to Ruth Bogart, "that's that."

The time, he saw, had changed again. It was quarter to twelve o'clock.

"I wish you wouldn't keep making that remark," she said. "Maybe that and that will add up to something else someday."

Her face looked drawn, which was not surprising, because pursuing the sun across the Pacific was always a tiring process.

"We may as well get a taxi to the hotel," he said, "and not wait for the limousine. Nobody around here seems interested in us."

"I hope you're right," she said. "I don't want to go into an act right now. My God, I'm tired."

He wished that he was feeling more alert himself because it was hard to trust decisions made under the strain of fatigue. He noticed that the main concourse at the airport was not crowded, except for the smallish group that had come to meet the plane, hotel and travel agents, and friends of the passengers. The faces, as he examined them swiftly, were Japanese, but there was none of the Gilbert and Sullivan quality that a stranger might have expected. The women were dressed in the same style that one might see in New York. The men, bareheaded, wore neat dark business suits, proving once again that the Japanese were, superficially at least, the most adaptable people in the world. Only a few generations, he was thinking, lay between the grotesque shadows of the double-sworded Samurai, who had once roamed the streets of Tokyo as symbols of total feudalism, and this entirely Western scene. The changes in that brief span were impossible for even a vivid imagination to encompass and they had ended in an adequate acquisition of all the skills of Western culture. Perhaps Japan's main ineffectiveness lay in the too rapid merging of past with present, but then there had been no time for a gradual change. It was no wonder that there was something bizarre even in the self-conscious drabness of that group waiting at the airport. No Western observer that Jack Rhyce had ever heard of, and no Japanese either as far as his reading went, had been able to rationalize all the conflicts of the Japanese spirit.

These thoughts all came to him hurriedly and added up to a sort of bafflement, as he faced the crowd.

"Taxicab?" he said to the porter.

The porter, dressed in coveralls with the airline's name stitched across it, smiled, shook his head.

"Limousine," he said. "All people go in big limousine. Will stop at all hotels."

"No, no," Jack Rhyce answered slowly. "The lady and me—taxicab."

He was just as tired as Ruth Bogart. He did not want to be in a crowded car, and he was so anxious to make his point that he was not aware that anyone had been watching until a small, middle-aged Japanese, dressed in a business suit of an unpleasant purplish blue color and wearing very yellow tan shoes, stepped toward him.

"Excuse me, sir," he said. His hair was grayish and close-clipped, and he bowed in the manner of an older generation. "Do I speak to Mr. Rhyce?"

Jack Rhyce had honestly thought until that moment that they were in the clear. He wished that his mind were moving faster, and that everything did not have the blurred quality that was so frequently the outgrowth of fa-

60

tigue. The main thing, he told himself, was not to appear too careful.

"Why, yes," he said, "I'm Mr. Rhyce."

The Japanese smiled again, and Jack Rhyce saw that both his upper incisor teeth were gold-covered.

"I am so very glad, sir. May I introduce myself?" His voice was high, and slightly monotonous. He gave a nervous deprecating laugh, and his hands moved with astonishing rapidity as he snatched a wallet from inside his purplish blue coat and whipped a name card out of it.

"Please," he said, holding out the card.

"Why, thanks," Jack Rhyce said as he took the card, "thanks a lot."

The thing to do was to take it slowly and clumsily. It was of great importance to exhibit no alertness or suspicion.

"I. A. MOTO," he said, reading aloud from the card. "Well, well, let's see—that name rings a bell somewhere." He did not want to overdo the slowness, but at the same time he did not wish to appear too bright; finally he allowed himself to break into a relieved smile. "Yes, I've got it now." He pulled out his own wallet and thumbed eagerly through papers and memoranda until he produced the card he had been given at Fisherman's Wharf.

"Yes, it's the same name," he said. "Moto. Yes, I've got it now. Your nephew gave me your name in San Francisco. Well, this is a real surprise." He turned to Ruth Bogart, smiling with fatuous enthusiasm. "You remember that nice Japanese boy on Fisherman's Wharf, don't you, Ruth dear, who told us about his uncle who might show us around the city?"

"Why, yes," Ruth Bogart said, and her face also grew radiant with delight. "Why, he must have sent over a cable. What a lovely thing of him to do."

It was quite a little scene, and Mr. Moto was laughing in courteous sympathy.

"Yes," he said, "my nephew. He sent a cable. Yes."

"Well," Jack Rhyce said. "It's a pleasure to meet you, Mr. Moto, and it's a mighty nice surprise to find you here, just when I was trying to tell the porter that I wanted a private taxicab to take us to the Imperial Hotel."

"Oh, yes," Mr. Moto said, "Teikoku Hotel."

61

"What's that one again?" Jack Rhyce asked.

"Teikoku," Mr. Moto said, "Japanese word for Imperial. We can get a taxicab downstairs. This way, please." And he spoke swiftly and eloquently to the porter.

"This is all mighty kind of you, Mr.—er—Moto," Jack Rhyce said. "This young lady and I are pretty tired. If you could just get us a taxi and tell the driver Imperial Hotel—then suppose you come around later and call my room at, say, six o'clock, and maybe we can talk over what you can show us in Tokyo. I'll be a little bit more on the ball by then."

"On the what?" Mr. Moto asked.

"On the ball," Jack Rhyce said, laughing at the small joke. "It's the American way of saying more wide-awake."

Mr. Moto looked delighted.

"On the ball," he said. "Oh, yes. Thank you so very much, and good-by until then. I will call at six o'clock, and we will both be more on the ball."

He laughed; Jack Rhyce and Ruth Bogart joined him.

They were silent in the taxi for the first few moments. There was no way of being sure about the driver's English. She put her hand over his and her fingers pressed quickly.

"Picked us up again."

"Yes," he signaled back, and at the same time he spoke aloud.

"Ruth, dear," he said, "it seems to me your face is on just a tiny bit crooked."

"Oh, Jack," she said, "why didn't you tell me sooner?" and she snatched her compact out of her handbag, and a moment later gave the signal of negative. No one was following, but then, why should there have been? They were going to the Imperial Hotel and the driver had been selected.

"Wasn't it nice of him to meet us, Jack?" she said.

"Yes," he answered, "it was very polite, wasn't it? I think it will be interesting to see more of him, don't you?"

"Yes," she said, "maybe. Well, I can't believe we're here, can you, Jack? So this is Tokyo. I must say it isn't so romantic as I thought it was going to be."

She was right. Tokyo was not a romantic city. It lay sprawling over a large area, divided by a muddy river and canals—a dusty, smoky city that sweltered in the summer and shivered in the winter. Except for the areas contiguous to the Imperial Palace, all the districts of that immense city were jumbled together planlessly like a deck of cards thrown on a table, so that dwellings, shops, temples and factories were shuffled into an indiscriminate confusion. There were districts, but there were no street names except for those that had been set up by the American Army of Occupation. He remembered a bright paragraph that had been written about Tokyo in a prewar guidebook. It was fortunate, the book had said, that most of the dwellings in Tokyo were of fragile frame construction, with paper windows, because they caught fire so easily in the winter, thus making better city planning possible when they were rebuilt. There had been ample opportunity to rebuild Tokyo. The great earthquake of 1923 almost razed the city, and during the war incendiary bombing had achieved virtually the same result—in fact, the modern business district in the vicinity of the Palace was about all that had withstood the bombing. Yet now there was hardly a sign of war. Tokyo was rebuilt again, in the same disorder as before, and with the same flimsiness and impermanence. The shops were back again, wide open to the street, displaying dried fish, vegetables, bolts of cloth, earthen and enamelware and banners in Japanese characters waved above them. You could buy anything in Tokyo, from raw tuna fish to a whole gamut of Western-style goods in the great department stores along the Ginza. Tokyo was itself again, but, as the Chief had said, there was a new veneer. There were signs advertising American toothpaste and American cosmetics, and the streets were as full of motor traffic as any American city, with driving that was even more aggressive. The variety of the vehicles on those teeming streets was a living and rather disturbing illustration of the efforts of the East to adjust itself to competition with the West.

Once when he was in Chungking, during the war, Jack Rhyce recalled having had a long conversation with a well-informed Chinese. It had taken place during an air raid, from which they had not bothered to seek shelter, and the words of his Oxford-educated acquaintance had been punctuated by the thudding of Japanese bombs. Industrialization, the Chinese had said, was not the private property of the Western world, but only a trick which the East could learn as easily as not, and perhaps this was so. Perhaps all learning, in the final analysis, was only a trick. Certainly the Japanese had learned industrialization, and they were still learning how to adapt it to their peculiar needs. The vehicles there in Tokyo were like illustrations for the Darwinian origin of species, and all the manufacturing nations in the world were represented in the picture. Japanese and English cycles, motor bikes, scooter bikes, pedicabs, small, three-wheeled private cars, larger three-wheeled trucks, heavy-duty Japanese trucks, small shiny Japanese cars that competed with the German Volkswagen, American light cars, American heavy cars, French and English and Italian motors—everything was there to answer any need, including rickshaws and hand-pushed barrows. Somehow this variety against the façades of the shops with their indecipherable signs managed to assume a monotony which he associated with the outskirts of any large city. But the Chief had been right. Where had the kimonos gone? And where were the wooden clogs called getas? There had been an effort everywhere to lift the face of Tokyo. There were strange echoes of New York, Chicago, and Hollywood. The American moving pictures and the GI's might have inspired the ball parks, beer halls and dance halls. But from the street, at any rate, there was no way of seeing behind the entrance doors, and the sliding windows, sanded or papered, of the wooden Japanese dwellings and inns along the main thoroughfare. There was only a suspicion, among all that modernity, of something older and more conventional, only an occasional, fleeting glimpse through a gateway of a dwarfed tree, or a pool or a rock garden. Nevertheless, as sure as fate, most of old Japan still lay behind those perishable façades, and it would remain at least for the foreseeable future.

"It's dreadfully noisy and crowded, isn't it?" Ruth Bogart said.

He remembered that she had never been there before, and that the noise and crowded feeling inspired by an astern City was different from the West. There was ore patience and adroitness and discipline because populations were denser and living space was smaller. Tokyo ve a sense of teeming millions that one never experienced in London or New York, but Jack Rhyce knew that ere was a peculiar peace behind those façades. Once ey had reached home, all the Japanese women, in their ew York cotton dresses and their high-heeled shoes, and the Japanese schoolgirls, in their navy-blue skirts and hite middy blouses, and all the men in their business its and all the Boy Scouts would move magically into other kind of life.

The shoes would be left outside. There would be straw atting underfoot. European clothes would be hung way, and there would be kimonos—no chairs, no beds; d still, perhaps, wooden blocks for pillows. There ould be cushions beside low tables, a charcoal brazier d tea, and *sushi* made of raw fish and rice, and a porlain jar of hot sake surrounded by minute cups. There ould be the family tub for the hot bath, and now that it as summer, an open window would afford a glimpse of a ny garden court, with goldfish in a lily pool. This picture ould vary with poverty or wealth, but everywhere in 'okyo the pattern would be the same. The old conventions still lay just behind the modern curtain and behind ie barrier of language. Every stranger, in his own way, as conscious of that older life. It must have been hard to ve two lives at once, as people always did in Tokyo.

"Are you sure we're going the right way?" she asked.

Of course he was sure. It was true that he had scarcely een in Japan, but as soon as he had been briefed on his resent assignment, he had spent so many hours on the 'okyo material that he could have found his way to any oint in the city, without asking directions.

"We'll be there before long," he said. "You'll see the mperial Palace grounds and the moat to your right in ist a minute."

"You do know a lot of fascinating facts," she said. "I ould have boned up on this, too, but I didn't know I as coming."

"It's going to be a great experience for you," he said. We're reaching the handsomest part of Tokyo now. It

might almost be Cleveland or Toledo, except for tl
Palace."

The Palace and the moat and the modern office buil⟨
ings that stood opposite, across the broad avenue, gave
vivid illustration of the colossal effort Japan had made ⟨
compete in a dangerous and changing world, and spo⟨
very eloquently of the cultural cleavage that had to⟨
Japan for a century. There was no place in Tokyo whe⟨
the pictures of old and new Japan appeared in more acc⟨
rate focus. The Palace grounds of Japan's Emperor we⟨
guarded by a moat and behind it by a grim, sloping, d⟨
masonry wall of black lava rock. At the wall's summ⟨
through the artificially contorted outlines of pine tree⟨
were the curving tiled roofs of ancient guardhouses. T⟨
area had been the citadel of the old Tokugawa fortres⟨
before the Emperor had moved there, after Perry's visit ⟨
Japan. The walls and moat were at least a thousand yea⟨
old, and the etiquette and spiritual qualities that they pr⟨
tected were vastly older. A part of the Palace had be⟨
destroyed by bombs, but the Emperor was still residi⟨
among the trees and gardens. Across the street the sk⟨
scraper buildings of banks and insurance companies, a⟨
the modern Nikatsu Hotel, made a dramatic contra⟨
Most of them were of a prewar vintage, and most of the⟨
had successfully survived the bombings. It was true, as ⟨
told Ruth Bogart, that when you saw them, you had t⟨
whole story of Japan, if you could manage to read it.

"Out there in the park by the Palace gates," he sa⟨
"is where the people gather in times of grief and mour⟨
ing. They say that there were thousands of them on t⟨
day of the surrender."

He thought that he could still feel echoes of that tin⟨
as they passed the Palace walls. The Emperor ha⟨
addressed his people over the radio that day, the first tin⟨
that his voice had ever been heard by the general publi⟨
and it was ironical that it had been difficult for many ⟨
his subjects to understand him because he spoke in the ⟨
alect of the old Court of Japan. It was a time, he sa⟨
when all must bear the unbearable; Japan had surre⟨
dered, and the subjects of Japan were asked to welcor⟨
their former enemies. And they had done so. They ha⟨
put large signs on the airstrips reading WELCOME, U.S.⟨

was still not difficult to imagine the park, filled with thousands of mourning Japanese, prostrate, beating their heads on the ground. Hundreds had disemboweled themselves before the walls that day, as a loyal gesture to the emperor.

"You see," Jack Rhyce said, "they are very loyal. That's the main thing to remember about Japanese. Loyalty is the essence of their religion, although they might not put it that way."

"How do you know so much about them," she asked, "if you've been here so little?"

"By reading," he said. "And in the war we took a prisoner now and then." But this was no time to talk about himself; they were driving up to the Imperial Hotel.

He heard her exclaim when she saw that low structure of yellowish volcanic stone, with its strange windows and angles. Although the hotel was designed by an American, it must have once represented the quintessence of Japanese aspirations. He had always thought it was one of the oddest buildings in the world, and he still thought so. While he went to register at the desk, he left Ruth Bogart standing by the baggage, staring bemused at the rough stone corridors and angles. The building had been completed in 1922, and, as a guidebook once put it, it was a maze of "terraces, loggias, porte-cocheres, turrets, inner gardens, glassed-in corridors and roof gardens . . . the salient architectural features of the exterior have been reproduced in the interior, where there are columns, edges, winding tile stairs and templelike effects."

He could not tell whether he was surprised or relieved when he found that their rooms on the third floor of the front wing had a connecting door. Gibson had made the arrangements, and the connecting door might possibly have been an attempt at humor, except that Jack Rhyce knew that Gibson seldom made jokes. Three Japanese boys walked ahead of them, carrying their luggage. He was almost sure that he had seen at least one of them when he had been at the Imperial during the Occupation. The hotel had seemed old and tired then. Now he knew that it would never be young again, because it represented a Japanese dream that was lost, a fantastic, disturbing dream of misplaced grandeur and conflicting taste. He

67

wondered, as he often had before, whether its famous architect, Mr. Frank Lloyd Wright, or some Japanese contractor had approved the final plans. He was inclined to settle for the contractor, because everything was too small and weirdly compact for Western taste. There was a Lilliputian quality about the rooms and everything inside them. The writing tables were too low, the wardrobes below normal height, and the walls of volcanic stone made everything look crowded.

"You can take either room you like," he said. "I don't really see much difference."

"Neither do I,' she said. "I'll take this one." And then he saw that she had noticed the connecting door. He did not wish to discuss it then, while he was busy giving orders about the baggage.

"I'd go to sleep if I were you," he said. "Knock on the door if you want anything."

Before he decided on any course of action, he had to make a routine examination of his room. The draperies the carpet, and the bed covering were all worn, and gave him again a melancholy feeling of creeping age. The bath tub was also too small. He had to bend his knees to reach the washbasin. He went carefully through the wardrobe and every drawer, looked behind the mirror and over every inch of the wall. He finally took off his coat and shoes and opened the door for a glance at the corridor, but there was no one there. The ubiquitous servants that he had remembered in the Occupation—the smiling maids obis and getas, and the boys in white uniforms—had disappeared somewhere into the past. On the whole he approved of the selection of the rooms. They each looked over the fantastic porte-cochere and the hotel driveway thus affording a view of all the hotel traffic. The walls were all thick, so that it would be possible to talk freely voices were kept low and all the locks were sound.

He knew the number he was to call, but he did not give it to the operator.

"I want to speak to Mr. William Gibson," he said, and he spelled the name out slowly, "at the Osaka Importing Company. If he asks who's calling, say it is Mr. John Rhyce," and he spelled the name carefully again, and put down the telephone.

It was half past one in the afternoon, but he did not feel hungry because of all the elapsed hours of the ocean flight. The sun of late June shone hot and strong on the lotus pool in front of the porte-cochere, and he stood at the room's small window looking at the pink and yellow lotus flowers while he waited for his call. He did not turn when he heard the door connecting the two rooms open, because he knew the sound of her step by then.

"Is everything all right in your place?" he asked.

"Yes," she said. "Everything's okay. So you knew this door was unlocked?"

"Yes," he said, "and the latch has been oiled, I think. Gibson must have wanted it that way."

"Well, let's keep it open for a while," she said. "It's awfully far away from everything here, isn't it? Do you like the way things are going?"

"No," he said, "not with that Jap meeting us at the plane. He looked to me as though he were in the business. When he reached into his pocket to take his wallet out, I almost thought he was going for a rod. You don't move that way without training. You just don't."

"So you're feeling jumpy, too, are you?"

"It's the trip," he answered. "I'll feel clearer just as soon as I get a little shut-eye. Im just contacting Gibson. They ought to call back any minute now. How would you like some tea?"

She shook her head.

"How about a drink? I've a flask of bourbon in my bag."

"You sure it won't take the razor edge off your mind?" he said.

"It isn't kind to kid me," he said, and he pulled a flask from the bottom of his bag. Just then the telephone rang.

"Here," he said, "mix two stiff ones while I'm talking."

VI

There was no mistaking the harsh quality of Bill Gibson'[s] voice. Jack Rhyce was tired, but he had to go into an ac[t] again.

"Say, Bill," he said, "guess who this is? Jack Rhyce."

"Why, *Jack*," Bill Gibson answered. There was no on[e] who could throw himself into a game better than Bil[l]. "Where did you ever drop from, you old buzzard, an[d] what are you doing in Tokyo?"

"I thought you'd be surprised," Jack Rhyce said. "I'[m] over here to write a report for the Asia Friendshi[p] League. And who do you think I've got with me, to hel[p] out? Ruth Bogart. You remember Ruth, don't you? She['s] right up in the room here now, mixing us both a good sti[ff] drink of bourbon. Why don't you drop everything, an[d] come on up, Bill?"

"There's nothing I'd rather do in the world," Bi[ll] Gibson said, "but right at the minute things are prett[y] busy in the office."

"Oh, now Bill," Jack Rhyce said, "can't you let thing[s] drop for just half an hour? It's been a long time no se[e] and—"

Bill Gibson's laugh interrupted him. It had just th[e] right warmth, and the proper tolerant affection.

"Oh, all right," he said, "all right. You always did hav[e] a bad influence on me, Jack. Sure, I'll break away. What['s] your room number?"

Now that the point of urgency was made, the convers[a]-tion was as good as over, but Bill Gibson's final remar[k] struck Jack Rhyce as disconcerting.

"Leave your door unlocked," he said, "and save m[e] some of that bourbon."

Ruth Bogart was standing close beside him, an[d]

Gibson's voice was loud enough so that she must have heard the conversation.

"Are you sure that was Gibson on the wire?" she asked.

He was sure it was Gibson's voice and he told her so. Besides there had been enough material in that conversation, innocuous though it had seemed, to afford a double-check.

"Why did he ask to leave the door unlocked?" she asked.

"I guess because he wants to get in in a hurry," he said. "Did you hear him say that things were pretty busy at the office?"

"Maybe I'm not going to have a nap after all," she said.

"It could be possible," he told her, "but how about that drink?"

The worst thing in the world for anyone in the business was to develop any dependence on alcohol, but he was sure that the whisky was good for both of them, under the circumstances. It was one of those few opportunities afforded them to be natural. They sat smiling at each other when they were not watching the unlocked door to the hall.

"Here's looking at you," she said. "I'd really like to have a hot bath and go to sleep."

"In a miniature tub?" he asked.

"Anything at all," she said. "Jack, are you carrying a rod?"

"Absolutely not," he said. "Are you?"

"I have one of those fountain pens," she said, "in my handbag."

"Well, never mind it now," he said. "I suppose you've been told that you're a very pretty girl."

"Yes," she said, and she looked prettier when she answered. "I've been told, but I'm glad you brought the subject up. And now do you mind if I make a remark about you, as long as we're being personal?"

"Why, no," he said, "anything at all."

But she hesitated before she answered, and the bright, efficient gaze left her face, making her look almost sad.

"I keep wondering what sort of a person you really are.

71

I mean, what you're like when you're being yourself, what your tastes are, what you want most and everything like that."

He felt depressed after she had finished speaking. He could think of a number of things he had lost in the course of time. Besides, he had to tell the truth, and the truth was something that had been bothering him lately.

"You know," he said, "I'm really beginning to forget what I used to be. That's the trouble with this business, isn't it?"

"Yes," she said. "It's beginning to be the same way with me. I keep forgetting. I wish we could have met on the outside. Have you ever thought of getting out of all of this?"

"I have thought along those lines," he said. "The trouble is, I don't know whether you ever can get outside, after you've been inside. Inside leaves a mark on you, and gives you disagreeable habits. I wouldn't know what I could do outside to earn my living any more. I was planning to be a lawyer before the war came—but that's all too late now."

"You could be a trustee," she said, "out front, in a bank with a marble floor. You wouldn't look half bad in a Brooks Brothers suit."

"Yes," he said, "or I could be a football coach; I used to play football. Or I could teach languages on the side, or maybe judo. I can drive a car pretty well—but I wouldn't want to do any of those things. If I ever were to get outside—"

He stopped because he had learned long ago that talking about one's self never added up to much.

"Go ahead," she said. "What would you do if you ever got outside?"

When he took another swallow of whisky, he felt more like himself than he had since Honolulu.

"Frankly, I wouldn't want to do anything immediately," he said. "I'd like to get a canoe and some canned goods and a tent. I'd paddle up through the lakes in Ontario until I got about a hundred miles from anywhere, and then I'd pitch the tent. And when I wasn't asleep I'd sit in the sun, doing absolutely nothing, just realizing that nobody could find me. But the main thing would be doing absolutely nothing—"

Just then the door opened. His mind was jerked from northern Ontario, and he realized he never should have been thinking of it. He was not surprised at the manner in which Bill Gibson entered the room, having seen Bill Gibson move fast before, on several occasions, although he had never understood how it could be done with excess weight and a sagging waistline. Bill Gibson was in a hurry, just as Jack Rhyce had said he might be. But even in a hurry, Bill Gibson looked the part he had played for years in Tokyo—a middle-aged American businessman who drank too much before lunch, who fell asleep at the club bridge table in the evening, who talked too much, and who had amorous proclivities which he could never suppress when he should. He was wearing a washable business suit. His jowls were heavy, with a blackish tinge, no matter how clean-shaven he might be. His black hair was brushed back in a pompadour, and he wore horn-rimmed spectacles. Although he had been in a hurry, he was not out of breath, and he had moved so silently that there had been no sound until the door opened.

"Hi," he said gently, and he nodded to Ruth. "Lock that door now, kid. I'm sorry to barge in this way, but I've had a hunch for the last few days that I'm hot as a pistol, and I don't want to be seen coming up here. There's no better place to play cops and robbers than the Imperial Hotel." He spoke easily and confidently, as he always did. "I'll take my weight off my feet and have a drink," he said, sitting down on the edge of the bed. "These rooms are all right to talk in. I've used them before. Well, what's the damn emergency, Buster? I thought I was to call you, and not you me."

Jack Rhyce nodded. He realized that he was being rebuked, and he knew Bill Gibson well enough to see that the situation was tense.

"That's right," he said. "I took the liberty, Bill. It's about Big Ben."

"All right," Bill Gibson said, "go ahead, and make it snappy if you don't mind."

"It's just a hunch," Jack Rhyce said, "but I have a feeling we've seen Big Ben."

He started with San Francisco and with the steps outside the door, and the singing of the tune, and then the other tune at Wake just as light was coming in the sky. He knew Bill Gibson well enough to make an interpolation.

"I've never been psychic," he said. "I never could tip tables, or write messages on a Ouija board, but when I heard that voice, it linked right up with that song in the hall. It wouldn't have given me a jolt if it had not been from the same show. The song in San Francisco was 'Every Day Is Ladies' Day with me,' and it was 'The Streets of New York' on Wake, but they're both out of *The Red Mill*."

"Did you sneak up on him?" Bill Gibson asked.

"I didn't want to try, on that terrain," Jack Rhyce said. "No, we just stood there, and I sang the same song back."

Bill Gibson took a generous drink of his bourbon.

"If I'm seen here it won't hurt to have the smell of American hooch on my breath," he said. "Well, describe him."

"He was in khaki trunks, old army-issue," Jack Rhyce said; "hair was wet, yellow to ginger-colored after his dip in the lagoon. Bushy eyebrows; wide forehead; big mobile mouth, and talking with a drawl, more Tidewater than Texas; and he was damn big, and a beautiful build—all big, especially his hands."

"Bigger than you?" Bill Gibson asked.

"Yes," Jack Rhyce said, "some. I'd hate to tangle with him. He has beautiful co-ordination."

"How did he react?" Bill Gibson asked.

"Friendly. Maybe a little too God-awful friendly. He thought maybe Ruth and I were new airline personnel, and then he asked if we were passengers on a world cruise. He indicated he had read about the world cruise group on Operations teletype. That's the one wrong move he made. I don't think the fact would come through Operations. My hunch would be that he picked it up in San Francisco the night he was singing 'Every Day Is Ladies' Day with Me.' "

Bill Gibson took another swallow of his whisky.

"Ruth dear," he said, "would you look out the window in a nice careful way and see if there's an old beat-up

74

Chevrolet out there—dark green, '51 model? Coupé, left front fender pretty well mashed in, a big dent on the left-hand door, and the door missing a handle. Let me know if you see it, will you dear? . . . So your hunch is he's on a plane crew—what?"

Jack Rhyce nodded.

"And I'll bet he's only a few hours out of here right now," he said.

"There isn't any Chevrolet outside yet," Ruth said.

"Well, thanks, sweetie," Bill Gibson said. "Keep on looking, will you? That Chevvy's been like Mary's little lamb to me the last few days. . . . Did you check up on him at Wake?"

"No," Jack Rhyce said. "It was a big temptation, but it might have been a giveaway, and you'll have to be careful how you handle it here—not that I want to give advice, Bill. He looked very impressive to me—an able, thoughtful character."

Bill Gibson whistled softly.

"Maybe you've got something, Buster," he said. "It's the first good lead on him I've seen for quite a while. I hadn't been thinking much about plane crews."

"If you don't mind," Jack said, "if you've got the time I'd like to add a little more."

"All the time in the world," Bill Gibson said, "so long as that Chevvy isn't there. Keep looking, will you, darling? And I can do with another drink."

Sometimes it was hard for Jack Rhyce to realize that Bill Gibson's mind and techniques were among the best in the office. While Bill listened, he took off his horn-rimmed glasses, and his face looked bloated without them, and his eyes rheumy and dull, but he was not missing anything. He was listening to the encounter with the Russians, about the old bank clerk at the table, and then about the Japanese who mentioned the words Big Ben.

"Cripes, Jack," he said, "this thing is closing in."

"And that isn't all," Jack Rhyce said. "There was this other one at the airport."

"Let's see his card." Bill Gibson held out his hand. "Come on, Buster."

He held the card and squinted at it, and put back his glasses.

"It's a phony, as far as I know," he said. "Moto isn't a Japanese name, it's only a suffix to a name, like Yamamoto, or Mikimoto, who puts pearls in the oysters—and maybe there'll be some Mikimoto pearls for you, Ruth dear, if you happen to see that Chevrolet." He finished his drink in a single gulp. "Well, well, kids," he said, "it looks as if we're going to get some action pretty quick out of this one. Would you guess this Moto boy was in touch with Wake?"

"I couldn't guess," Jack said, "but the thought has crossed my mind, Bill."

Bill Gibson cleared his throat and looked at the empty glass on the floor beside him.

"No," he said, "no, I won't have another, thanks. Well, this has been very interesting to me, kids, because it ties up with some other stuff that's just come in. We have a few people ourselves who get around, you know. Big Ben is around, all right. I've a hell of a lot of things I've got to do, and I can't brief you now. It could spill everything if I were seen up here, but we've got to get together somewhere. Now here's what I want—"

He stood up. It was amazing how quickly he could pull himself off the bed, fat abdomen, jowls and everything.

"Now get this." He looked very much like a sales manager addressing a convention, or a coach, exhorting a team between the halves. "I want you two to take all tomorrow to get your cover sweetened with this Asia Friendship League. I also want you two to make damn fools of yourselves about each other. I'm glad to see you have the connecting door open already—not because I believe in sex, but because, under the circumstances, sex is the safest thing for you. That's why, the day after tomorrow, you're going on a shack-up job to a resort hotel up in the mountains. It's a real off-the-record honeymoon retreat, and no one will notice you, if you just keep interested in each other. I'll be up there Saturday night. You'll see me at the bar at six o'clock, but don't pay any attention to me. Go to the big dance that night and have a good time. My room will be in a cottage called Chrysanthemum Rest. It's near the ballroom. At ten o'clock, leave the ballroom as if you were going out in the dark to smooch. There'll be so much noise and music, no one will
76

hear us talking, or care, but I don't want us to be seen together in Tokyo. I'm too damn hot. Have you got it, Jack?"

Jack was aware again that his mind was not working as accurately as it should. Bill Gibson had asked if he had got it, and the truth was that he had been getting too much in the last few hours. Granted that he had been trained until most of his reactions were instinctive, a craving for rest was beginning to keep his mind from facts.

"Well, Bill," he said, "you've handed me quite a lot since you've been here."

"I've been concise," Bill Gibson answered, "but I'm in a hell of a hurry, Jack."

"This hotel," Jack Rhyce said. He was trying to get things into order, but if he could not get some rest, as sure as fate he would slip up on something, and once you made a slip, with circumstances the way they looked you seldom were given a chance to recover. "Where is it, and how do I get there?"

"In Miyanoshita, up in the mountains. Here's the name."

Bill Gibson scribbled the name on the back page of a notebook, and tore out the page. "The army used it during the Occupation. Officers and their wives spend the week ends there, and unattached young men and their Japanese and other girl friends. It's a peculiar place, like Japan, torn between two worlds, but comfortable and friendly."

"All right," Jack Rhyce said, "but if everything's so hot, why don't you give us the whole fill-in for everything right now?"

"There's not time," Bill Gibson said. "I mustn't be identified with you. But I'll tell you this, it's dangerous as hell. It's confirmed today. They are planning a political assassination—"

He did not complete his sentence because Ruth Bogart, standing by the window, interrupted him.

"A Chevrolet with a dented fender is driving up," she said.

Bill Gibson was on his feet in an instant, and again it was surprising how quickly he could move.

"All right," he said. "Persistent bastards, aren't they?

Let me know what whoever gets out looks like, but tell me later. Good luck. You've got everything?"

"Yes, Bill," Jack said. "We'll be seeing you."

"Right," Bill Gibson said. "Don't get in touch with me again, and remember: *safety in sex.*"

He was gone, so quietly that the closing of the room door hardly made a sound. The incongruity of some of the things Bill Gibson had said only occurred to Jack Rhyce later. One obeyed orders and there was no reasoning why in the business. There was no time to discuss whether he or Ruth Bogart liked the situation in which they had been ordered to participate. You were never yourself in the business, and you did what you were told.

Ruth Bogart was speaking to him from her place by the window.

"Only one man in the Chevrolet," she said. "He's parked, and getting out. Man, thirty-five or six, sun glasses, brown hair, balding at temples. Height five feet ten. Weight maybe one seventy. Pale face, professorial type. Aloha shirt with goldfish on it. Trousers white silk. Shoes, white buckskin trimmed with brown leather. He's entering the hotel. He seems American and harmless-looking."

Jack Rhyce did not move to the window to confirm because it seemed like a professional and accurate description.

"Right," he said. "You'd better go and lie down for a bit, Ruth, and order up something to eat if you want it."

"I don't want anything to eat now," she said, "but hadn't we better talk things over? Bill Gibson looked upset."

"You take a nap first," he answered. "I'm afraid we're going to have a lot of time to talk things over."

"Afraid?" she repeated after him, and he could not help thinking that she looked the way she might have on the outside, but it was not the time or place to let one's mind wander.

"Forget it," he said. "I didn't mean it personally."

"All right," she said, "I'll forget it. God, you really are a pro."

She was obviously not saying it in a complimentary way, and for a second her words gave him an accurate
78

and devastating picture of himself, but one he could excuse.

"Yes," he said, "I'm a pro. We all have to be, don't we? Now go and lie down."

"Yes," she said, and she smiled at him although a smile was not necessary. "I'm a pro, too, a poor, tired pro."

She kicked off her shoes, and it seemed to him that their heels were too high for efficiency. Then she tossed herself inelegantly on the bed, indicating there was not much reason for reticences when you were in the business.

"I'll draw your curtains," he said.

"Thanks," she said, "and move my handbag near me, will you? Thanks, Jack."

He believed that she was already asleep when he closed the door to the adjoining room, and he envied her because instinct told him that one of them must stay awake until there was some assurance that things were moving in a settled groove; the Chevrolet outside was curious and disturbing. He stood by the window looking at it—an inconspicuous American car, one of thousands of its vintage, and one which must have had several owners. It was exactly the sort of car he would have picked if he had wanted to tail someone. He was still gazing out of the window, and wondering whether it would be wiser to stray down and take a closer look when someone knocked loudly on the door.

His reaction of annoyance was a measure of his fatigue. The necessity for being alert again was difficult to face, but it was an absolute necessity because he could not imagine who would disturb him, and the knock had been too loud for hotel servants. It was no time to be careless, and also no time to be furtive. He walked to the door promptly and opened it, seemingly carelessly, but with a few technical precautions. He was too tired for further shocks, but he had to face another. Standing outside in the rather narrow corridor was the man whom Ruth Bogart had described—in the Aloha shirt with the goldfish on it.

He had taken off his sun glasses, but there was no mistaking the shirt, or the trousers of heavy Shantung silk, or the white buckskin shoes trimmed with tan, or the closely clipped brown hair, receding at the temples. Ruth Bogart had said he had a professional look, and she had been correct. He had the look which Jack Rhyce had begun to associate with hundreds of individuals sent out by the government to work on helpful commissions and projects—the eager and at the same time self-satisfied expression of someone who knew he knew the answers.

"Hello," the man in the Aloha shirt said, and he had a warm hail-fellow voice that fitted his professional expression. "You're Mr. Rhyce, aren't you? They said downstairs that you were still in your room."

Jack knew that the face of the man in the Aloha shirt was important and he catalogued it immediately—darkish, intellectual, brown eyes, high cheekboness, longish nose, pointed jaw, thin-lipped mouth, good teeth. These observations took only an instant as Jack Rhyce returned the other's smile.

"Well," he said, "the name is Rhyce, and I'm here all right, just off the plane."

"Well, it's a real pleasure to welcome you to Tokyo, Jack Rhyce," the man in the Aloha shirt said. "My name's Harry Pender, running the shop here for Asia Friendship, replacing Jules Blake, who was called home last week. Chas. Harrington wired you were coming in today. Seriously, it's fine to have you aboard."

Seriously, it was difficult to lapse into the cover again, and to give the proper illusion of delight when all sorts of thoughts and questions were moving in the background.

"Well, Harry Pender," Jack Rhyce said, "this is mighty kind of you to look me up so promptly. I was on the point of lying down and taking a little snooze. That plane trip has, frankly, left me a bit woozy, but come on in. You've woken me up already."

It was true that Harry Pender had woken him up. There were certain thoughts that demanded strict attention. Pender was undoubtedly the man in the Chevrolet, and why was it he had not called on the house telephone? How long had he been outside in the hall? Then, on top of those questions Jack Rhyce had another thought. The Chief had made a mistake for once. If the Chevrolet with the battered fender had been following Bill Gibson, how about the Asia Friendship League? For a fraction of a
80

second Jack Rhyce wished that the Chief were there to know that it was not harmless.

"I won't take a minute of your time," Mr. Harry Pender said. "Of course you're not oriented to Japan yet. No one ever is. I should have met you at the airport, but frankly, we're going to have a conference of Japanese writers tomorrow, and I've been unusually busy as a consequence, and also, all the office cars were in use. All that was left was our old Chevvy, and I've had to use it all morning, buzzing around."

"Meeting planes is always a problem," Jack Rhyce said. "You mustn't have me on your mind at all. I'm just here to look things over and do this report, you know. I can hardly wait to see the office tomorrow, and I'd like to sit in on that writers' conference."

Mr. Pender nodded enthusiastically. "Chas. Harrington indicated that you'd be right in here pitching," he said, "and the whole place is open to you, Jack Rhyce. Nothing up our sleeves or anything like that." He laughed heartily. "And I don't know any way in which you can get the spirit of what we're up to here more than by sitting in at the table with some of our Japanese writers. They're lovable people, the Japanese—I mean, when you get to know them."

"How do you mean—lovable?" Jack Rhyce asked.

"You'll see," Mr. Pender said. "You'll see. You'll get their spirit, given time. They're basically only a bunch of mixed-up kids, but lovable at heart. You'll see."

Jack Rhyce nodded in a respectful, sympathetic manner,

"I suppose I'm somewhat prejudiced in my point of view about the Japanese," he said. "You see, I was in the Pacific during the war."

For one mad moment he could not recollect whether or not his war service had been mentioned in that first letter to Mr. Harrington of the Asia Friendship League, but he was sure that it had been when Mr. Pender made a grave gesture of agreement.

"I know," Mr. Pender said. "I know the superb record that you made with the paratroopers in Burma. I wish I might have been with you, but I had to serve in a more sheltered branch myself, due to being in the Four F category—the U.S.O."

"Oh," Jack Rhyce said, "so you were in the U.S.O.?"

It was only because he was very tired. He could have kicked himself the moment he had said it. The U.S.O. and Big Ben might come together somewhere and he never should have betrayed interest. He almost thought there was a sharpening in Mr. Pender's brown eyes, but it might very well have been his imagination.

"It used to hurt at times," Mr. Pender said, "not to be able to be up forward with you boys, but then we did our best in our small way. I was in a singing troupe."

"That must have been fun," Jack Rhyce said, "and believe me, I'd like to have been able to change places with you at some points. I always did like singing. What sort of songs did you do?"

"Oh," Mr. Pender said. "we had a name. We called our group the Song Caravan, and they were a fine dedicated bunch in it—you know, boys and gals with a smattering of semiprofessional experience from the summer theaters and whatnot, lots of whom finally joined more active branches of the service. We sang all the popular numbers. We would just ask the crowd to holler for a number and we'd sing it. You might have seen us out in the Pacific if you hadn't been in Burma. We did get to Chungking once. Were you ever in Chungking?"

"Oh, yes," Jack Rhyce said, "once or twice, but only very briefly. Quite a place—Chungking."

"It was," Mr. Pender said. "It always seemed to me a very fascinating page of social history—Chungking; we must have a good long talk about it sometime, but it's all water over the dam now. We mustn't forget that we are entering into a new era of reconstruction and not destruction. I know you are going to agree with me—the Japanese basically are nothing but a bunch of mixed-up kids—but lovable." His glance traveled about the room with a casualness which could have been overelaborate. "Oh, by the way, the young lady who was coming over to assist you—is there anything I can do for her? What is her name? It's gone out of my head."

"Bogart," Jack Rhyce said, "Ruth Bogart. She's asleep, I think."

82

"I certainly don't blame her," Mr. Pender said. "But bring her over to the office tomorrow morning. The more the merrier. We'll only have the one day—until Monday—because we close things over the week ends, but we'll think up some program for you over Saturday and Sunday."

"Why, thanks," Jack Rhyce said, and to his surprise he felt genuinely self-conscious. "As a matter of fact," he paused and cleared his throat, "I'd sort of promised to take Miss Bogart to that hotel up in the hills where they have the hot springs at—where is it—Miyanoshita. You see, this is her first glimpse of Japan."

"Oh," Mr. Pender said, "I forgot to ask—were you here during the Occupation?"

"Only passing through for a day or two," Jack Rhyce said, and far from appearing watchful, Mr. Pender looked relaxed and tolerantly genial.

"We're going to have a lot of things to talk about, you and me," he said, "and I know you're going to like our bunch out here, and everything we're doing. And now, before I go, is there anything you want?"

"Well, no," Jack Rhyce said, "except maybe a little sleep, but thanks a lot for asking."

"Yes, sir," Mr. Pender said. "You and I are going to have a lot of fun together. I can feel it in my bones." He held out his hand again. His muscle tone was excellent. "Well, so long. How about up at the office at half past nine sharp tomorrow? You have the address, haven't you?"

"Oh, yes," Jack Rhyce said, "and thanks again a whole lot for dropping in."

After Mr. Pender had left, Jack Rhyce stood unobtrusively by his window watching the parked Chevrolet. In two and a half minutes Mr. Pender had reached it—approximately the time it should have taken him to walk down the staircases of the Imperial, across the lobby and out of its front door. Jack turned from the window and very gently opened the door of Ruth's room. She was wide awake, her head propped up on the pillow.

"I'm sorry if we've kept you awake," he said. "It was the man in the Aloha shirt."

83

She smiled at him, and again she looked very much as she might have on the outside.

"You didn't keep me awake," she said. "I went down and took a look at the car."

"That was a very good girl," he said, "provided you got away with it."

"I think I did," she said. "I'm pretty good with cars. There was nothing except a rod in the glove compartment."

"Oh," Jack Rhyce said. "What kind?"

"Beretta," she said, "all loaded."

"Oh," he said, "Beretta."

It was interesting that anyone in Mr. Pender's position should have been carrying an Italian officer's pistol. Pender had brown eyes but he did not look like an Italian.

"And now," she said, "go away and let me sleep, and you'd better, too. I think things are going to be quiet for a while."

They did not mention Mr. Pender again, but there was no need at the moment. They both had their own ideas about him—the same idea.

It was exasperating to discover the desire for sleep had left him, much as he needed it. He draped his coat over one of the small chairs, stretched out on his bed and tried to relax. The street sounds of Tokyo were nearly indistinguishable, now, from those of a European city, but he could not rid himself from watchful tension or from the intuitions which no one could help developing in the business. He was full of the old malaise that told him that a net was closing. The elderly man in San Francisco and the Nisei Japanese boy were parts of it, and so was the middle-aged Japanese named Moto who had picked him up at the airport. You developed a seventh sense for spotting opposite numbers; he would have bet his last dollar that Mr. Moto was in the business, except for the clumsy use of a name that, as Bill Gibson had pointed out, was not a name at all. It was so obvious that it might have been a signal, but there was no way of being sure. And then Pender was another strand of the net. If he had not said that he was a former U.S.O. entertainer, the Beretta in the car was indicative, and besides, there was the fact that Bill Gibson was on the run. The net was closing on

Bill Gibson, and Bill knew it, but it might be, Jack Rhyce thought, that he and Ruth Bogart were still out of it. He was almost positive that Mr. Pender had accepted them.

Mr. Moto was due to call at six. There would be a chance then to evaluate and handle him, and until six there was nothing to do but rest. Then suddenly he realized he had forgotten something, and immediately he pushed open the adjoining door. Ruth Bogart was asleep. The hardness which he had occasionally noticed on her face was gone. The tenseness about her mouth had relaxed. Although her eyes were closed, she had a half-cheerful, half-expectant look. She was a very pretty girl now that she was asleep, the way she would have looked on the outside, and he was sure that her dreams had taken her there. He was sorry to bring her back into the business.

"Sorry," he said. "Just one thing, Ruth."

You could tell that she had been at the girl's branch of the Farm from the way she awakened. A second before she had been on the outside; now her right hand had moved toward her handbag, but it was only a half-conscious gesture.

"Okay," she said softly. "What?"

"This Moto character who's calling at six," he said. "I think he'll ring the house telephone and not barge up like Pender. I'll leave our door open. The bell will wake you. Get up and close the door but listen, and keep that fountain pen handy. It might just be we'll have to use it. Do you follow me, Ruth?"

"Yes," she said. "I'd have covered you anyway, Buster. Now go and relax or you'll be fidgety when he comes, and leave the door wide open. Don't be so delicate. I need company."

He could not tell whether she was being friendly or not, when she called him Buster; but he felt a twinge of annoyance because he had never liked the name, and also the mere fact that he was annoyed worried him. He would not have given the matter any thought if he had not been tired.

VII

He still could not sleep when he lay down again. The truth had begun to dawn on him that he was not physically the man he had been, that his old resilience and iron were wearing thin, and that he would have been better even three years earlier. Everyone in the business burned out eventually. Either their physical reflexes slowed up first, or their ability to keep concentrated on a single line. He knew it was the worst possible time to put his thoughts on a personal basis. It had been the girl's face that looked so young and happy in its sleep that had disturbed him. He began thinking, just when he should not have, of the outside. If he had stayed on the outside he would undoubtedly be married by now. He would have been in the law. He would have had a home and children, and he would have been a decent man—warm-hearted and genuine—not a suspicious, machine-tooled robot who had been through too much, a man who had played under so many covers that it was becoming impossible to guess what he could have been.

Of course there had always been people like himself who could not easily adjust to civil life after having faced the violences of war. There had been wonderful moments and triumphs. There was always the satisfaction of knowing that in ten years he had made a place for himself in a highly exacting profession, but in the end, what was there of real value? Very little, except what might lie in a set of disconnected memories, very little of which to be proud. And what was he in the end? He was a spy, or a secret agent, if you cared for a politer word, trained to live a life of lying and of subterfuge; trained to submerge his individuality into something he was not—to be a sneak, and if necessary a betrayer; trained to run from danger and let his best friend get it, if it helped the business; to kill or be killed inconspicuously; to die with his mouth shut, in the dark. There was only one loyalty—loyalty to the business. It was, by outside standards, a contemptible profession, and in the end, everybody in the business paid, because deceit was the same as erosion of character.

Why had he not gotten out of it, before it was too late? He raised himself on his elbow. The whisky flask was in his bag and the glasses were on the table. He could even see the traces of Ruth Bogart's lipstick on her glass. She should have been more careful. He sat up, with his eyes still on the bag, but then he leaned back again. Drinking was always dangerous in the business—it was far safer to indulge in bitter thoughts. It was too late for him to leave the business now. He remembered what she had called him a while ago—a pro; and you could not get from the inside to the outside once you were a pro. He wished to heaven he could sleep as she did. It meant that she still could get out of the business; he hoped she would. He resolved to tell her so, if they came out of this safe. He must have been thinking of what he would say to her just as he fell asleep.

He was convinced that he was not the man he had been once, when the telephone awakened him. He heard Ruth Bogart close the adjoining door before he was on his feet. First he had not been able to sleep. Then he had slept too heavily, and like Ruth Bogart, he must have been on the outside, too, in his dreams. It was something that should never happen in the field.

"Hello," he said. "Jack Rhyce speaking."

At any rate, he was back under his cover again, hearty voice and everything. The time on his wrist watch was six to the dot. He was feeling very hungry, and also rested. He was on the beam again.

"Please." It was undoubtedly Mr. Moto speaking. There was the slow, gentle modulation he remembered, and also the monotony of speech that even excellent Japanese linguists sometimes found hard to escape. "I hope I did not awaken you, Mr. Rhyce."

"Oh, it's you, is it?" Jack Rhyce said. "Do I sound sleepy?"

There was a nervous laugh that went with conventional politeness.

"Just a little in your voice, Mr. Rhyce."

He had to admit that the man downstairs was a damned smart Jap, and when they were, it was hard to find anything smarter.

"Well, you win, as a matter of fact," Jack Rhyce said. "I have been having a little shut-eye. But come on right up, you've got the room number, haven't you?"

"The room number? Oh, yes."

It was a needless question. Of course he had the number. There was time for Jack Rhyce to tie his shoes, and put on his seersucker coat. As he did so he realized he had not unpacked anything. He hastily opened his Valpak and pulled some clothes out, because he did not want to give the impression that he might leave at any moment. Then he left the door to the hall half open because a locked door might be conspicuous, and then his heart gave a startled jump. He had completely forgotten the three glasses on the table, but as he moved toward them he saw that only two were there, one with the lipstick smears, and another. Ruth Bogart must have been in when he was asleep, and he felt very much ashamed. He should have thought of the two glasses himself—one of them with lipstick.

The tap on the door was gentle and discreet. Jack Rhyce was accustomed to Japanese manners, and he had listened for many wearisome hours to lectures by social anthropologists on Japanese psychology, but from his own experience in the cruder arena of combat intelligence, he doubted the correctness of many of the lecturers' conclusions. The background and the thought process of Japan were so different from his own that he had always avoided a confident appraisal. When Mr. Moto knocked, Jack felt a species of nervousness. He knew too much about Japan, yet he must not show it. Japanese were always sensitive.

"Well, well," Jack Rhyce said, "step right in. You're right on the dot, I see." He spoke loudly and deliberately, as one should to a foreigner.

Mr. Moto's features were finely chiseled. His hands were slender and graceful. In native dress, he would have been a fine figure of a trusted Samurai, and it was very possible that his family had held that feudal rank. But the hideous, purplish blue business suit, aggressively pressed and arrogantly neat, ruined this romantic picture, and so did the very light tan shoes. Mr. Moto was more a figure of low comedy than a representative of old Japan. Then a startling idea came to Jack Rhyce—that he and Mr. Moto might both be impersonating clumsy people. If you took it one way, the hissing intake of Mr. Moto's breath had a Weber and Fields quality that was too loud and too comic. The same was true of his speech, yet Jack Rhyce could not definitely tell.

"So nice of you to receive me," Mr. Moto said. "You have enjoyed your sleep, I hope."

"Yes, sir," Jack Rhyce said. "I had a real nice shut-eye, thanks, and I feel very much the better for it, Mr.—excuse me. I forget your name."

"Moto," Mr. Moto said. He laughed again, but there was no way of telling whether or not his politeness was deliberately overdrawn.

"Moto," Jack Rhyce said. If they were playing a Mr. Japan and Mr. America game, both of them knew their business. "I've got that straight now, and I hope you'll excuse it, Mr. Moto. Japanese names are tough for me to remember, and I suppose my name is hard for you—Rhyce."

"Oh, no," Mr. Moto said. "R is easy in Japan. We have trouble when we pronounce your letter rell. See—I cannot say it. Ha-ha-ha."

It was hard for Jack Rhyce to decide whether or not Mr. Moto was having deliberate trouble with his *l*'s It was true that the *l* sound was difficult for Japanese to accomplish, although good linguists could manage it. In the Pacific during the War, Jack Rhyce remembered, there had been a sea area christened "Alligator Lipstick." The term had been invented because the area was frequently mentioned by voice over the air and "Alligator Lipstick" was a jawbreaker for the average Japanese. It seemed to Jack Rhyce that sometimes Mr. Moto was having no trouble with his *l*'s at all.

"That is comical, when you come to think of it," Jack Rhyce said, "but it takes all kinds to make a world, doesn't it? You know, I'm kind of hungry after that plane ride.

I wonder if we could get some bacon and shirred eggs and tea. Maybe you can make the room boy understand in Japanese better than I can in English. Ha-ha-ha."

As he spoke he felt sorry for Ruth Bogart listening at the connecting door, and he added, "A whole flock of bacon and eggs and tea."

"Oh, yes," Mr. Moto said. "I shall call up room service. Everything is up to date at the Imperial Hote-ru. Excuse me when I cannot say the *l*."

There was no breaking the law of averages. Sooner or later there would be a slip of the tongue, or else a careless gesture might become a chain reaction that ruined everything. Mr. Moto had slipped, and Jack Rhyce was sure that he was unaware of it. Mr. Moto had surmounted that stumbling block of the Japanese tongue by pronouncing the letter *l* with a subconscious fluency, indicating that he could speak a better brand of English than he was using. When he picked up the hotel telephone and asked for room service in Japanese, his accent was crisp and educated. There was something in the careless way in which he handled the instrument that was not Japanese, or English, or German, and certainly not Russian. His posture was very good, as he stood speaking into the receiver, showing that he had done his tour of military duty—the army, Jack Rhyce guessed, rather than navy; and if it was the army, he might have been in the fanatical wing that started the war. His face showed no passion or arrogance, but it was hard to classify Japanese features. When Mr. Moto gave the order, he asked for bacon and eggs and coffee—not tea; and Jack Rhyce was certain he had mentioned tea. He could not suppress a quiet satisfaction as he sat and listened to Mr. Moto's Japanese. He felt rested, and Mr. Moto had lost a trick in pronouncing the letter *l*.

"Everything will be right up," Mr. Moto said. "Chop-chop, as they say in China. Ha-ha."

"That's mighty kind of you," Jack Rhyce said. "This language barrier is a pretty tough thing, isn't it? Sit down, won't you please? And I do hope the food does come up chop-chop, as you say. I could certainly do with a cup of coffee."

You were bound to fall flat on your face at one time or

another. He could have bitten off his tongue the moment he mentioned coffee, but already it was too late. There was nothing to do but go ahead, without showing a trace of embarrassment.

"You know you've come at just the right time, Mr. Moto," he said. "I'm here to do a piece of work for an organization known as the Asia Friendship League, something in the nature of a report, and the more I think of it, the more sure I am that I'll need somebody like you to show me around."

Mr. Moto's glance had turned toward the glasses on the table; Jack Rhyce had a feeling that tension had relaxed when Mr. Moto saw them. There might have been some truth in that phrase of Bill Gibson's—safety in sex. You could discount a good deal of potential menace in a man if you saw a glass with lipstick smears in his bedroom.

"The Asia Friendship League," Mr. Moto said. "How very, very nice. The United States is such a kind nation, after the war, to do such nice things for Japan. The Asia Friendship League is known to me, and Mr. Pender, its new head, is such a good, nice man."

"So you know Mr. Pender?" Jack Rhyce said. "Well, that's fine. I've already had a warm and really constructive talk with him. He's going to show me around the shop tomorrow, and so I'm afraid I'll be pretty much engaged tomorrow. By the way, how about a little drink, Mr. Moto? Oh-oh . . . I've got to rinse the glasses."

"Oh, no," Mr. Moto said, "not for me. But you—prease, you help yourself."

Jack Rhyce took his flask from his open kit-bag and poured himself another drink.

"I suppose the tap water's all right in Tokyo?" he asked.

"Oh, yes," Mr. Moto said. "You see, the American Army has been here."

"Oh, yes," Jack Rhyce said. "Well, as I was saying, I'm going to be busy tomorrow, but Saturday and Sunday I shall need a little rest and relaxation. You know—maybe you've got a saying in Japan like ours in the States—all work and no play makes Jack a dull boy? And the nice thing about that little maxim is, my first name happens to be Jack."

Jack Rhyce smiled fatuously and sipped his drink. He was almost sure that Mr. Moto was smiling sympathetically.

"There are lots of amusements in Tokyo and its vicinity," Mr. Moto said. "I would be so preased to show geisha girls or anything, Mr. Rhyce."

Jack Rhyce laughed easily.

"That would be swell sometime later," he said. "But this Saturday and Sunday I was thinking of taking a spin into the country. You see, I was here in the Occupation for a day or two, and the army had taken over a hotel up in the mountains. I've got the name of the place written down. It's in Mio—Mio—"

"Oh," Mr. Moto said, "Miyanoshita. Very nice."

Jack Rhyce took another sip from his drink, and gave Mr. Moto a man-to-man look.

"Well, I thought if you could rent me a good car, and a driver, I might go up there, and well—you know, take a girl along."

Mr. Moto nodded and tactfully drew in his breath.

"Oh, yes," he said. "I can drive myself. I can get a good car for you, and very nice girl."

"That's it," Jack Rhyce said. "That's the spirit, Mr. Moto. I had a hunch, right when I saw you at the airport, that you'd be broadminded. A man has to have fun sometime, doesn't he?"

"Oh, yes," Mr. Moto said. "Oh, yes. If you wish, I can find four or five girls and you can make a choice."

"Well, that's fine," Jack Rhyce said, "but you supply the car, and I'll supply the young lady. Be around here at nine o'clock on Saturday morning."

"Oh, yes," Mr. Moto said, "and we can see Kamakura—many interesting things. The Daibutsu Buddha—very big and very old, and Eno-shima—very rovery, very many things."

There was a knock on the door. It was a waiter with bacon and eggs and coffee. Mr. Moto rose and bowed. The bow was old-fashioned, belonging more to the older than the newer generation. "Nine, Saturday," he said. "Big, fine American car. Everything first-crass. You will be satisfied, I am sure, and thank you very much. Good night then, Mr. Rhyce."

92

It had been a long while since Jack Rhyce had been so unsure of his cover work. He could not tell exactly what anything was about, except that there had been that atmosphere of tenseness, and a combat of minds. That slip of his still worried him. There was no need to exaggerate its potential danger. His expression must have disturbed Ruth Bogart when he called her to come in.

"What went wrong?" she asked. "You sounded so terrific, you almost made me feel sick to my stomach."

Jack Rhyce pointed to the table and the tray.

"Sit down and eat it," he said. "I'll order up some more from room service." He stopped and imitated Mr. Moto's voice. "Everything is up to date in the Imperial Hote-ru."

"But what is worrying you?" she asked.

"The coffee," he answered, and he told her.

"Well, it's over now," she said. "I didn't know you knew a word of Japanese. You said you'd hardly ever been in Japan."

There was nothing to do, and time stretched ahead of them uninterruptedly until the next morning. There was actually no reason why he should not talk about himself, or why they should not be reasonable human beings for a while.

"Frankly," he said. "I did live in Japan from the age zero to five. Japanese servants are devoted to kids, and I was speaking the language all the time. My father was a missionary, and the moral of that story is always to look out for missionaries' sons."

"You're too conscientious for me to have to look out for you," she said. "Why didn't you lose that Japanese when you went back to the States?"

He had not talked about the outside to anyone for several years. It was an unfamiliar and rather agreeable experience, to be sitting there in Tokyo, thinking of the outside.

"My father wanted me to keep it up," he said, "and he made me for quite a while. You see—don't laugh—he wanted me to be a missionary, too. It's peculiar what parents want their children to be, isn't it? The language came right back to me in the war at language school."

He stopped and passed the flask to her.

"We may as well finish this," he said, "and you heard

93

what our friend told us—tap water's good in Tokyo. And thanks for doing that about the glasses. Thanks a lot."

"Don't mention it," she said. "You can't be a mastermind all the time, you know. Did he notice?"

"Oh, yes," he said, "he noticed. You wait until you see more of him. I'm afraid he's very smart."

"Afraid?" she repeated.

"That's right," he said. "I don't know where he fits in—not to mention this man Pender in the Chevrolet." He had forgotten that she did not know about Harry Pender.

"We're still in the clear with him, I think," he said, "or he wouldn't have told about that U.S.O. singing caravan. But we're running into something."

Her manner changed as she listened. All the outlines of her face had hardened. Her eyes were still very pretty, but they had hardened, too.

"Yes," she said, "we're walking into something, but let's not take it too big, if you know what I mean."

"I wish I could place the Jap," he said. "It's what I tell you I can't make out where he fits."

"All right," she said. "We'll find out. We're walking into it, but don't take it too big."

"There's the second time you've said that. Just what do you mean?" he asked.

She thought for a moment before she answered, and the hardness had not left her face.

"I suppose I'll have to be personal," she said. "We're teamed up on this, and we've got to stick together, and you're running the show, of course. I don't know as much as you do, but I've seen enough to like the way you work. There's only one thing about you that makes me nervous."

From the way that he reacted he knew that his nerves were still edgy, and he found it difficult to keep annoyance out of his voice.

"I'm sorry if I make you nervous," he told her. "Go ahead and tell me why."

"Because, as I was saying, you're too damned conscientious, Jack," she told him. "You try to think of everything, and no one can. Why not try to just think of one or

94

two things tonight, and put the rest out of your head? It will be back in the morning."

"All right," he said. "Name the one or two things."

"Well, I'll name one," she answered. "How about thinking about me for a while? I wish you wouldn't take me as another responsibility. I'm really not as bad as that. Remember about the glasses?"

When she smiled at him his nerves were not on edge any longer.

"I mean," she said, "let's try to be friends as well as business associates. I think it would help the cover if we found out a little more about each other—what we really are, I mean, and not what we're pretending to be. We can pick that up again tomorrow."

"That's true," he said. "We don't know much about each other, do we? And maybe you're right. Maybe it wouldn't be a bad idea."

"Then go ahead and be yourself," she said. "Say anything, but for heaven's sake let's be ourselves. For instance, say something about Japan that isn't a free lecture. Just go ahead and say something."

Her mood, it struck him, was the same as his had been before he had fallen asleep. He understood exactly what she meant, and it saddened him that it was an effort to do what she asked. Instinctive caution was all around him. He had been in the business too long.

"Well," he said, "I suppose childhood is an impressionable age. Even if you can't remember the details, they are all back in your mind somewhere. I haven't been back to Japan since I was five, except for a few days in the Occupation, but it's all familiar. I can feel at home in it because I used to go to the mission school. I used to play with the gardener's boy." He paused and cleared his throat. "Is that the conversational line you wanted?"

"Yes," she said, "it is, and it's the first time you've been natural since I've seen you. Now I know quite a lot about you, but you don't know anything about me."

"No," he said, "but you don't have to tell me, Ruth."

"But aren't you curious about me?" she asked. "Guess what I was outside? Aren't you curious enough to guess?"

He was surprised that she asked the question because girls in the business seldom cared to talk about their pasts. It was a safe bet they all had them, and rather lurid ones, or they would not have been in the business. There was always some tragedy of love, or a broken home, or some hate or some frustration that was requited by the business. As his glance met hers, and as she raised her eyebrows slightly, he honestly preferred to take her as she was, without knowing any more.

"Why, yes," he said, "I could make an educated guess about you, but I don't know that you'd like it."

Her glance met his again, and then shifted.

"You're such a damn pro—aren't you?" she asked—"you know everything."

He was sorry to detect an undertone of antagonism in what she said. Antagonism, or clash of personality, would seriously interfere with their working smoothly together. He knew that she must be tired by the trip, and by Bill Gibson's hurried call, and by the Japanese; the appearance of Mr. Pender in the dented Chevrolet did not help to soothe one's nerves. The truth was that neither of them did know anything about the other, and in his opinion it was better that way, when working with a woman in the business. It was better to keep things on an impersonal basis, if possible, and not to quarrel or be unkind; but the strain of the day had told on him, too. Otherwise, he would not have been led further into the conversation.

"I'm sorry if I've displeased you," he said. "I've got a lot on my mind, you know. Of course I don't know everything, but maybe I've been around more than you have, and I've been acquainted with a lot of girls in the business—some good and some not. I know how they look and how they act, and I've often had to check their backgrounds. Naturally I can make an educated guess about you. Naturally I've made one to myself already."

He was sorry to notice that her face had flushed.

"So you think I'm just another tramp," she said. "Is that what you're trying to tell me?"

"No," he said, "I'm not trying to tell you anything. There's no cause for you to lose your temper, Ruth."

"I'm not losing my temper," she answered. He knew this was not true. "But I do think if two people are going to work together they understand each other better if they know something about each other, and if they're friends

96

nd not acquaintances. Suppose you tell me what you
hink you know about me, and I'll tell you if you're
ight."

"Why don't we keep what we think about each other to
urselves?" he said. "It might save a lot of trouble, but if
ou want it your way, I'll go along."

There was no use antagonizing her just when work was
tarting, but she had challenged his professional pride.

"If you stay in this racket," he said, "as long as I've
een in it, you'll naturally learn to notice things about
eople, and not let them get on your nerves. You'll get
urther if you just sit quietly and look. All right, if you
vant the professor to give you an analysis—in the first
lace, you're not in the tramp class, and you never will
e. You're too well bred. You have too much background
nd character to be a tramp."

"That's nice to know," she answered. "Go ahead, what
lse?"

He was no longer reluctant to go ahead. He had finally
ecome interested in his ideas. If he had any gifts, his best
ad always been analysis of people.

"Now most girls in your position," he said, "always tell
he same story. All of them are always born of wealthy
arents, usually living on Southern plantations. Then
long came a business failure, or else they married an un-
esirable man. The undesirable man is usually correct—
ut in your case the rest of it is true. You come from an
xcellent background. You were brought up in a large
American city, but I can't tell which, from your accent.
Jpper-class accents are reasonably interchangeable."

"Go ahead," she said. "What else?"

"You never spent all the year in the city." He had for-
otten Tokyo. He was always interested in blocking out a
haracter. "You spent a lot of your time, while you were
rowing up, in the country—a riding country, but not the
Vest. You schooled and jumped horses once."

There was a flicker of interest in her glance.

"What made you make that guess?" she asked.

"Your posture," he said, "but mainly your hands. You
ave beautiful hands, but they are strong above the aver-
ge. They are riding hands."

"All right," she said. "You hit that one. Go ahead."

"All right," he said, "if you'll excuse my being personal. One or two things you said on this trip make me think you've been used to attention, and expect a good deal from people. You should, because you're exceedingly good-looking."

"Why, thanks," she said.

"I'm a man," he answered. "It's obvious; but I don't think I've been influenced by it."

"And, believe me, I haven't tried to influence you," she said. "And don't worry. I won't. So you think I was spoiled, do you? All right, I was, by the family and the servants."

"I'd also guess that you're an only child," he said. "That's only an educated guess. I'd say your father had great personal charm. Drinkers do, and I'm afraid he was a drunk. I've noticed how your expression changes every time I pick up my glass. You loved him and he disappointed you—so you were disillusioned by the father image. He died, I imagine, while you were away at a fashionable boarding school. Your mother married again, and you were on the loose with an independent income—bright, popular girl. You went to college, and I'll bet was nearer to Bryn Mawr than Goucher. You fell in love and the boy friend left you flat. He wasn't killed in Korea or anything. He left you flat."

"What makes you say that?" she asked.

"From the way you act with a man," he said. "You don't trust men. Then you met the Chief. The Chief good at spotting material, and he found that you were natural at the business. You were rattling around loose just the way I was when the Chief found me, and that about all."

When he had finished he knew he had been very close to being right, from the cool suspicious way in which she looked at him.

"Just how did you happen to see my file?" she asked. "I thought those things were confidential."

He shook his head slowly.

"No file," he said. "I've only found out about you by minding my own business, watching you. You asked for it."

She was looking at him with a new respect. At least he

antagonism had gone. Suddenly she smiled at him, and he knew that they were friends.

"You make me feel naked," she said, "or like the tattooed woman in the circus. I didn't know I had everything written on me in fine print. Actually, in case you want to know, we owned a place in Virginia. In fact, I own it still."

"Now, listen," he said, "you don't have to tell me anything more about yourself. It doesn't help the general situation, and we shouldn't be talking like this. It's too dangerous, Ruth."

She shook her head in an exasperated way.

"You're always damn careful, aren't you?" she said. "How do you mean—too dangerous?"

"When you get talking this way you get interested," he said. "It's dangerous to get interested, or like anyone too much in the business, Ruth. You might have to ditch me, or I might have to ditch you tomorrow. You know that."

His hand rested on her shoulder, and she had not moved away, and he was right that it was dangerous.

"Well, thank heaven you have a human side," she said. "And I'm glad we've talked this way, and to hell with the business until tomorrow." She brushed his hand off and stood up. "Look, we haven't had anything to eat. Call for a room waiter since everything's so modern at the Imperial Hotel, and these eggs are cold, and everything. And I have another flask in my suitcase. After all, you're supposed to be crazy about me, Jack."

He was right that the whole thing was dangerous. He knew all the rules about women and emotional involvement. He knew that he was at least coming very close to breaking several of them, but he had never realized that the prospect could be so pleasant. For a moment or two, at any rate, he felt he was himself again, exactly as he had been on the outside. It was a transient sensation, but at the same time, it was a revelation, because he had never believed that clocks turned back.

"Let's save your flask for some other time," he said. "I'm having a good time without it. In fact—"

He stopped because his training was back with him.

"In fact, what?" she asked.

That twinge of caution was gone when he looked at her. He knew he was saying what a great many others had said before him, and yet he did not care.

"Maybe it won't hurt if we took a little time off," he said.

VIII

A great deal of the business was very dull, but that ensuing Friday was one of the most irksome that Jack Rhyce could remember. His hours with the Asia Friendship League had a fatuous quality that demanded every bit of his patience in order to fall into the mood of the dedicated people in the Friendship office, and still not miss a trick. He could not tell, in the space of a day, exactly how dedicated all of them were. He could get only a general picture in his mind, yet he was reasonably sure that most of them had honest intentions and felt that they were engaged in a great work. His thoughts went back a dozen times that day to the briefing the Chief had given him in Washington, on the great American strength and weakness—the persistent belief that good will and good fellowship could conquer everything.

He wished that he could make up his mind as to whether or not Mr. Harry Pender honestly shared this viewpoint, but he had to set down the whole Pender problem as unfinished business. Mr. Pender made himself so hospitable and charming that no time was left for analysis. Besides, it was a time to be very, very careful, until he had told Bill Gibson his ideas. It was a time to be naïve and to convey emphatically the utter harmlessness of himself and Ruth Bogart. It was a time to be enthusiastic but dumb, in an openhanded way. It was also a time to show by a series of skillful shadings a picture of growing attachment between himself and Miss Bogart—one of those half-furtive, half-fleeting romances between two well-meaning people that burgeoned more rapidly in the Orient than anywhere else. All these details had kept Jack Rhyce very busy.

"Of course this is only a very quick fill-in," Mr. Pender

kept saying. "You can't really start getting your teeth into anything until Monday, Jack."

Inevitably they had reached a first-name basis in a very few minutes.

"I can't wait to get the bit in my teeth, Harry," Jack Rhyce said, "and possibly to be of some help with the wonderful things you are doing here. I had no idea that you had such an inspiring picture to show me, or such lovely and artistic offices."

"You just wait," Harry Pender said. "These are only temporary quarters."

Temporary or not, the Asia Friendship League occupied, already, half the floor of a postwar office building in the neighborhood of the Ginza. Mr. Pender, as the head of the Japan branch, had a truly beautiful office looking over a large section of the city, furnished with new Japanese furniture that had been adapted to the European fashion. The furniture had been designed right in the Friendship League; desks, chairs, coffee tables and everything were made by Japanese craftsmen, with authentic Japanese spirit, but also were suited to both Easterners and Westerners. A lot of leading Japanese artists and merchants had been consulted, and had been generous with their help, Mr. Pender explained, and the result had surely been worth the hours of conferences. All you had to do was to look at the lovely Oriental woods, turned out along chaste, modernistic lines, to realize that here the Friendship League had made an important good-will contribution. Its furniture was already on display in a number of Tokyo department stores; several exporters were expressing practical interest. In fact, it might very well start a new vogue, Mr. Pender said, and this was just a small example of what the Asia Friendship League was up to. The League's motto might in one word be termed Interest. Mr. Pender did not mean financial interest, but an honest interest in the other fellow out here in the East. Well, this interest was now flowing in all sorts of directions. There was a group in the office for example, studying the new Japanese films. Then there was the sports group. And this afternoon, as Mr. Pender had said, there would be a panel discussion on writing in the conference auditorium. One of the Foundation's own girls, Miss Kettleback, was going to deliver a lecture to some young Japanese writers on the American novel. It was amazing, Mr. Pender said, how eager these intellectuals were for American culture. Just wait—the auditorium hall would be filled half an hour before the lecture started.

There was not really time, Mr. Pender said, to give a full runover of all the projects, but there was one which was a particular pet of his—the Friendly Pen Pals. Up to this point Jack Rhyce had listened brightly, but now his interest quickened.

"What's that again, Harry?" he asked.

"Well, it's an idea that is purely my own," Mr. Pender said, "and I hope you'll play it up big in your report, Jack. You've heard of Pen Pals in the States and Europe? Well, it just came over me—why not do it here? Why not get a lot of these Japanese kids in school and the universities to swap ideas and news with their own age groups back home? It would seem to me to be the very essence of the cultural interchange we're looking for, and it's working already. You'd be surprised."

Mr. Harry Pender was watching him expectantly when he finished, seemingly waiting for pleased surprise as the idea dawned, and Jack Rhyce nodded slowly. He was beginning to wonder how he had overlooked Mr. Pender in his research back in the states. The data might be in his notes at the hotel, but he could not remember the name or description, and he could not see how the Chief had overlooked him either. The idea of Pen Pals was original, and could form the basis of an excellent message center.

"There's only one thing I don't get," Jack Rhyce said. "I don't exactly see how they write to each other without a common language."

"That's right, Jack. That's the difficulty," Mr. Pender said. "I began playing around with that problem just as soon as I took over the center here, and then it came over me, just a week or two ago—why not set up a translation post right here in the League—just an informal unscrambling of the Tower of Babel, and translate the kids' letters? It's not so tough as you'd think. You'd be surprised at the number of Japanese around who can read or write English—and there's unemployment for a lot of intelli-

103

gentsia. The translation center kills two birds with one stone. We have two big rooms now. Would you like to see them?"

Mr. Pender pushed back his chair, but Jack Rhyce shook his head. It was better not to be overcurious, and besides, Bill Gibson knew the ground. Bill could never have missed the Friendship League for a moment, or this new man who was running it, and Bill would give the orders.

"Thanks, Harry," Jack Rhyce said. "I would be fascinated to see this project next week because I can begin to see already what a real thought there is behind it. But right now, how about some more on the organization's setup, before I go after the details?"

Mr. Pender nodded. "I think you're very wise, Jack," he said. "Take the whole thing slowly. You'll be able to get your teeth into everything beginning Monday. Of course, our basic trouble as I see it is getting personnel out here who are imbued with the right ideas in the social sense . . ."

Harry Pender was a good, fast talker when he discussed the problem of personnel. As Jack Rhyce listened, occasionally nodding in agreement when a cogent point was made, he constantly made mental notes of Mr. Pender's facial expressions and mannerisms. The type was familiar, the intellectual, professorial features, the pale skin, the brown eyes, the receding hair line. There was a fine photographic collection back in Washington of all known people in the business, and Jack Rhyce racked his memory for photographs of the Pender type, but he could make no identification. The trouble with the business recently was that new faces and new talents were continually appearing, and the photograph files were getting a year or two behind the contemporary parade.

He glanced across the office at Ruth Bogart.

"You're getting full notes on this, aren't you, Ruth?" he asked.

"Oh, yes," she said. "It's very fascinating, Mr. Pender."

His one anxiety was not to make a mistake, which might disturb the picture. That was one of the hardest things to learn—to keep things quiet.

It was late in the afternoon when entirely by accident Jack Rhyce picked up another piece of information that interested him. They had made a tour of the offices while Mr. Pender poured forth facts. The man, Jack Rhyce was thinking, must have been at some time the recipient of a Ph.D. degree, and he must have worked as an instructor, presumably in sociology in some college in the States; there was a depth and charm to his voice that fitted well with the U.S.O. Song Caravan.

"You see," Mr. Pender was saying, "this job here is a real challenge to me, Jack. I don't know why Chas. Harrington thought I was suitable for it. There I was, just running our settlement house on Pnompenh not six weeks ago—and along came the news that the League board had selected me for Tokyo. It's a big jump from a little settlement house in a one-horse town to a place like this."

"Pnompenh," Jack Rhyce said slowly, "I don't think I've ever heard of Pnompenh."

It was not true, what he had said, but this was not a time to be bright.

"I don't blame you," Mr. Pender said. "It's in Cambodia, and not many people get there now; but the Cambodians are very lovable people."

It was also an excellent place from which to communicate with China, but it was never wise to appear too interested. Jack Rhyce glanced unobstrusively at his wrist watch.

"This has been a very full and fascinating day, Harry," he said, "and I can't be too grateful to you for giving us all this time. But now maybe Ruth and I had better leave you and call things off until Monday, or else we'll lose perspective. We can get a taxi, can't we?"

"Oh, don't do that," Mr. Pender said. "Why don't we all go to a real Japanese restaurant for supper, and see night life in Tokyo?"

Jack Rhyce glanced at Ruth Bogart and shook his head.

"Let's make it sometime next week," he said. "I think Ruth's still tired from the trip. Aren't you, Ruth?"

"Well, yes," she said. "I am a little, Jack."

"I'll just take her for a walk along the Ginza," Jack Rhyce said. "I can find my way all right, thanks, Harry.

I'm curious to see the Ginza. It was quite a shambles back in '47."

Mr. Pender smiled at them as they moved toward his office door.

"You won't recognize it now," he said. "It's everything it used to be, and more so. Well—" his smile grew broader and more tolerant—"have fun, kids, but come back to school on Monday."

The offices of the Friendship League had been air-conditioned, so that the heat on the street outside made one catch one's breath.

"That office and that damned Aloha shirt," she said.

"It was a fresh one since yesterday," he told her. "The fish were red yesterday. They were blue today. Did you notice?"

"Oh, yes," she said. "I'm a dumb girl, but I noticed quite a lot besides the fish."

"How much else?" he asked.

"Enough to know we'd better be careful," she told him.

"That's why we're walking down the Ginza," he said. "If anyone's tailing us . . . I agree, we'll have to be damn careful."

Every large city in the world was bound to have a characteristic street or square, and Jack Rhyce had seen enough of these to make intelligent comparisons. It seemed to him that the Ginza was the most vital of them all; it best expressed the *Geist*—he had to use a German word—of the people who had made it, although it was not a beautiful street, any more than Broadway was beautiful. The only civic decoration connected with it were the willows on either side of the thoroughfare that were peculiar to the Ginza district. He did not know what they symbolized. Perhaps they were supposed to illustrate the old saying of the supple tree bending before the wind, and perhaps they delivered a quiet, reassuring message of patience and of waiting to the crowds that thronged past them. It was a tawdry street, but very gay, with all the resilience and adaptability of its sidewalk trees. There were huge department stores, and smaller shops filled with garish, highly colored Japanese goods. There were motion picture houses displaying the latest Hollywood films as well as Japanese-made pictures. There were beer halls, cabarets and billboards, jewelry and cultured pearls. There was something for everyone on the Ginza. Though many of its shops had the impermanent construction which he associated with a Western mining town, the whole combination was a tribute to the indomitable spirit of a people anxious to be in the front rank of what was perhaps erroneously known as progress. The startling vigor of Japan was reflected in the burgeoning of manufactured articles that ran from celluloid and plastic toys up to vacuum cleaners and electric refrigerators. And where was Japan going to sell this glittering and sometimes meretricious output? This was one of the world's new, restive questions, and the world's future might be hanging on the answer. The motion picture houses, the beer halls and the cabarets with their beckoning invitations in English also showed the versatility of Japan. It was too early for the neon signs, but once they were turned on, the Ginza would be another Broadway, a center of national aspirations. Actually it was more significant than New York's Broadway of the present, because Broadway was tired, worldly-wise and cynical, whereas the Ginza was full of a naïve, unfaltering hope. Now and then you could believe that you were on Broadway except for the Japanese features and the voices speaking a strange tongue, and the Japanese characters above the shops.

"It's a little spooky here, isn't it?" Ruth Bogart said.

"How do you mean?" he asked. "There aren't spooks around at four in the afternoon."

"I mean, it's half home, and half not," Ruth Bogart said. "I wonder whether the Japanese feel any more at home here than we do."

It was one of those interesting thoughts that could never be answered, and it showed that she was not anybody's fool. The truth was, he was thinking, he was growing too interested in her reactions, but it was pleasant to turn his attention to her after a difficult day.

"The beer halls are air-conditioned," he said. "Would you like to go in and have some beer and listen to some jazz?"

107

"No, thanks," she answered. "Let's walk. It's hot as hell, but I like to see the show. It isn't like Piccadilly, is it?"

"No," he said, "it isn't like anywhere else. Would you like some raw fish and rice? There must be some good *sushi* places down the side streets."

"Not raw fish," she said, "and don't try to be an informative guide using words for local color. To hell with the *sushi* places. Let's just walk along."

"I could show you quite a lot if I wanted to use the language," he said.

"I'd say we're seeing enough the way it is," she said. "I wouldn't say we had a tail on us. Would you?"

"No," he said. "I wouldn't. Between us we should have spotted one by now."

She smiled at him, and he smiled back because he shared her temporary relief.

"Then let's go back to the hotel and have a drink in the bar," she said. "And you can make eyes at me in front of the bar boys and the barflies, just to build the cover, darling—just to build the cover. They have an air-conditioned bar at the hotel. Did you know it?"

"We'll go there pretty soon," he said, "but there's one place I'd like to take you first. It's quite a distance, but we can get a taxi!"

"Oh, no," she said, "not any more sights today. I never did like sights."

"It won't take long," he told her, "and perhaps we can pick up some ideas."

Along the Ginza it was simple enough to find a taxi driver who could speak a little English.

"Street with all the bookstores." Jack Rhyce said. He took a paper from his pocket and pretended to read the name of the district from it, with a clumsy pronunciation.

"Bookstores?" she said, as soon as the cab had started on its way. "For heaven's sake, why bookstores?"

"You'll be surprised," he said, "at how many people are reading in Japan."

There were districts in every city where dealers in new and secondhand books congregated, but few were larger than the book street in Tokyo. The bookshops extended for block after block, and, like Ginza, they offered a

108

little bit of everything. The wide-open doorways leading to the brightly lighted interiors displayed stacks of new paper-backed editions, translations from all over the world, the classical literature of Japan, and current fiction. Also older works were displayed in the show windows—books of art, court ceremonial and religious writings—but the books in English were more provocative than any. There was, for instance, in one shop window, a handsome set of leather volumes on the birds of northern Britain, published some years before Perry had anchored off Japan; an early set of the Waverley novels; a handsome edition of Emerson's essays; a book on navigation dated 1810; and *The Parent's Assistant* by Maria Edgeworth. These timeworn volumes each had its untold and unknown story of its ending in an Oriental bookstall. You could not help wondering who had first brought them to Japan. Had they been owned once by someone in the British Embassy, or by an American missionary, or had they come from the library of a once rich Japanese, impoverished by the war? No one would ever know the answer any more than one could guess who would eventually read them. The past, the present and the future were all implicit in the bookstores.

Most of them were filled with customers, many of whom were reading as much of a volume as possible in the hope of getting the gist of it before they had to buy, but no one disturbed the furtive readers. No one interrupted Ruth Bogart or Jack Rhyce either, as they moved from shop to shop. The displays of periodicals were what interested him most, particularly the large numbers that dealt with Russia and Red China. These—some in Russian, some in English, some in Japanese—were crude but effective projections of American formats. Except for some scurrilous pictures of Uncle Sam and heavily armed gentlemen with dollar signs on their waistcoats who whipped starving workers into factories, everyone was happy in the pictures. Fat Chinese peasants were smilingly learning to read. Farmers were proudly operating tractors. Soldiers carrying the Freedom Flag of the Hammer and Sickle gave candy to little children.

"You see," he said, "how it rounds out the picture of the day?"

"Yes, naturally I see," she said, taking his arm and pressing it urgently. "But let's go. We shouldn't have come here."

"Why not?" he asked her. "What's the hurry?"

"Buy some cheap American magazine," she said, "and get out of here."

He did not ask her again what the matter was until they stood on the curb waving to a taxi.

"We're in the clear," he said. "There was nothing queer in any of those shops."

She shook her head impatiently.

"No," she said, "but we are. We were the only foreigners and everyone remembers foreigners. Where would you keep a lookout for new operators? Put yourself in their position, Jack."

He felt deeply mortified that he had not thought of her point himself. Too many small mistakes too often added up to something fatal, and there was no way of knowing how great a margin of error they possessed. A taxi had halted.

"There are some people looking at us," she said.

"What sort?" he asked.

"I don't know," she answered. "Little men."

"But, darling," he said, and he laughed loudly. Then he put his arm through hers and took her hand. At least he could leave the impression of love and dalliance if anyone was watching. "This country is full of little men. Insufficient food in infancy—and the large intestine of a Japanese is two feet longer than that of his opposite number in Europe. Did you know that?"

"No," she said. "How fascinating!" But she leaned against him and laughed up at him applaudingly.

When they were in the taxicab he put his arm around her. As Bill Gibson had said, there was safety in sex. They had only been two people in love looking for a copy of *Hollywood True Romances*.

"Oh, Jack," she said, and she giggled.

The taxi driver, if anyone asked him, would remember.

"Honey," he said, "I'll get you a nice cool drink in that nice cool bar. Frankly, I can't wait."

But she had been right. He had been a fool to be examining Red literature in Tokyo.

The bar of the Imperial Hotel was aggressively modern and so over-air-conditioned that Jack Rhyce felt for a moment that they were locked inside a refrigerator. They sat next to a sealed plate-glass window that looked out on a small Japanese garden containing a marble bust of an elderly man in the top half of a frock coat. Nearly all the tables were filled, some with prosperous Japanese businessmen, but most with rather weary-looking Europeans who appeared as peculiarly assorted as the English books they had seen exposed for sale. People were looking at them with the friendly curiosity with which foreigners in the Orient regard new strangers. There was nothing professional about anyone there, nothing technically disturbing. It was becoming easier and easier to appear conspicuously interested in Ruth Bogart.

"What would you like, sweet?" he asked, when the bar boy came to the table.

"Scotch on the rocks, darling," she said.

They gazed at each other fatuously for a while after the bar boy left, and then they both begun to laugh, and it was the first time in several weeks that he had been genuinely amused.

"Did you know, sweet," he said, "that rats are very adaptable creatures?"

"Why no, darling," she answered, "but what makes you think of rats?"

"The extreme coldness of this room," he said. "Once when I was crossing the ocean, the ship's captain asked me to a cocktail party. Have you ever been to a ship's captain's cocktail party?"

"Yes, darling," she said. "That's one reason why I travel by air."

"Well, this was a very nice ship's captain," Jack Rhyce said, "and he told an anecdote about a rat. It seems that this rat was locked up by mistake in the ship's refrigerator. He stayed there for four weeks and he didn't freeze to death. When they caught him he had a coat as heavy as mink. That's why I say rats are adaptable."

"Is there any moral to that story?" she asked.

"No," he said, "no. It's just an off-the-record story."

"Well," she said, "it's the first off-the-record story you've ever told to date."

"Yes," he said, "that's so. I'm afraid you're a bad influence on me."

"I hope I am," she said. "I really do, and I hope you'll tell some more."

He realized that he was happy, and happiness was such a rare sensation that he was suspicious of it, but the more he examined his mood, the more certain he was that it was genuine. He could discover no particular reason for it, and he did not particularly care. He only knew that it was something that made the whole day worth while.

"You know," he said, "I think you're a pretty clever girl."

"Why, thanks a lot," she said. "Coming from you, I must be."

The mood had not left him yet. He could even enjoy looking at the bust of the old man in the garden.

"In fact, maybe you are smarter than I am," he said. "You were right about those bookstores."

"I like to have you wrong sometimes," she said. "It shows that maybe you are human."

"Why, thanks a lot," he said, "but believe me, it's better not to be."

She smiled at him, ironically, but very pleasantly.

"You remind me of a poem of Whittier's," she said.

"What poem?" he asked.

"About the boy and the girl at the schoolhouse," she said. " 'I'm sorry that I spelt the word: I hate to go above you, because,'—the brown eyes lower fell,—'Because, you see, I love you!' "

"Yes," he said, "but I don't like what comes later. *Dear girl! the grasses on her grave Have forty years been growing.*"

"I don't like that either," she said, "and I wish you hadn't brought it up."

But even so, nothing changed his mood.

"You know," he said, "I don't see why we shouldn't have a nice time going there tomorrow."

When she smiled at him again, it was exactly as though they were on the outside.

"Please," she said, "please let's, Jack."

IX

Jack Rhyce glanced at his wrist watch as they stood beneath the porte-cochère of the Imperial Hotel. The time was 9:05 exactly. They had brought box luncheons, and they could make a leisurely trip, spending the whole day if they liked. Mr. Moto had done very well with the car. It was a vintage Buick limousine, with the chauffeur's seat separated by glass from the owner's.

"Thirty thousand yen to keep for week end," Mr. Moto said. "Me, automobile, and glass for privacy, everything. It is not too expensive, I hope."

"Oh, no," Jack Rhyce said, "not for this once. Everything's just swell, and here are some yens on account—just so you'll know I've got them, Mr. Moto."

He laughed heartily, and Mr. Moto laughed back. There was one good thing about the business. Money was never an obstacle, and nobody audited expense accounts if you happened to get home. Their suitcases were locked in the trunk behind. Everything was ready.

"All right," he said, "let's go"—and he smiled at Ruth Bogart affectionately for the benefit of the doorman. "That is, if you've remembered everything, sweet?"

"Silly," she said. "Of course I've remembered everything."

The mood of the afternoon before was still with him, and he felt no sensation of tenseness or discomfort. He was sure that they were not being watched or followed, and that they were still in the clear.

"By the way," he said, rolling down the glass partition, "we might stop for a few minutes at the Memorial Temple—the one for the soldiers, I mean. Miss Bogart might like to see it."

113

She looked at him questioningly, but he was sure that he was right about the temple. His asking to go there established them as sightseers, and for some reason the Japanese felt no resentment at Americans visiting the shrine of their war dead. The pine-shaded area of the temple's grounds stood in one of Tokyo's heavily populated districts, making a sharp contrast with the surging traffic on the street outside.

"Wait, please," Jack Rhyce said to Mr. Moto. "We won't be long"—and Mr. Moto smiled.

In plan, the temple was typical of all the shrines of Japan dedicated to the Shinto sect, which was more of a national loyalty than a religion. The arched stone-lined causeway leading to the red-lacquer pavilions, and also the smaller paths that diverged beneath the dark pines, had undoubtedly been adapted, like so much Japanese culture, from early Chinese religious structures; but time had added dignity to this adaptation until Japanese shrines possessed an austere beauty entirely their own. There was a Spartan simplicity in the repression of design, as well as in the repression of the people, mostly elderly, who moved about the grounds, stopping now and then before a pavilion, clapping their hands and bowing their heads in prayer. The ashes of soldiers who had died for the Emperor were preserved there, and where there were not ashes there were names.

"I come here," he said, "because I'm responsible for several of these names."

There was no necessity, he realized, to have given her this explanation.

"How many?" she asked.

"I don't know," he answered. "Twenty-thirty. More, perhaps. You can't always tell everything that a machine gun or a hand grenade does. And you see, most of them preferred to die."

They walked back to the car in silence, and he hoped he had taught her something about Japan that was both important and unfathomable. It was hard to realize that all the city streets had been torn by war, and that every person walking on them had lost some near relation, because the signs of war had almost disappeared, both from

114

Tokyo and the faces of its people. It was valuable to understand that nothing was forgotten.

Even during the journey, Jack Rhyce knew that he would never forget the motor rides to Miyanoshita. It was one of those unrelated lapses that come into one's life when least expected, a sudden unalloyed period of beauty that became something more than memory. It was dangerous to feel as he was beginning to about the girl in the car beside him, but as he looked back over that long day he could not experience a single qualm of regret. Actually there had been no need for any, because there was nothing that he or she could have done about anything until they made contact with Bill Gibson at the hotel that night. There was no necessity to think or plan, and no immediate harm in being beguiled; and besides, all they did was part of the cover.

It was part of the cover to be conscious of her nearness and to hope that the car would soon take another curve so that she would lean against him. It was as though they were both on the outside, that day, and it was more of a fact than an illusion. It was a part of his business to know perfumes. The first instant he had met her he knew that she used Guerlain's and he had identified the variety, but there was nothing technical about the Guerlain any longer. He had immediately recognized her as beautiful, but now everything about her was subjective, not objective any longer, just as it might have been on the outside. The way a draft of air blew a wisp of hair across her forehead was beautiful, and so was the austere perfection of her profile when softened by a smile, and so were the quick gestures of her strong but delicate hands. A pair of white gloves lay across her lap, but she did not wear them, and she wore no rings, no jewelry at all except a plain gold clip.

"It's just as though we were on the outside," he said.

"Yes," she answered, "and please let's keep it that way." And she did not move away when he took her hand.

In a way that ride to Miyanoshita had everything. Later he could unroll it in his memory as one did a Chinese scroll painting, which should be seen in parts and never all at once.

Their ride took them past the area of heavy industry that surrounded Yokohama, then along the sea and finally into the country. Except for the heavy traffic on the roads, the disruptions of the machine age were gone once they reached the country. The thatched farmhouses, the jade-green of the rice plants reflected in the shallow water of the checkerboard squares of the paddies, the bamboo windbreaks, the farmers in their huge straw hats meticulously tending each rice shoot, the jagged mountains in the background were part of an eternal picture of a way of life that could survive all change. Yes, the ride had everything. There was the immense Daibutsu Buddha and the island of Enoshima, with its crowded inns and its shops of seashell ornaments, the scene of the most masterly satire yet written on Japan. *The Honorable Picnic*. This was a book which had been banned before the war, but was now on sale everywhere. Had the war taught the Japanese to laugh at themselves? Like all those questions, there was no definite answer, except that the humor of Japan was as detailed and specialized as its ornamental ivories.

Nothing that Ruth Bogart said or did was discordant. She had great adaptability, but Jack Rhyce was also sure that they both honestly liked the same things and were impressed by the same details. There were two incidents that day that were more vivid than the rest. The first was the sight of two wounded soldiers, on the path leading to one of the shrines at Kamakura. Each had an artificial hand, and each an artificial leg. They were dressed in well-washed khaki without insignia. When he stopped and gave them a fifty-yen note, they came to attention and saluted, and he had returned their salute before he recollected that he was in civilian clothes. They had spotted him as a soldier, too, and for a second all three of them must have been moving into the past. Now that the war was over, there was a lack of resentment impossible for a Westerner to understand.

Then there was the fortuneteller who had his concession just beyond the alms-seeking soldiers, an emaciated elderly man who smiled and beckoned the moment Jack Rhyce and Ruth Bogart betrayed interest. On a stand near him was a miniature red-lacquer temple with three

116

small black-and-yellow birds Perched in front of it—gold-finches, Jack Rhyce believed. He had never been good about birds. But, going back to his early childhood, he remembered tame birds looking just like them that would sing and fly and return to their cage at a whistle. The fortuneteller was clearly used to Americans, because he whipped out from his pocket a typewritten explanation.

"Give any bird a fifty-yen folded note," Jack read. "Bird will drop it in the cash box, fly to temple door, ring bell, enter temple, get fortune on folded paper and bring back same."

"It might be worth fifty yen," Jack said.

"Yes," she said, "but let me pay for it. I want it to be my fortune." She handed the old man a folded note. He held it in front of one of the birds, and just as the explanation said, the bird took it in its beak and dropped it in a tiny money chest.

"Come on, Joe," the old man chanted, "come on Chollie, go on Joe."

The birds and their owner repeated a pattern that Jack Rhyce had seen in nearly every city in the world. That act of fortunetelling must have dated back to temple necromancy, but here the words were new. They had an unfamiliar ring beneath the hot Japanese sky, telling their tale of lonely American soldiers on leave, back at home now, or dead perhaps in Korea.

"Come on Chollie; come on Joe."

The tiny black and yellow bird cocked its head and its beady eye was remarkably intelligent. It fluttered from its perch to a tiny ladder that led to the temple porch. It pushed a small bell smartly with its beak, and the bell tinkled with a miniature clarity that completely rounded out the illusion. Then the bird disappeared inside the toy temple and emerged carrying a folded bit of paper.

Then the bird fluttered back to its perch, and Ruth Bogart took the paper from its beak.

"Don't be afraid to read it," Jack Rhyce said. "They only have good fortunes here."

He had meant to speak lightly, but he was disturbed by her intent look.

"Yes, I know it's rigged," she said, "but I want it to be true."

The strip of paper resembled one of those fortunes that one used to find as a child inside a snapper at a birthday party. She glanced at the words and handed it to him.

"Once you were unhappy," he read, "but you are very happy now."

"That's true, you know," she said. "Absolutely true."

"Well," he told her, "you wanted it to be."

"I don't have to want it. It's here," she said. "And you're happy too, aren't you? I mean for just now?"

"Oh, yes," he said, "I'm happy."

She laughed. She was watching the outlines of the rock pines against the cloudless sky.

"I was afraid you were going to say you were too happy," she said. "I love it when you're not careful, and you haven't been all day."

"If you want to know," he told her, "it's pleasant for a change."

"There's only one catch about it," she said. "It says I'm happy now but it doesn't say how long, and I want it to be long-term. Would you like it long-term?"

She had said she liked it when he was not too careful—and he was not careful then. With her standing close beside him in that place, so far removed from anything that was familiar to either of them, it would have been impossible for him to measure everything he said, and he would have hated himself afterwards if he had done so.

"Yes," he said. "You couldn't possibly know how much I want it that way."

That was all that either of them said, and it was all that was necessary. They both knew that the moment would be transient, but a weight was lifted from him. He felt a grateful relief that he was alive, but this relief had nothing to do with any of the cruder gratitudes for survival that he had experienced more recently. As it happened, neither of them had time to embroider on what they had said, because he heard a footstep behind them before she did, and he was back from the outside to the inside, turning slowly and accurately on his heel. Nothing was ever gained by appearing startled or suspicious.

He did not know that Mr. Moto had followed them until then, nor was there any sure way of telling how long Mr. Moto had been behind them or what he might have heard—not that what they might have said would have affected any situation. There was nothing harder, Jack Rhyce was thinking, than to tread softly on a graveled walk, and only that single footstep had attracted his attention.

"Oh, hello," Jack Rhyce said. "Have we been staying here too long?"

"Oh, no," Mr. Moto said, "but there is still a great distance to go, and many things to see."

"All right," Jack said. He put a slight edge to his words because he wanted to make it clear that he had not approved of that gentle approach. "Go on back to the car. We'll be with you in a minute." When Mr. Moto moved away, Jack Rhyce waited deliberately until the purple suit and tan shoes were a hundred yards in front of them.

"Have you noticed one queer thing about him today?" Ruth Bogart asked.

"I've noticed several," Jack Rhyce said. "Which one did you notice?"

"He said he was a guide," she said, "but all day long he hasn't tried to explain one single thing to us. Did you ever see a guide like that?"

"That's right," he said, "but he's an A-1 driver. He has to be, with all the crazy driving on these roads."

It was one of the few moments when they were both inside that day.

"You're right about his being in the business," she said.

"He was once, anyway," he answered.

"Do you think he knows what we are?" she asked.

"Let's not worry right now," he said. "We'll know better when we see Bill tonight. Let's still try to be happy. I enjoy making the effort, as long as you do, too."

They had been in no hurry, and there were long cool shadows across the road as they began to climb into the hills. The trees of the carefully tended forests that had replaced the rice farms in the landscape were the ginkgo, the feathery cryptomeria, trees that looked out of place when in a Western land, but fitted perfectly into the Japanese landscape. They would be at the hotel at half-past five or six.

There were hot springs at the hotel, and a swimming

119

pool, he told her. The rooms were very comfortable, and the food and service were very good.

"But I'd rather stay at a Japanese inn," he said. "I'll take you to one sometime."

"I'd like it," she said, but he knew she was thinking of something else. "Jack?"

"Yes," he said.

"Jack, will you promise me something?"

"Promise what?" he asked.

"Don't be so cagey," she said. "If we get out of this, let's try to live on the outside. And promise me you'll get out of the business if I don't come back."

"Listen," he said, "have you got a hunch about something, Ruth?"

"No," she said, "no. But I'd like to have you promise before it gets you, Jack."

"Let's talk about it later," he said, "but I'm glad you like me that much."

"Yes, I like you that much," she said.

It must have been at that moment that the peacefulness of the day ended. It was time to drop a curtain on the day and think about the evening, and it was time to heed the warning of common sense. He looked through the plate glass at the back of Mr. Moto's head. The man's age, he was thinking again, was about fifty, but his reflexes were still excellent, and his driving on the switch-back turns of the mountainous road superb. Actually Jack Rhyce had not bothered to see whether the car was wired for sound, because nothing they had said was of any importance except those last speeches, but even a microphone would hardly have carried above the outside noises of the traffic on the heavily traveled road. He heard her laugh beside him.

"Don't worry," she said. "The car's all clean."

If she said so, she was correct, and it was not necessary to ask how she knew, or how she had made the opportunity to find out.

X

The town was on a slope of the winding road that led to
Lake Hakone and, farther, toward the sacred Mount Fuji.
The hot springs and the scenery had made it a resort for a
great many years, patronized by the old nobility and
wealthy people from Tokyo, many of whom had owned
houses there; and the Japanese inns were excellent. The
hotel to which they drove had been designed as a concession to European tastes, long before the war; time, plus
the imagination of its proprietors, had given it an exotic
Eurasian charm. Its grounds on the mountain slope were
watered by rills from natural springs that made a continued merry sound of running water. The season was too
late for the azaleas and some of the exotic blooms, but
the hotel gardens were still very beautiful. The Japanese
had ancient ways with plants and flowers which were different from those of other gardeners. They lavished a
watchful care and patience on every shrub and even on
the surrounding trees, so that everything, even if seemingly wild, was actually in order, even down to the arrangements of wind- and waterworn rocks.

The spirit conveyed by the hotel was agreeable. It had
frankly been designed as a place for a happy holiday, and
it had brought peace and happiness to many travelers.
There were highly European swimming pools and tennis
courts, but the public rooms, stiff with formal furniture,
reminded him that even the most adaptable Japanese had
trouble in selecting suitable assortments of Western
chairs, tables and carpets. Yet in spite of a cleavage in
taste that was hard to bridge, on the whole the hotel had
succeeded; the reason for its success might have been its
rambling informality, growing from a profusion of halls,
staircases, outside galleries and connecting ells that had

121

happy names in English with an Oriental lilt—Plum Blossom Cottage. Cozy Nook. The Peach Bloom.

Due to the crowded week end, the parking spaces along the driveway were already filled with the cars of United States naval and air force personnel, and bellboys clad in white ducks were very busy with the luggage. The day was still warm but the air was cooler and fresher than it had been in Tokyo. Mr. Moto was speaking authoritatively to the Japanese concierge, and Jack Rhyce was contented to hear him say that his passengers were good people who would appreciate attention.

"I will take the car," Mr. Moto said, "but I will call later for orders and to see if all is right."

"You don't have to until tomorrow," Jack Rhyce told him. "It's been a very fine day, and thanks a lot."

The sunlight had grown softer and the shadows longer. He did not need to consult his wrist watch to know it was somewhat before six, but there was still plenty of time before dark to stroll about the grounds and to locate the cottage called Chrysanthemum Rest, where Bill Gibson would be staying. Nevertheless, he was afraid it would take more time than was available to be as familiar as he would wish to be with the halls and connecting passages of the rambling buildings.

"It's a mixed-up place, isn't it?" Ruth Bogart said, as they followed the boy with their bags. Being built on the side of a hill, the hotel had several levels. They were passing through an arcade, lined with display cases of silks, lacquer, ivories and porcelains, and occasionally they encountered a direction arrow pointing to HOT BATHS, MAIN BAR and DINING ROOM.

"Yes," he said, "this would be quite a place to play cops and robbers in, wouldn't it?"

He was ashamed of his lack of caution the instant he said it, but it was not such a bad estimate of the situation. There were many places where you could lose yourself, and too many exits and entrances for one ever to be at ease.

As Bill Gibson had said, a room had been reserved for them, very comfortable, as the clerk anxiously pointed out, with a bath, in a quiet section of the hotel known as Cozy Nook. Jack Rhyce did not know exactly what had been said or through whom the reservation had been made, but he found the solicitude of the clerk disturbing. Still, he only had to tell himself that nobody knew his business better than Bill Gibson in order to set his own mind at rest. When they followed the boy with their luggage along further passageways to the upper level of the hotel, he realized that in spite of years of practice in many places, the ground plan of this building was too much for him, and he greatly disliked the sensation of not being oriented. In consequence, his first task, he told himself, would be to get entrances and exits straight. Also the friendly smiles of the desk clerks had brought home to him again the necessity for cover, since the management seemed to be so clearly aware that he and Ruth Bogart had arrived for an off-the-record week end. Although this could not have struck the hotel staff as unusual for two Americans, it was of the utmost importance to keep up the illusion. And now, facing the prospect, Jack Rhyce encountered in himself an embarrassment that made him very formal, especially when the boy opened the door to a spacious double bedroom. There was a 10 per cent service charge, about which Japanese hotel employees were far more conscientious than their European counterparts, but still he gave a liberal tip and spoke enthusiastically as the boy backed out, bowing.

"This is a nice room, isn't it, dear?" he asked. "I think perhaps I'd better take the bed by the doorway, don't you?"

It did not help his sense of uneasiness to find that she was laughing at him.

"And if you want to bathe or anything," he said, "I'll go out for half an hour and stroll around. The hot water comes directly from a hot spring, I believe, in case you'd like to know."

"Listen," she said, "you've traveled around considerably, haven't you? Haven't you ever been alone in a hotel bedroom with a girl before?"

"Well, yes," he said, "occasionally, now you ask me, but not exactly in this way, Ruth."

"Well," she said, "I don't see such a great difference and don't take it so seriously, for heaven's sake, even if

123

your father was a missionary. I'm going to take a bath, and you'd better, too. Do you snore, darling?"

"No," he told her, and he lowered his voice, "you ought to know I don't; not in this business, Ruth."

She tossed her suitcase on the bed next to the wall and snapped it open. The easy way that she moved her luggage showed that she was much stronger than she looked.

"For heaven's sake," she said, but she lowered her voice just as carefully as he had, "the more we forget the business while we're in here, the better. Darling, aren't you going to give me a kiss or anything, after you've brought me all this way?"

She raised her voice when she asked that last question and looked at him meaningly.

"Why, dear," he said, "I've been waiting for this for hours."

"Oh, darling," she said, and then she whispered, "there's someone in the hall outside. We have the privacy of goldfish in this room."

His first instinct was to tiptoe to the door and snatch it open, but she held him and shook her head.

"No, no," she whispered, "maybe it isn't anything, but we'd better act damned silly. I think this place is spooky, Jack."

She was right about the room. There was a transom above the door and he especially disliked transoms. Two windows at the foot of the twin beds, both of them open now, looked over the carefully tended grounds at the rear of the hotel. The third window in the bathroom with ground glass obviously opened on the corridor, and now that the bathroom door was open, a sound of footsteps made a rhythmic beat along the corridor's jute carpet. They were the staccato steps of an Oriental, one of the hotel boys, he was very certain. Nevertheless, he quickly closed the bathroom door.

"Thanks," he said. "I seem to be losing my grip, what with one thing and another."

It was a mistake, he realized immediately, to have said such a thing out loud. He believed in holding a positive thought; as soon as one became overworried and overanxious, accidents frequently occurred. He stepped to the open window, examined the shades and curtains and then

124

made a thorough inventory of the bedroom, which would have been unusually attractive under other circumstances. The Japanese prints on the wall seemed surprisingly good, although he was not a connoisseur of that sort of thing: pictures of strange bent-kneed men with staffs and heavy burdens on their backs, climbing mountains, crossing narrow-arched bridges, or laboring on farmsteads. The curtains that could be drawn before the windows were of heavy cotton, green and yellow with the bamboo motif so favored by Japanese textile designers. The twin beds with comfortable box-spring mattresses were in simple European taste, matching the large mirrored bureau and the taller dresser. Each was covered with a yellowish green spread of raw silk, and the walls had a matching greenish tint. Whoever had decorated the room had good taste. But there was one disturbing feature. The lock on the door was an old and clumsy contraption which any well-trained operator could pick in a matter of seconds. The bathroom was commodious, and the tub, made out of marble slabs, gave it an old-fashioned charm.

Ruth Bogart had turned on the bathtub taps and the noise of the running water made a cheerful sound.

"I suppose we'll have to look nice but informal," she said, "if we're going to that dance." She was taking out clothing from her neatly packed bag. "I'll wear my light green silk."

"Better put on the dark green or a dark blue if you have it," he told her. "Remember, we are going to go outside."

"Right, I forgot," she said. "I wonder whether Gibson's got here yet."

"That's his problem," he told her. "I'm going out to walk around while you take your bath."

"You don't have to, you know," she said, "and I wish you'd put on something else besides that seersucker suit."

"I'll put on my blue one tonight," he said, "but haven't you noticed that everyone who does kind things for backward peoples customarily wears a seersucker suit?"

"Oh, dear," she said, and she smiled at him. "I wish we were really staying here and that there could be just two people in this room instead of four. I'm sick of split personalities."

She was still unpacking and hanging things in the bedroom closet as though they were going to stay there for an indefinite period. Her confident unpacking and the running water in the bath contrived to make a new bond in their relationship. The voices from the hotel guests came gaily through the open windows from the grounds outside. People were calling to each other at the swimming pool; army and navy mothers called to their children, and single men far away from home talked to their sweethearts. It was a tolerant hotel, a long way from anywhere, both moral and amoral, but agreeably enough the voices all sounded happy. Up by the swimming pool someone was singing, and then in the distance someone began whistling a tune that made Jack look at Ruth Bogart.

Both their faces had assumed their old watchful look because it was the tune they had last heard before the break of day at Wake Island.

> *You cannot see in gay Paree, in London or in Cork!
> The queens you'll meet on any street in old New York.*

"Well, well," he said softly, "our old favorite, isn't it?"

There was no reason, his common sense told him, to be unduly startled. The melodies from *The Red Mill* were always cropping up on modern records, and they were good, despite the lapse of time.

"It's no favorite of mine," she said. "I told you this place was spooky."

There was no one outside whom he recognized—only a stream of tennis players and of bathers coming down from the pool to dress for dinner.

"Well," he said, "go ahead and take your bath. I'd better go down there and see what I can see."

She shook her head emphatically.

"I'm not going to stay here alone," she said. "I'll go right down with you, and go dirty. That damn song. Frankly, it makes me frightened."

They walked around the grounds for a while, arm in arm, hanging on each other's words, laughing at each other's jests. They walked up the hill to the swimming pool, which was almost deserted now that the sun was

126

low. They observed the empty tennis courts and the hotel greenhouses with their potted azaleas and their cyclamen and fuchsias. They stood in the shade of a giant cryptomeria which must have been at least four hundred years old. They wandered heedlessly past Chrysanthemum Rest—a small cottage, which sure enough was not much more than a hundred and fifty feet away from the ballroom ell. Bill Gibson could not have picked a better place for a private conversation because, as he had said, the noise of the orchestra would drown out anything else. Then they stopped at the fish pond and watched children feeding bread crumbs to the giant goldfish.

"You know," she said, "I wouldn't mind being a fish myself, right now. No wonder they live a hundred years."

"Don't wish that, sweet," he said loudly enough so that everyone could hear, because there was safety in sex. "Just compromise and be a mermaid."

"All right, if you say so," she answered, "you old seadog, you."

He gave an involuntary shudder at her remark, but still, the cover was not so bad as he thought it was going to be.

"Just don't overplay," he whispered to her amorously.

"All right," she said, "you old seadog, you." And then she laughed.

There was reassurance in her laughter; it meant that, like him, she had noticed nothing out of the ordinary. All they saw were happy people, young, carefree, many of them handsome, all concerned only with each other. It was very much like another musical comedy song—"Love is Sweeping the Country"—at that kindly hotel at sunset.

"Hold my hand," she said. "It looks better, and now maybe we'd better go up and get ready for dinner."

"Let's go to that place called the Main Bar," he said. "We haven't seen it, and there may be something new there."

The Main Bar was on the hotel's lower level. The inspiration for its decoration must have been derived from foreign influence close to the turn of the century, because it had the earmarks of another happier age, and its spiritual quality, if such a thing could be attributed to a bar,

127

was remarkable close to the music of Victor Herbert. Its dark woodwork was like the Old New York where the peach crop was always fine. Its comfortable chairs and tables were not crowded too closely together. The bar itself, with its magnificent array of glass, was almost as long and hospitable as the now mythical bar in Shanghai that was once believed to be the longest bar in the world. The only concession to a changing world lay in the new bar stools, those importations from the French *bistro* that had reached America at the end of Prohibition. A dozen happy couples, now that the dinner hour was approaching, were taking over the tables in groups of fours and twos, and several unaccompanied men were seated at the bar. Still, the room was large enough so that it gave a quiet, half-empty impression; the voices of its patrons were partially absorbed by its spaciousness.

"It's awfully Gothic, isn't it?" she said. "Like a church."

"I'm not carried away by the resemblance," he told her. He beckoned to a waiter. "Would you like a gin and tonic, dear?"

They had selected a table in a far corner from which the whole room was visible. He was already giving the people a mental screening even while he was thinking that he was tired of this sort of watchful analysis.

"Scotch and water," she answered, "and I hope we can get bathed and ready for dinner pretty soon. Everybody here looks very cool and comfortable, and though you're smarter than I am, I can't locate any types."

"Don't try too hard. Don't forget we're in love," he said. He leaned back and sipped his drink. She was right that there was no one who showed interesting signs. If it had not been for that tune, he would have believed that the place was wholly antiseptic, and of course Bill Gibson must have thought so, too, or he would not have named it as a contact point.

"That's right," she said. "I've got to keep remembering. You look handsomer tonight than you did yesterday, but you could do with a clean shirt, and I'd like it, at any rate, if you could get your seersucker suit pressed."

"Oh, don't say that," he told her. "It makes me look

128

informal, feeble and good-natured. Nobody cares what happens to a man in a seersucker suit."

"I care at the moment," she said, "if only because I don't want to be left alone in this rat-race. Oh, Jack! Look across the room."

His glance followed hers to the entrance by the bar.

"Well, well," he said; "now things are looking up."

He had to admit that he felt as Livingstone and Stanley must have when they encountered each other in the interior of Africa. At least things were moving according to plan, because Bill Gibson had entered the room, and there was no mistaking what Bill was. He was a tired, middle-aged American exporter from Tokyo out for a good time over the week end. He was obviously having one, and he must have had a good time at the hotel on previous occasions because he waved to a group at one table and sat down with a couple at another, putting his arm playfully around the girl's waist.

"Where's Dorothy?" they heard him say. "Why didn't you bring Dorothy?"

No one in the business was more consummate than Bill Gibson. In fact, his appearance gave Jack Rhyce a slight spasm of professional envy. Bill's loud Aloha shirt was art. The paunchy roll of his walk and the slump of his shoulders were beautiful. He sauntered in an aimless way about the room, just as a lonely man with a few drinks should. He walked close by the table where Jack and Ruth Bogart sat, and Jack was exasperated by the obviousness of the contact. Bill was his senior in the business, but that was no reason to treat his junior like an amateur with such a clumsy check-in. For a second Jack thought he might be given some sort of signal, but nothing in Bill's expression changed as he passed the table, no warning gesture, no signal of anxiety. The truth was that Bill Gibson could not have noticed anything off color either, or he would not have moved so carelessly. His face was flushed as though he had been in the sun by the swimming pool. His jowls had their old purplish tinge, his eyes their deceptive glazed expression. He passed their table and ambled to the bar, hoisted himself on one of the stools; Jack heard him calling happily:

"Another Scotch and soda, and make it a double this time, Boy-san."

"Listen," Ruth Bogart said, "school's out now, isn't it? Can't we please go up and get a bath?"

"You go ahead," Jack Rhyce said. "Maybe I ought to stick around here a few minutes."

"No," she answered. "All those corridors . . . I won't go up there alone."

"Now, listen," he began, "I don't think there's a cough in a carload here." And then he checked himself, and his voice dropped to a whisper. "Fasten your seat belt," he whispered, "and for God's sake let's be natural. Boy!" He raised his voice and waved to the bar waiter. "Two more, please. You'll have another, won't you, dear?"

"Oh," she said, "yes, if you'd honestly like me to get tight, darling."

XI

She was a good girl, back in the act again. She had glanced for only a fraction of a second at the doorway to the bar, but the instant had been long enough for her to see what he had seen. There was no mistaking the sandy hair, the bushy eyebrows, the clear-eyed glance, the easy walk, the lazily swinging arms, and the characteristic half bend of the fingers of the man who had just entered. Once you had seen Big Ben, you could not miss him. He was wearing khaki trousers, army issue, and he, too, wore an Aloha shirt, and even in that moment of impact Jack Rhyce made a mental note that the shirt had a fish design similar to the shirt of Mr. Harry Pender at the Asia Friendship League.

"The fish," she whispered.

"Yes," he answered. "For God's sake let's be 'natural.' ... You look awfully sweet tonight, honey."

After all, there were plenty of fish designs on plenty of Aloha shirts, but still there was the coincidence. He saw Bill Gibson at the bar tossing off his double Scotch and soda. Bill had the description and Bill never missed anything. He must have seen, of course; he and Jack Rhyce must both have shared the same surprise and consternation, and also the same exalted sense you always had when the game was getting hot—because anything might happen now, anything, or nothing. It was unsafe to rely on intuition, and just as unsafe to discount it absolutely, but things had gone beyond the intuitive stage in Jack Rhyce's reasoning. The coincidences had gone so far that there was scarcely a reasonable doubt any longer that the man was Big Ben. His appearance at the hotel at just this time confirmed the fact. Bill Gibson's mind must have been moving in the same channels, but he continued drinking his whisky without a glance at the doorway. After all, there was nothing else to do. There was only one question hanging in the air, unanswered by the voices around them: *How much did Big Ben know?* Did he know who Bill Gibson was? Did he know who they were? There as no immediate answer to those questions, but very soon there was bound to be one.

There was bound to be because, as Big Ben stood by the door, their glances met, and Jack saw that he had recognized them. He could feel it in the nerves of his neck before his reason confirmed the fact. The light was on Big Ben and as far as Jack could see there was no blankness or surprise. The face was mobile. Honest pleasure rippled over it. The corners of the wide, expressive mouth turned upward, yet that was not all. Big Ben waved to them from across the room. Jack Rhyce waved back and beckoned, at the same time lifting his gin and tonic glass.

"Darling," he said loudly, "just look who's coming over! Ships that pass in the night, darling!" And then he lowered his voice, "Don't forget, for God's sake, that we're in love."

Big Ben sauntered toward them. Jack did not like to think that the physical sensation he experienced was one of fear; in fact, he was fairly convinced that it was not. It was rather a state of intense warning and watchfulness that set all his perceptions at concert pitch, with the result that he had seldom experienced such complete awareness. It might have been his mood, which Ruth Bogart had detected when she had told him once not to take it too big, but he was not unsure of himself. There was nothing easier to detect than over-anxiety or overinquisitiveness, but he knew that he would not overplay. All that bothered him was the perennial pitfall of an unconsidered word or gesture; there was nothing which could prevent this contingency except hoping for the best. He pushed back his chair and stood up, smiling.

"Well, hello, troops," Big Ben said.

"Why, hello yourself," Jack Rhyce said. "If it isn't our sweet singer from Wake. Remember, Ruth? *In old New York! In old New York!*"

He was even able to put the lilt of the tune in his voice.

"I certainly do remember," Ruth Bogart said. She

smiled in just the right way, invitingly, but at the same time not seekingly. "It was terribly romantic out there before dawn, and you had such a lovely voice."

"Gee, thanks," Big Ben said. "It was quite a surprise to me to hear the *boy friend* . . ." He underlined the words with gentle humor, and smiled tolerantly at them.

"Oh, now," Jack Rhyce said, "come. What an implication! We were just out for a stroll at Wake, weren't we, Ruth?"

". . . to hear the boy friend," Big Ben repeated with a chuckle, "answer right back from nowhere—it almost made me jump out of my swim trunks."

"We certainly owe you a drink if I did that," Jack said. "Take a chair and take the weight off your feet, and give your order to the waiter. It ought to be a double or a triple for a boy as big as you."

"Aw, come on," Big Ben said, and his hands relaxed on the table in front of him and he smiled at them both. "You're not such a peewee yourself, fella. I'll bet you played football in your time."

"Is that so?" Jack said. "Well, you win. Mr. Holmes, I played right half for Oberlin. Where did you play?"

"Oh, shucks," Big Ben said. "I was never in the big time like that. I only played for a jerk-water Southern Baptist college."

His words trailed off apologetically, and then he gave his order to the waiter.

"You savvy what's called Bloody Mary, Boy-san? Vodka and tomato juice, nice and cold and big. Sorry, folks, if I'm unconventional, but you see, this is my playtime."

Jack had never watched or listened more carefully, but he could detect no flaw. The Baptist college explained that Southern accent; there was no uneasiness anywhere. He could assume very safely now that he and Ruth were accepted for what they appeared to be and that they were in the clear. He was so sure of this that he had to fight down a rising sense of elation, because they were in an advantageous position as long as the position lasted.

"Seriously," Jack Rhyce said, "this is a real pleasure, meeting you. I suppose we ought to introduce ourselves. My name's Rhyce—Jack Rhyce, and this is Ruth Bogart.

133

We're just traveling through—out here to make a survey for one of these foundations."

"Oh, yes," Big Ben said. "Seems you mentioned the name of it back there at Wake. Seems to me it had the name of Friendship in it."

"You really have some memory," Jack Rhyce said, "and it's mighty flattering that we made such an impression on you during our brief visit. The name's the Asia Friendship League."

"That's it," Big Ben said. "Say, it's a pleasure to meet you two nice people again, Jack Rhyce and Ruth Bogart. My name's Ben Bushman. Just old Flight Engineer Bushman, at the present time. Our crew lays over at Tokyo about ten days out of every month, and Bushman comes up here for ease and relaxation." He chuckled happily. "Just the way Jack Rhyce and Ruth Bogart have come up to study Asia Friendship. Am I right, or am I right?"

"Well now, I don't exactly know how to answer that one," Jack Rhyce said. He laughed self-consciously, and so did Ruth Bogart.

"But you must admit it is a friendly place here, Mr. Bushman," she said, and smiled at him dazzlingly.

"Now, now, honey," Big Ben said, "let's cut out the Bushman part. You call me Ben, and just remember I'm tolerant as hell, and I don't blame Jack here, for one minute, but any time if two isn't company and there isn't a crowd, just kind of look around for me, will you? We might sing some old songs, or something. I'm nuts for old songs."

"Why, that will be splendid, Ben," Ruth Bogart said. "Jack loves old songs, too, and he has a lovely voice, if I do say so . . . but if he gets preachy or tiresome, I'll know where to turn, and two will still be company, won't it. Ben?"

"Oh, now, Ruth," Jack Rhyce said. He wished that her flirtatiousness did not sound so genuine, but she was right as far as the business went. "I'm not as bad as all that, am I? But she's right, Ben. I do like a jam session sometimes."

"Well, maybe we can have one tonight," Big Ben said. "There's always a few groups here who like to sing, later in the evening. Just drop down here into the bar sometime later, say eleven—that is, if you haven't something better to do."

He smiled in a very friendly way.

"Oh, come," Jack Rhyce said, "you mustn't kid us, Ben."

Big Ben slapped him affectionately on the shoulder and stood up.

"I'm not kidding you, boy," he said, "I'm envying you. Well, see you later, I hope. And now I've got to be gittin'."

"What's your hurry?" Jack said. "Have another drink. Don't go."

Big Ben shook his head.

"Thanks," he said, "but I want to get cleaned up for this dancing party, and maybe I can find a girl myself. You two make me lonely. Well, I'll see you later, troops."

Jack Rhyce heard Ruth Bogart sigh. He drew a deep breath himself, but his abnormal consciousness of life and motion was still with him as he watched Big Ben. The man's walk was lazily loose-jointed, but at the same time perfectly coordinated. It was the gait of the highly proficient all-round athlete who could move from an eight-oar shell to the tennis courts, the boxing ring, the baseball diamond, or the football field with no need for conscious adjustment. You could not help admiring him because he was aesthetically magnificent. He sauntered past the bar without stopping, shoulders carelessly squared and arms swinging easily. If Bill Gibson had not seen him come in, Bill had surely seen him by now. Jack's first instinct was to deliver some sort of warning, but this would have been superfluous, and besides it had become more important than ever that neither he nor Ruth Bogart should be connected with Bill Gibson. Things were moving so fast that everything at any moment might pour itself into a barrel and go over Niagara Falls.

"It was all so natural, wasn't it?" she said, and her words echoed exactly what he had been thinking.

That conversation with Big Ben had been so frank and real, so entirely in keeping with the guises they had assumed, and so banal and dull, that he could nearly believe that it had been true, but actually it had been interwoven with threads of truth. Football at Oberlin, song fests be-

135

cause both of them honestly loved to sing, and even his growing interest in Ruth Bogart had all contributed to honesty. That piece about the Southern Baptist college was especially appealing. It was the one bit of really tangible revelation that had come through to him; its hidden tones had been touching in their frankness. It had all been small-time, Big Ben said, and Jack Rhyce could recall a lingering note of sadness. The Baptist college must have been true, just as there must have been some sort of social frustration there similar to what everyone faced in one's adolescent years, and to which most people had learned to adjust. There had been something in that unknown Southern Baptist college that Big Ben could not handle yet, although later he had traveled to more sophisticated fields. Jack Rhyce could see the place in his imagination. Small institutions for higher learning were apt to have a dreary similarity in the South. He could imagine a quadrangle of decrepit dormitories, a chapel in bad repair, a lecture hall, a tiny library with its carefully culled collection of deserving books, a football field with its goal posts and bare bleachers, and long-needled pines covering a flat sandy country in the background. It all could have fitted into the composition of a Benton picture. The pinch of poverty would be over it, but at the same time lines of social demarcation would be etched more strongly by the poverty, making them far harsher than any differentiations existing in the North. Distinction would be more than just the other side of the tracks in such a place; there was a quality in Big Ben's voice and gait that told its own story. *White trash* was the name for it, that unhappy phrase which was applied to people living in the clearings behind the pine-grown old fields, who had not solved for generations any of their economic problems. No matter what he had done at football, no matter about his singing town or in a great city. As he put the theoretical story to-voice, Big Ben had been white trash once; and it was not hard to project imagination further, and see him in a mill gether. Jack Rhyce believed that the Chief in Washington had been right, if not about the missionary, at least about the religious background. Big Ben's father might very possibly have been one of those itinerant preachers. The contagion of pulpit inflection still remained in Big Ben's voice. It was a hymn-singing voice which Jack Rhyce could readily identify, since in many ways he and Big Ben had sprung from a common background, sharing many of the same repressions and simplicities. A minister's son could spot a minister's son. The saying was not wholly a joke.

He felt her hand on his arm, shaking him insistently.

"Darling, you've got to talk to me," she said—"that is, if we're going to keep sitting in this damn place, or else if you keep sitting like a wooden Indian everybody will begin to think we've had a fight. What have you been thinking about, Jack?"

"You ought to know," he said, "about You-Know-Who, and you needn't have given him such a big glad eye."

"You-Know-Whom, you mean," she said. "At least you don't know everything, do you, Fearless Fosdick?"

"Maybe Fosdick knows a little about You-Know-Whom," he said.

"And maybe Miss Fosdick does, too," she answered, "and Miss Fosdick knows she can make him in about five minutes, if necessary. Maybe we should have registered as Mr. and Mrs. Fosdick. Do you think he was poor white trash, Jack?"

The mere fact that their minds had reached the same place independently gave his theory added substance.

"Yes," he said, "I shouldn't wonder. I didn't know you knew the South."

"There were Southern girls in boarding school," she said. "My roommate was a Southern girl—deep South, very deep. People like him are apt to go off the track somewhere. I ought to know, because I've been off myself. Were you ever off it?"

"I was on two drops into Burma during the war," he said. "There weren't any tracks at all there. I'm sort of used to being off the rails."

They were leaning toward each other, ostensibly absorbed in each other's words, and they had waited long enough in the bar. They both had known, without saying so, that they should not leave the place directly on Big Ben's heels. Jack signaled to a waiter, and paid the check.

"Well," she said, "thank goodness. Does this mean we

can bathe and change? Or have you got some other thought?"

The double bedroom, as she had said, afforded all the privacy of a goldfish bowl.

"Anyway," he said, "we may be able to talk with your bath water running."

"And we can talk with me splashing in it," she said. "You don't have to look, but I'm going to have a bath."

They were another eager happy couple when they left the bar, as they walked hand in hand following the signs along the hotel corridor that pointed to the ell called Cozy Nook.

"You know, darling," he told her, "I was just thinking of another one of those *Red Mill* songs. Ben might just as well have sung it at Wake."

"Oh, sing it now, dear," she said, "softly, just for me."

He drew her closer to him. They made a very pretty abstraction, flushed with their drinks from the Main Bar, on their way to Cozy Nook.

> *Not that you are fair, dear,*
> *Not that you are true,*
> *Not your golden hair, dear,*
> *Not your eyes of blue.*

He stopped and laughed.

"It doesn't fit, does it?" he said. "Your hair is too dark, dear, and your eyes are grayish green."

"Never mind," she said. "I approve of the general scheme. Go ahead and finish it."

As a matter of fact, when he finished it he approved of the general scheme himself.

> *When we ask the reason,*
> *Words are all too few!*
> *So I know I love you, dear,*
> *Because you're you.*

"I wish to goodness," she said, and her voice had a catch in it, "that I could be me again, or I, or whatever damn way you want to have it."

138

It was the old lament again, and there was no solution to it, or certainly not then. Besides, there was not time to discuss it then because they had reached their room door, and he was pulling the clumsy outmoded key from his coat pocket.

"Why, say," he said in the bemused tone that one should use after a session with the girl of one's choice at the Main Bar, "it's unlocked. I thought I'd locked it. Didn't you think I had, honey?"

"Why, yes, darling," she answered. "I kind of thought so." And then she giggled. "But I did have other things on my mind."

"Well, it all goes to show," he said, "that I'm losing my memory in my old age."

They both laughed like two college freshmen. Then they hastily opened the door, using the standard Farm precautions.

Mr. Moto was standing in the center of the room. The dust had been brushed from his light tan oxfords, his purplish blue suit had been freshly pressed. Jack Rhyce was not entirely surprised to see him, but he hoped that he acted surprised. The illusion was helped when Ruth Bogart suppressed a startled scream that sounded technically genuine.

"Well, how the hell did you get in here?" Jack Rhyce asked, assuming the correct badgering tone of an honest American dealing with a wily Oriental.

"So sorry," Mr. Moto said, and Jack Rhyce was interested to see that his hands shook with artificial agitation. "The door was unlocked. So sorry."

The door had not been unlocked, and it was a safe assumption that Mr. Moto knew he knew it. The only solution for the problem was to become more confused, to raise one's voice a hectoring octave higher.

"And if the door was unlocked—so what?" Jack Rhyce said. "Does that mean you should walk inside?"

"Excuse," Mr. Moto said, and his hands fluttered placatingly, "but the door was wide open. More better, I thought, to wait for your return. Then things would not be stolen. Such old-fashioned doors in this hotel."

"That's funny," Jack Rhyce said in a more reasonable tone. "I thought I'd locked that door, but you never can

139

tell, can you? Anyway, it doesn't look as if anybody had got into the suitcases, and you had your handbag down at the bar with you, didn't you, sweet?"

"Yes," Ruth Bogart said. "My gold clip would have been the only thing that really mattered anyway. I think it was very thoughtful of Mr. Moto to wait here for us."

He wished to heaven that he could place Mr. Moto, who was becoming an annoyingly loose end to the problem.

"Of course I'm grateful to Mr. Moto too, sweet," he said. "I was only sort of startled at first, seeing him there, that's all. Excuse it, Mr. Moto. What did you want to see me for?"

Mr. Moto bobbed his head and rubbed his hands together. Once more Jack Rhyce had the impression of a character that was too Japanese to be true.

"First, may I ask you if all is right here, and proper?" Mr. Moto asked.

It did not alleviate Jack Rhyce's frustration when Ruth Bogart giggled softly at the word "proper." He even wondered whether Mr. Moto had used it intentionally, but then "proper" was a favorite Oriental word with many shades of meaning.

"Everything is swell, thanks," he answered.

"And your wishes for tomorrow?" Mr. Moto asked. "So many things to see. Might I suggest a picnic and a ride toward the base of Mount Fuji? And Lake Hakone is so very beautiful. But this means start early."

If it wasn't one problem, it was another. In the light of recent events, he should have rented a car and driven it himself, so that it would have been parked outside the hotel at all hours, if they needed to get away, but now his mobility was controlled by the Japanese in front of him. Bill Gibson, he was thinking, would not approve of what he had done about the car.

"I tell you what," he said. "You be waiting outside with the car at seven o'clock tomorrow morning, and then we'll decide what we want to do."

"Seven o'clock," Mr. Moto repeated, and Jack Rhyce could not tell whether it was a repetition or a question. It was a ridiculously early hour, out of keeping with a

140

peaceful week end, but it might be that they would badly need the car.

"Maybe it's a little early," Jack said, "but I was thinking we might climb some of the mountains." He smiled at Ruth Bogart affectionately. "You want to see as much of everything as you can, don't you, dear—that is, if you're not too sleepy in the morning?"

"Jack," she said, "I honestly don't know how I'll feel in the morning."

Jack Rhyce smiled at her patiently.

"Of course, dear, if you don't feel like it in the morning," he said, "we can change everything. But it won't hurt to have him here early, just in case, now will it?"

"All right," she said, "as long as it's just in case."

"Well, that's settled," Jack Rhyce said, smiling in a man-to-man way at Mr. Moto. "Let's make it eight, and thanks, and forgive anything I said about your being in the room. I'll see the door's locked next time."

XII

He stood close to the closed door listening to the sound of Mr. Moto's footsteps retreating down the hall in a clumsy noisy rhythm wholly different from the soft step on the gravel by the temple. The footsteps indicated as plainly as words that Mr. Moto knew he would be listening. Ruth Bogart crossed the room, making a quick noiseless check of the suitcases. She shook her head as a signal that nothing had been disturbed. He moved to the window and peered out. The afterglow had left the sky, and the electric lights had been turned on along the paths of the hotel grounds. He drew the curtains carefully.

"Turn on the water in the tub," he whispered.

"Oh, Jack," she called as she turned the water on, "hasn't it been a wonderful day, darling?"

It was not the right adjective to describe it, and besides, the day was only just beginning. She moved close to him and rested her head on his shoulder, and he was glad to put his arms around her. He had seldom felt so grateful for companionship.

"My God," she said, "it's really started now."

"Yes," he said, "it's moving. What do you know about Skirov?"

"Skirov . . ." she repeated vaguely.

He could not blame her much when her whole mind must have been on the present.

"Yes," he said. "Skirov, the Russian who's running the Communist show here—the masterminder whom our boy makes contact with. The Chief briefed you on him, didn't he?"

"Oh, yes," she said. "I'm sorry, Jack. I was thinking about the Jap and the big goon down in the bar and ev-

142

erything. Yes, Skirov. I saw him in Vienna once—Cossack descent, I think."

"You saw him?" Jack Rhyce said. "Then you can tell me if I have his description straight. Middle forties, five feet five, one hundred twelve, thin, agile, delicate hands and feet, Mongoloid features."

"Yes," she said, "that's him."

Jack Rhyce lowered his voice, not because he was afraid of being overheard, but because he dreaded that his idea might not be right.

"All right," he said, "what about this Moto? Is he Skirov playing a Jap?"

He was conscious of his anxiety while he waited for her reaction. It had been one of those swift inspirations which he had learned to suspect, but if he were right, they might be able to end the show that evening, because they would have worked out the whole scheme of the apparatus. It would be Gibson's job to make the ultimate decision regarding Skirov, but from their point of view, the mission would be accomplished. The prospect of completing a mission always had its alluring side; he had never before been so desperately anxious to end one, not so much because of himself as because of her.

She was still considering his question. Her forehead was wrinkled and she gazed straight ahead of her. He was aware both of her nearness and her beauty, which annoyed him because his mind should have been concentrated on abstractions.

Finally she looked up at him, not enthusiastically, but with respect.

"I guess I was wrong in thinking that big handsome boys like you are dumb," she said. "I like your thought. I wish I could buy it all."

He had already developed the thought further, while she was speaking.

"Maybe it's more reasonable than it sounds at first," he said. "Take it this way." He began to speak in a whisper, in spite of the running water. "They looked us over in San Francisco. They've got us down as innocent bystanders. They think we're absolutely pure."

"Yes," she said. "I check with that. I think we're clear to date. I had that feeling in the bar."

"Right," he said, and his enthusiasm rose. "Then what could be better than using us as a cover? Wouldn't you do it if you were on their side of the fence? Skirov and Big Ben want to meet. They know we're greenhorns. What's better than having Skirov as a Japanese chauffeur? That explains his being in the room—just to make a final check." He stopped and laughed quietly.

"What's so funny?" she asked.

"The two contacts," he said. "Us doing the same thing—coming up here for a meeting. It's like a convention in Atlantic City, isn't it?"

"Yes," she said, but she did not look amused. "It's funny if true. The trouble is, it's too good to be true. Life isn't made that way. It's too damned easy, darling."

Her criticism confirmed his own inner dread. She was right, that life never ran that way, and nothing ever came easy in the business.

"Besides, Jack," she said, "he simply isn't Skirov."

"You don't know Japs as well as I do," he answered. "This one's like something on the stage."

"I've got eyes too, dear," she said. "Perhaps he's trying to hide his rank or education, but I know he isn't Skirov."

"Well, if he isn't," Jack Rhyce asked, "who is he?"

She shook her head slowly, and her expression reminded him of the Whittier's poem about the schoolhouse.

"It's too bad—because it fits—but he just isn't," she said. "He's in the business, all right; I can spot that as well as you can—but he isn't Moscow-trained. You know he isn't, darling. You know how that Moscow school sticks out all over them. You can spot them a mile away, as easily as you can a German Volkswagen. Skirov is a Moscow boy. This one just isn't."

Jack Rhyce sighed.

"All right," he said. "But I still want Bill Gibson's reaction. Since you can spot them—what about Big Ben? Was he on the Moscow squad?"

"Yes," she said.

"I don't agree," he said. "But what makes you think so?"

"You'd have noticed it in the bar," she said, "if you hadn't been concentrating on the dialogue, darling. That Paul Robeson, Old Man River manner, that lift-that-bale, we'll-all-land-in-jail manner. It's late Moscow. It's still being taught there by their prewar American imports. They must have rather a quaint American section."

"I've got to watch him some more," Jack said. "He doesn't look much like it to me. He looks as American as all get-out."

He wanted to go on and tell her about his reconstruction of Big Ben's college days, but it would have to wait until later.

"Of course he's as American as all get-out," she said. "A lot of very American Americans have gone to Moscow. Jack Reed went and he's in the Red Square now, if they haven't moved him. Now unzip my dress, will you? I'm going to have that bath, but I'll leave the door open, if you have any more ideas."

He had a number of ideas as he sat in an easy chair near the window and listened to her splashing in the tub, but he had learned long ago that it was folly to spread ideas around. No one should ever know more than necessary in the business; the less you knew the less you could tell if they caught you. It occurred to him that he should not even have told her his idea about Skirov. His having done so went to show that he was talking too much, and besides he might be obliged to revise all his thinking after his meeting with Bill Gibson. Bill would have the whole story straight, while he and Ruth Bogart were still only on the fringes of it. Nevertheless, he was already getting his general shape and structure so clearly that a question of policy was beginning to arise. Should the apparatus be smashed, or should it be left alone in the hope of locating Skirov? But Bill Gibson, not he, would make the ultimate decision. The main thing was to get the picture straight.

He wished that he did not have to see Bill Gibson that night, now that the dangers of the meeting had measurably increased with Big Ben on the scene. However, the importance of an immediate meeting had increased correspondingly, but now the contact must be made more carefully than ever. The room was growing dark. He rose and switched on the light that stood on the small table separating the twin beds.

"Jack," she called, "are you all right?"

"Yes," he said, "I'm fine."

"I thought you were going to tell me some new ideas."

"You know that's bad technique, to tell too much," he said; "and you know the reason, Ruth."

"Yes," she said, "I know."

She was out of the bathroom, brushing her hair by the mirror with quick, brisk, almost savage strokes. She was wearing an oldish cotton print robe.

"I'll buy you a kimono tomorrow," he said. "You'd look well in a kimono, green and blue."

"Thanks," she said, "I'm sorry about the thing I have on. I didn't know there was going to be a bedroom scene. I've started your bath for you."

"Thanks," he said. He began taking things from his suitcase, putting his brushes and toilet articles on the tall dresser, laying his blue suit carefully over the foot of the bed and his dark black shoes with their composition soles on the floor beneath it. Both he and she were neat as pins, as you were bound to be in the business.

"I was thinking about tonight," he said.

"Were you?" she said. "Well, you aren't the only one."

They looked at each other thoughtfully for a second.

"You know you're right about that goon," he said. "From the way he looked at you I think maybe you could take Big Ben—if you keep on ecouraging him."

"Yes, I know I can," she answered.

"But at the same time it makes me mad," he said. "But maybe it's a good thing for tonight."

"Why for tonight?" she asked.

He hesitated before he answered, and she must have guessed what was running through his mind. Nevertheless, it was part of the business.

"I want Ben's mind to be off things for about an hour. You do it and I'll see Gibson," he said. "It's necessary to box that boy off. He mustn't worry where I am, and only be glad I'm not where he is. It's the best way of handling things, don't you think?"

Her face grew stiff and wooden. She did not answer.

"What is it, Ruth?" he asked. He spoke more gently. "Are you afraid of him?"

"No, I don't think so," she said, "but I hated that mental undressing way he looked at me, and you'd have to be mighty convincing with a man like that."

146

It was the business, it was what she was there for, and they both knew it, but still he felt his face redden.

"I didn't mean anything serious," he said. "Just a walk downtown or a ride up the mountain in his car."

The set expression left her face and she smiled.

"It's nice to know you're human occasionally," she said. "I'm glad the proposition doesn't appeal to you personally, but I don't think it would be a good one, anyway. It's too damned obvious, Jack, and he's a very smart man."

"Yes, he's smart," Jack said.

"It's just the thing we'd be expected to do," she said. "Don't you see it would tell him right away that there was something wrong with us? You've got to be jealous and difficult. It would look better if I simply let him know he was attractive to me—and made him want to get me away from you."

She moved closer to him and put her hands on his shoulders.

"Now listen, Ruth," he said, "I'm ashamed I made that proposition, but it was business, Ruth."

"Never mind the proposition, Jack," she told him, her grip on his shoulders tightening. "Just get it through your head that I want to stay with you tonight. I don't want to see you get a shiv in your back."

"If anybody's watching," he said, "it's going to be harder for two to get up to that cottage than one."

"Jack," she said, and she moved closer to him, "please—all right, I'm frightened. I'm scared as hell. All right, he's scared me, on your account more than mine, Jack. I promise I won't let you down."

He bent over and kissed her. Even as he did so he knew that under any circumstances he was being very foolish.

"All right," he said, "but put on a dark dress, and let's go down to dinner."

"Darling," she said again, "I won't let you down. You'd be surprised. I'm wonderful in the dark."

Jack Rhyce had often thought that any ballroom anywhere in the world was interchangeable with any other. There was every reason why this should be so, since the ballroom and the dances derived from it were a part of Western civilization that should have interested Spengler. If you thought of it in purely historical terms, the decline of the West—and he believed that in many ways the West was declining—could be interestingly illustrated by ballrooms and modern music. The time and place that night made thoughts like those more natural then usual because the ballroom of the hotel was an incongruity, like its native orchestra. The jazz and the people had no evolutionary place in the Japanese starlit night. They were only there as part of the flotsam on the wave of history. At almost any time the European dancers might be whisked away, but the dance convention would be left behind because of its social, sensual and selective attributes. In fact, with the leisure of the machine age, how could people get on without dancing? They are no longer physically tired, and the imponderables of life are heavier, and with them grows the need to escape reality.

A great many couples were escaping in their different ways on the hotel dance floor at shortly before ten o'clock that night. They whirled with fancy steps that they had learned on other dance floors. No one noticed the elaborate Japanese paper decorations on the high ceiling. They were all following the uninspired rhythms of the Japanese orchestra, which did its best, in costume and manner, to follow the American tradition. The music was mediocre, and most of it dated, but everyone who danced lost part of his or her individuality in the pervading sound. The girls, both European and Japanese, were pretty. The men seemed to find it harder to surrender themselves to the pleasures of the evening. Their faces, as they danced, looked less forgetful and more careworn than their partners'. Tall windows on both sides of the room opened directly on the hotel grounds so that the dancing was almost in the open air, but even so the orchestra sounded surprisingly loud. Its members, though small men, were eager, conscientious and vigorous.

She was a light and beautiful dancer, much better than he, but they were both of them good enough, in that rather pedestrian company, to be disturbingly outstanding. Their steps had a professional exactness, and they both looked well—she in her dark green and he in his conserv-

148

atively cut blue suit. He was aware that they were attracting approving attention, which was something he could have dispensed with that night.

"Don't do anything fancy," he told her. "Just dance in a mediocre way. You're too good-looking as it is."

"That's what I thought about you when I saw you first," she said. "You're too good-looking for the business. You look like the answer to a maiden's prayer in this crowd."

"Do you see him anywhere?" he asked.

She smiled and shook her head.

"I wish he were here so we could keep an eye on him," he said. "We've been dancing about half an hour, haven't we?"

"Yes," she said. "Don't you like it?"

"I would under other circumstances," he told her, "but Bill's going to get nervous pretty soon. I wonder where he is."

"Bill?" she asked.

"No, no," he said. "The Big Boy. I gathered he was going to the dance tonight from the way he was talking in the bar."

He felt her shiver, and she shook her head.

"I wish you'd get him off your mind," she said, "or at least look as though you were having a good time so people won't wonder what we're going to do when we go outside. Hold me closer. Don't forget, we're supposed to be in love."

It was another half hour before he saw Big Ben. He had stepped in from the grounds outside. Instead of his Aloha shirt and khaki trousers, he wore a charcoal flannel suit, black shoes and a dark tie. He appeared very young to Jack Rhyce in that formal attire with his unruly sandy hair, his heavy eyebrows; only his eyes gave his age away. Eyes and hands were something that nobody ever could disguise.

"Good," Jack said. "There he is, coming in from outside."

He felt her shiver again.

"Is he looking for us?" she asked.

"Yes," he said, "I think so."

"If he cuts in," she said, "cut back soon. Please, Jack."

149

"All right," he said, "but don't discourage him. It won't hurt to have him fall for you."

Big Ben smiled pleasantly while his glance roved over the dancers. Jack Rhyce noticed that he pulled his coat straight, although it had not been disarranged. Then Big Ben took a handkerchief and passed it lightly over his forehead, though he had not been dancing, and then made a gesture with his hands as though he were ridding them of imaginary dust.

"He sees us now," she said. "He's coming over."

"All right," Jack Rhyce said, "and when he cuts in, smile."

Big Ben was moving toward them through the dancers, a head taller than most of the men. A second later he slapped Jack Rhyce on the shoulder. It was a friendly, good-natured slap.

"Hello, Oberlin," he said.

"Why, hello," Jack Rhyce answered, "Alabama Baptist U."

Big Ben's laugh was infectious.

"Your guessing cap's on crooked, boy," he said. "Not Alabama, Mississippi."

"Oh, come now," Jack Rhyce said, "your accent isn't thick enough. Let's make it Carolina."

"Okay," Big Ben said. "Carolina Baptist. And now may I relieve you of your lovely burden, Oberlin, just for a little while?"

"You mean you want to dance with my girl?" Jack Rhyce asked him. "All right, but just remember—only for a little while."

"Oh, now," Ruth Bogart said, "don't pretend to act so jealous, Jack. I'd love to dance with Ben just as long as he wants." She sighed, giving Big Ben another of her dazzling smiles. "Maybe I need a change. . . ."

Jack Rhyce walked to an open doorway and watched them. Like many large men, Big Ben danced very well, even to the nervous jiggling beat of the orchestra.

"Hold me closer," she had said. "Don't forget that we are supposed to be in love."

You had to be able to estimate degrees of physical attraction, and to observe and capitalize on the onslaughts of desire, if you wanted to be successful in the business. It was a sordid matter, standing there watching Ruth Bogart and the big man dancing. He was ashamed of playing a part in that ugly scene, but it was business. Seeing them dance was like watching the merging of two different worlds, a world of grace, gentility and refinement with another of ruthless, dynamic force. It occurred to him that Big Ben might never before have had the experience of dancing with anyone like Ruth Bogart. She had never looked more delicate or more a perfect product of gentle upbringing than when Big Ben held her in his arms. He saw her lips move in some smiling remark. He saw Big Ben answer, and he did not care to guess what they had said.

In the beginning he had entertained a technical fear, which she had expressed in their room upstairs, that her approach might have been too obvious. It had been necessary for her to move fast but, at the same time, Big Ben was a clever man. There was always the question, in such encounters, as to the exact moment when intellectual objectiveness could be discounted. He realized, as soon as he saw them dancing, that Ruth Bogart must have considered this matter also. There was that saying that the desire of woman is to be desired, and a woman could instinctively estimate a man's desire. Rapid though the interplay had been, and obvious as it had seemed to Jack Rhyce as an observer, from what he could see as he stood watching Ruth Bogart had been right about Big Ben. They were a handsome couple on the dance floor. He was certain now that she was something new in his experience. It was certain that he would not forget. Those things did not take long when certain instincts were in the balance.

In its essence, jazz was not happy music. It was restless and lacking in order, reflecting very accurately the spirit of the era which had brought it into being. The world was unhappy and Jack Rhyce was in a better position than most of his contemporaries to know because it had been his business in many places to observe and deal with violence. All his generation had been born and nurtured in an age of discontent, but he was not able to explain the reason for it, unless that a system or a way of life was approaching dissolution. Logically there were less reasons for unhappiness today in any part of the world than there had been fifty years before. The cleavage between wealth and poverty had been greater then, and the voice of social conscience had only been a whisper. Communication and industrial advance had been negligible compared with the present, and so had public health and expectancy of life; yet back in that harder day the world had been much happier. There had been security then in that everyone knew what to expect. There had been strength and order, which perhaps were the attributes that mankind most desired. What was it that had palsied the hand of the political system which had ruled the world at the time of Rudyard Kipling, in as benign and enlightened a manner as many political thinkers were attempting to rule it now? What was it that had opened the Pandora box and the floodgates of discontent? What was it that had allowed minorities to give such a loud voice to their grievances that they could upset the lives of persons ten thousand miles away? And what was the basis of the nationalism that made all nations truculent? Why, in fact, was it that individuals all over the world were disturbed, overpopulating the mental institutions, rebelling against conventions, filling the streets with juvenile delinquents? Why was it that no firm hand could any longer quell a social riot? He knew it had been different once, before his time, and he knew that the answer to these questions lay in what was known as the phenomenon of change.

The same questions must have arisen when the Roman Empire was falling. They had been asked also in the briefer and turbulent dynasties of China, and in eighteenth-century France. Volumes had been written about the course of the disease, but its cause was still in doubt. There was no doubt at all, however, regarding the ultimate result, and in the world as he saw it, both in the East and in the West, the result was just around the corner, eager and waiting. Anarchy might rule for a while in North Africa, Egypt or Persia might upset the Near East balance. Neutralism might reign in India, but still the result was just around the corner, just what it always had been—the ruthless oppression of absolute rule. It was now called "the dictatorship of the proletariat," but its end was the old dictatorship. The proletariat, with their agitators and their discontented, would be whipped back to their places, and order would be restored more merciless than the order of the Pax Romana or Britannica. And again there would be discontent, simply because man was a discontented being. The cycle would go on.

He realized that it was not the time or place to think of such things, but at least these thoughts made him a part of the stream of history. He and his generation were children of discontent. The drives of discontent had put him where he was, watching the dancers, and at the same time looking at the dark hotel grounds in order to memorize the shadowy places and the plan of the lighted paths. It was curious to think that the same drives which had placed him there had acted in such a different way upon Big Ben, who was still dancing with Ruth Bogart. Given different childhoods and different backgrounds, he and Big Ben might easily have swapped places. Tolerance was one of the troubles of the present. You knew, or you thought you knew, so much about human motivation that, in the end, you could not blame anyone for anything. And in the end rules and laws lost meaning. Perhaps it was this universal tolerance that was weakening the hand of order.

He looked into the night again. The cottage called Chrysanthemum Rest was completely visible. Though its shades and curtains were drawn, he could see that its rooms were lighted, as was the path that led straight toward it from one of the hotel verandas. But if one were to follow another path up toward the greenhouses, there would be shadow and concealment. He could not plan the full approach from where he stood. He would have to improvise after he had started. A glance at his wrist watch told him it was time—10:20 already. Ruth Bogart had been right in believing that it would look better if they walked out into the shadowy grounds together, and it was time to start now. He moved across the room to where she was dancing with Big Ben.

"Okay, Baptist," Jack said, "time for the praying colonels to go to the showers—the half is over."

"Aw, gee, coach," Big Ben said, "nobody's even blown the whistle. Well, thanks a lot, honey. And how about us

153

all meeting in the bar in a while? I'm going there right now to drown my frustrations, honey."

Ruth Bogart giggled appreciatively.

"I don't know whether Jack has frustrations or not," she said, "but whatever he does have, he always seems to be all for the drowning process. We'll be there whether I like it or not, won't we, darling?"

"Oh, come on," Jack said. He put his arm playfully around her. "You're going to have ginger ale, sweet. We'll see you down there, Ben."

"We'll dance a few minutes first," Ruth said, "and then I want to go out and get a breath of fresh air. It's awfully hot in here."

Big Ben laughed uproariously.

"And I bet you're getting a headache, too," he said. "How come? You didn't want fresh air when I asked you three minutes ago, honey? Well, no hard feelings. So long, troops."

They danced for a minute or two without speaking.

"He's gone all right," Jack said, "and he hasn't gone outside, either."

"That's so," she said. "I think you're right. I don't believe he's on to us at all."

"What makes you say that?" Jack asked her.

"Oh," she said. "Girls can tell about those things. If you want to know—from the way he tried to make me. It was an all-out and very clumsy effort, darling."

"It could be that we're barking up the wrong tree," Jack Rhyce said. "It could be that he's just a lonely soul on an airship. The world is full of them these days."

"It could be," she said. "But there was one queer thing about him."

"What?" he asked.

"He hadn't been dancing, had he?" she said. "But he was all in a glow, wringing wet with perspiration, darling. Did you notice him dust his hands and wipe his forehead when he came in? Whatever he was doing, he was exercising."

"Maybe he was playing Tarzan in the trees," Jack Rhyce said.

"His hands are so damned big," she said, "and his palms were sweating."

154

"Well, he's gone now," Jack Rhyce said. "Let's go out and look at the moon."

"Oh, Jack," she said, and the music had stopped so that everyone around could hear her, "who told you that there was a moon?"

XIII

They walked outside and toward the greenhouses, laughing and talking softly, only one of a number of other couples who were wandering about the grounds. While they walked they examined Chrysanthemum Rest from all angles. There was a clump of bamboo by its door, which was the only cover near it. Still talking softly, they examined the taller fir trees near the greenhouse. Jack was as sure as a fallible human being could be that he had missed nothing, having reconnoitered too many places not to be intensely aware of atmosphere. He had been able to tell for a long while, from his own physical reactions, whether or not a place was being watched. There was always a sort of tenseness in the air and an awareness of other people. He could swear that Chrysanthemum Rest was clear. They sat for a while close together on a bench in the shadow of an old cryptomeria, two lovers in case anyone should notice.

"Does it look all right to you?" he asked.

"Yes," she said. "There's only one offbeat thing. We've been out here for fifteen minutes, and have you noticed no one's moved inside the house? Not a shadow against the curtains—nothing. Perhaps he isn't there."

"He's being still," Jack said, "because he wants it to look as if he weren't there. Bill's a smart operator. Anything else?"

"No," she said. "I don't think we're being watched."

All that was left was the unavoidable danger that someone, by sheer inadvertence, might notice them entering Chrysanthemum Rest, a calculated risk which the bamboo thicket by the door would minimize. If they walked affectionately past the cottage, the thicket would conceal them from anyone standing higher up from the hill, and its

156

hadow would partially protect them from anyone who would be looking from the hotel windows. Of course the oor would be unlocked. There would only be the crucial econd when they crossed the threshold. Nevertheless, he elayed for a while, with his attention glued on the Chrysanthemum cottage. It was a white frame building of European style, similar to the cottage annexes that urrounded summer hotels at home. It stood peacefully at he foot of the slope of lawn that led from the tree under which they sat. He wished he could be sure that Big Ben was in the bar. He even thought of making a check, but is feeling that the cottage was not under observation made him dismiss the idea.

"Come on. Let's go," he said. "We'll know a lot more fter we've talked to Bill."

The brass of the dance orchestra blared across the awn, interspersed with its drummer's beat. They were nly a couple returning to the dance as they walked to Chrysanthemum Rest. His arm tightened around her waist s they reached the bamboo thicket.

"Follow me quick," he whispered.

They were inside the house in a twinkling, because they were both trained operators; the door was closed behind hem without a sound and without a fingerprint on its nob, either. The place, as he had observed, was fully ghted. They were in a small entrance hall furnished with European umbrella stand and a row of wooden pegs for oats and hats. A single open door showed a lighted oom, comfortably furnished with wicker easy chairs and couch. There was a Chinese rug on the floor and gay apanese prints decorated the walls. The room, to Jack hyce's surprise, was empty; so they stood for a moment, reaths held, listening. He could detect no sound except he blare of the dance music. He raised his eyebrows and estured to Ruth Bogart. She understood his signal and hey moved along the wall so that their shadows would ot show on the drawn curtains. It never paid to hurry.

Later, he never could recall what it was that made him ure that something was wrong in Chrysanthemum Rest.

"Bill," he whispered. What with the noise of the music, e might have spoken aloud, but in any case he already ad the conviction that he would not be answered.

157

The bedroom door was also open. The lights were on there, too. He tiptoed to the doorway with Ruth Bogart just behind him. Bill Gibson, in a clean pair of shantung silk pajamas, lay beneath the covers of his bed, eyes closed, head resting on his pillow, his clothes neatly folded on a chair at the end of the room. A glass, a half empty bottle of whisky and a pill bottle stood under the lamp on the bedside table. His restful posture gave every indication that he was sound asleep, but he was not breathing. Bill Gibson was stone dead.

"Okay," Jack Rhyce whispered to her. He felt in his pocket and drew on a pair of gloves. "Better go through his suitcase, Ruth. Look for anything. Anything." But even as he spoke he knew there would not be anything they wanted.

While she moved noiselessly about the room, he stood still for a minute gazing at the body of Bill Gibson, trying to estimate the strengths and weaknesses of this new situation in much the same way a bridge player might assess the possibilities in dummy when the cards were on the board. Now that Bill Gibson was dead, a whole new line of action was required. He was still in the grip of shock, but he was able to see at once that he was looking at a professional, almost a classic job of elimination. If Bill Gibson had been breathing, Jack Rhyce himself would have thought that it was an overdose of sleeping pills, and after all, suicide due to strain or melancholia had always been a factor in the business. The only trouble was that they had come too early. Bill Gibson should have been discovered in the morning for the job to have been perfect, and doubtless that had been the intention. This was an encouraging thought for Jack Rhyce, in that it showed as plain as print that no one knew that Bill Gibson was there for a meeting. It meant as clearly as a certified document that he and Ruth Bogart were not suspected yet.

There was another plain fact. The decision must have been made some time previously that Bill Gibson should be put out of the way, since the whole job was one that had obviously required meticulous planning. It also betrayed an anxiety to keep things quiet which was completely understandable to anyone in the business, when

158

iolent ways of taking out a man, no matter how carefully
worked, always offered embarrassing complications. On
he other hand, the danger of complication at Chrysanthe-
num Rest was very small indeed. Success only required
hat the body be discovered in the morning. Without his
eing familiar with Japanese medical procedure, Jack
Rhyce did not believe that a doctor called in the morning
would make more than a perfunctory examination with
he evidence before him; no doubt if a more thorough ex-
mination should be made this contingency would have
een provided for. He picked up the pill bottle, which still
eld three yellow capsules, a very pretty touch in itself
when added to a glimpse of the cork which had fallen to
he floor. A drunken man had accidentally taken an over-
lose of sleeping pills. From the color of the capsules, and
without reading the label he could guess that the drug was
ne of the better-known barbiturates of American manu-
acture, and he could guess from a minute abrasion at the
orner of Bill Gibson's mouth that a lethal dose was
afely in the stomach. There were several ways to make
eluctant people swallow.

Jack Rhyce set down the pill bottle and sniffed of Bill
Gibson's lips. There was the requisite odor of whisky to
explain the half-empty whisky bottle on the table. The
whisky had been applied overliberally to the lips, but no
ne would have noticed in the morning. Professionally it
was a job which had only one unavoidable drawback, and
ven this presupposed the presence of another professional, which indicated again that he and Ruth Bogart
were not suspected yet. Like every killing in the business,
his one had its signature, and this was ridiculously easy
o decipher once you knew it was a killing. The job pre-
upposed enormous and expert strength. It had required
omeone who could take care of Bill Gibson as gently and
ffortlessly as a nurse might handle a baby, and Bill
Gibson was no weakling. He touched Bill Gibson's hand
oftly. The body was still warm. He slipped his hand under the head. The mark of a hypodermic was barely visi-
le in the hair at the base of the neck. If one had not
nown exactly where to look, the mark could easily have
one unnoticed. He lowered the head very gently because
t was all a very private matter in which he and his op-

posite numbers shared the same anxiety to keep it quiet to keep it clean, to keep it above suspicion.

Ruth Bogart was looking at him from across the room and he nodded slowly in answer to her unspoken question.

"Yes," he said, "Ben was here all right. I wish I could have the privilege of polishing off that son-of-a-bitch. I always thought a lot of Bill."

"Yes, so did I," she said.

But when you were gone you were gone, in the business. His attention turned to the neatly folded clothes. Even the shoes by the chair were in meticulous alignment. The bedclothes were carelessly disarranged just as a man who was drunk might have moved them. The folded clothes were an error, or still better, an oversight. Bill Gibson must have folded them himself. He must have planned to meet them in pajamas and a dressing gown. Jack Rhyce peered into the bathroom. A burgundy silk dressing gown was hung from a hook on the bathroom door. He examined the back and sleeves. There was slight tear at the right elbow, and the silk was scuffed and a few tiny hairs of woolen lint were mingled with the fabric. It was the blue piling from a carpet, and the Chinese carpet in the living room was blue.

Ruth Bogart had finished with Bill Gibson's baggage and with the contents of his pockets. She shook her head when he nodded to her—but then, Bill Gibson would have been careful to have nothing on him except cover identification.

"Where did it happen?" she asked.

"The living room," he said. "He must have grabbed Bill right by the front door. I'd like to polish off that son-of-a-bitch."

He walked gingerly to the living room and she followed him. Of course there had been a struggle. How was it she had put it—that Big Ben had been all of a glow, and he hadn't been dancing? Yet the signs had been eliminated and nothing had been broken. However, the impersonal orderliness of the room told its own story of rearrangement. He could reconstruct what had happened as though it were going on now before his eyes—Big Ben in a noiseless bound, towering over Bill Gibson, the jolt in the solar

160

plexus that knocked out the wind. Strangulation was not necessary if you knew the trick. Big Ben's arms wrapped around the smaller man's gasping body . . . the fighting for breath . . . the expert hands lowering the struggling man to the floor . . . The sleeping pills with the suitable label would have been in Big Ben's pocket.

"When you danced with him," he said to Ruth Bogart, "was there anything in his coat?"

"I think so," she said.

It would have been the hypodermic, but this would not have been bulky. The piling of the carpet was scuffed and trampled near the door—not markedly so, but still the evidence was there once you guessed the story.

"They don't know about us yet," he said, "or they wouldn't have pulled it this way, do you think?"

"I think you're right," she said. "You're pretty smart sometimes, Jack."

"Okay," he said. "We'd better get out of here, and brace yourself. There's one thing more that's going to be tough tonight."

"How do you mean? What else?" she asked, and for the first time since they had entered Chrysanthemum Rest he saw that her nerves were shaken.

"We've got to keep in the clear," he said. "We've got to go and meet that bastard in the bar."

"Oh, no," she said, "not that."

"Oh, yes," he said. "Just that, and we'd better be in the mood for it, too, because he's a smart Joe, dear. Muss yourself up a little. Kiss me. Put some lipstick on my cheek. He's got to know we've been out in the garden making love."

No matter what happened in the business you had to go on with the show. When they got theirs, you let them go, and the show had to go on, if only because you knew you had to get yours sometime in some sordid corner or some cellar of some prison, and you would try to take it without a prayer for mercy, if you were in the business. You learned how to dish it out and to take it, too, if you were in the business. The scene which had taken place in Chrysanthemum Rest was still in Jack Rhyce's mind when they left the small detached building. His arm was around her, and they stopped and kissed shamelessly directly underneath a light on the path to the hotel. After all, the hour—which was just past eleven now—was growing late enough so that inhibitions should be breaking if boys were to be boys and girls girls. But even then he realized that their abandon had a quality that was partially genuine.

"Darling," he said loudly, "you're adorable." She giggled. She was very good at that girlish giggle which must have been a vestige of the outside.

"Darling," she said, "not again. Not *here*. Everyone will see us."

She said it exactly as though they were not intending that any even remotely interested parties should see them. At some points there were lighter moments in the business. But their words and actions were only a shadow on his deeper thoughts. He did not have ice water in his veins any more than she, and he had not recovered from the impact of that pseudo-quiet death in Chrysanthemum Rest. His creative projections into Big Ben's character all added to the acuteness of his upset. In his imagination he could hear Big Ben's voice behind his own and hers, and the gentle drawl had a nauseating quality in his memory. He could hear Big Ben speaking as he pinned Bill Gibson down, gasping and helpless. The voice would be kind, since in the end personal animosity ought never to obtrude itself in the business, and if your emotions got the better of you it was time to resign and be a salesman of fancy motor cars. Jack Rhyce knew that the scene in Chrysanthemum Rest was playing on his emotions, which was not right. He could hear Big Ben's voice in his imagination.

"You're goin' out in a minute, friend," he could hear Big Ben saying. "You might as well go out easy and not fight, mightn't you, since you're goin' out anyway, friend? Easy's better than hard, isn't it? And I've got no hard feelings. I'll he'p you if you go out easy, and I'll be right with you, friend. Now swallow these pills. They won't hurt nobody. Just get them down or I have to make you. Swallow them, and then there'll be the needle, and you and I know that it won't hurt at all. Don't make me be rough, Mac, because it won't gain you anything. I know that poison kit you folks carry. In case you're curious, it's what you call Shot Number Two."

The soft imaginary voice of Big Ben mingled with the music from the ballroom, and Jack Rhyce knew it was time to pull himself together.

"I'm against alcohol as a crutch on general principles," he said, "but I think you and I could do with two good doubles in that bar right now, don't you?"

"I agree with you for once, darling," she said. He felt her shiver, and he shook her in a rough playful way.

"For God's sake pull yourself together," he said. "The show's on the road."

"All right," she said. "So it's on the road, and stop being a space cadet."

He straightened his blue coat and felt his belt. He might not be carrying a weapon but, given the showdown, a properly fixed belt was a good substitute. His was fixed. He wished that he could slash his belt across Big Ben's face just once. Twice would be better—twice and Big Ben's closest relative wouldn't know him.

XIV

The atmosphere in the Main Bar had changed since he
and Ruth Bogart had been there last, for the better as far
as hotel receipts were concerned. There was no doubt any
longer, if there ever had been previously, that the patrons—aside from their Japanese girl friends, who were
trying to enter into the fun as vigorously as Madame But-
terfly had in another generation—realized that they were
far away from home. Their loneliness plus the dancing
and the drinks had begun drawing them together, so that
an alcoholic affection, plus an undercurrent of companionship in misery formed the motif for the now crowded
bar. The flyers, the officers of the ground forces, the Navy
personnel, the American civilians in and out of government jobs, and even a few Europeanized Japanese had
begun to realize that they were all members of the Legion
of the Lost Ones. No one had as yet started to sing
"Gentlemen Rankers" or "The Road to Mandalay," but
several men by the bar were already drunk, and an American girl was doing a dramatic recitation in a corner to
which no one in her party listened. A sea of smoke and
spilled drinks and voices washed like a wave over Jack
Rhyce and Ruth Bogart.

"All right, honey," he said, "we're tight and full of fun,
and we've got to check in here, honey, in a big way, and
this is our night off. Why, lookit—there's Big Ben, just
where he said he'd be." He leaned down until her hair
brushed his cheek. "Just remember, he doesn't know who
we are," he whispered. "Just hold that thought, sweet,
and give me another kiss. It's better that I'm all lipsticked
up tonight."

It was common sense aside from anything else. There
could never be anything sinister about a man if he was

smeared with lipstick, and what was it Bill Gibson had said? There was safety in sex. Perhaps if Bill had practiced that maxim himself he would not have been a corpse in Chrysanthemum Rest.

"Oh, Jack," Ruth Bogart said, and her voice had the shrill note that fitted with that happy evening, "look at Ben. He's got a man with a squeeze box with him. Aren't you glad we haven't gone to bed yet, darling?"

It gave him an unpleasant twinge to observe the number of amused faces that turned toward them after Ruth Bogart had asked her last question. Naturally she did not need to tell him to look at Big Ben. Big Ben stood in the middle of a noisy group near the center of the room, and sure enough, a man with an accordion was with him. He had learned the tricks of holding attention that could only have been derived from the theater. In fact, at the moment Big Ben might have been master of ceremonies in a night club, and perhaps he had held such a position once.

"Jack," she whispered, "he's changed his shirt."

She did not have to tell him. He had been wearing a white shirt when he had cut in on them on the dance floor, but now his shirt was blue.

"That's right," Jack said. "He's been having a busy evening, sweet. Wave to him. He's seen us now."

"Hi, Ben," she called.

"Why, sweetness," Big Ben called, and he shook his finger at her. "Say, whatever have you been doing to Oberlin? Honest, I couldn't guess."

Ruth glanced at Jack's face. She gave a stifled scream.

"Oh, Jack," she said, "I'm sorry. They told me in the States that it wouldn't come off, darling."

Jack Rhyce grinned self-consciously at Big Ben and the boys and girls around him, then he pulled out a pocket handkerchief, wiped his cheeks and lips, and shook his head.

"I guess the trouble is, dear, this isn't the States. Maybe nothing's kiss-proof in Japan."

It was a pretty good line, considering, and the laugh that greeted it confirmed this impression. A man with lipstick on him couldn't help but be a nice guy, especially in a bar.

The effort he was making made Jack Rhyce afraid that he might be overdoing things, until he saw there was no sharpness in Big Ben's glance.

"Say, boy," Big Ben said, "come on over here. Let's do a song number for the crowd. This fellow can really sing, folks."

"Oh, now," Jack said. "I might break my larynx."

Now that they knew he had a comic streak everything he said was funny. Ruth Bogart gave him a playful push.

"Oh, go ahead, Jack," she said. "You can sing just as well as he can."

There is nothing harder in the world than to give a convincing imitation of being drunk. Jack Rhyce was wise enough not to try.

"Well, let me have a double Scotch first," he said, "so I can halfway catch up with things."

Big Ben gave a hearty whoop of laughter. Jack Rhyce tossed off the drink when it was handed to him in three quick swallows. He did not need to ask for another because someone immediately thrust a second into his hand, but those two quick slugs had surprisingly little effect. They only served to make everything more hideously grotesque, at the same time bringing the faces around him into clearer definition. Big Ben was holding a half-empty highball glass in exactly the expert way that an abstemious person handles a drink at a cocktail party. You could always pick a drinker from a nondrinker from the way he held his glass. Big Ben, in spite of all his noise, was cold sober, but his sobriety had been hard to detect because his spirits and elation were not normal. Elation was exactly the word, the sort that came after emergence from danger. The truth was that Big Ben was happy, and also he must have felt completely safe. Like Jack Rhyce, he must have examined the hotel guests and must have concluded that there was not a cough in a carload.

"Well, I do feel better not," Jack said.

Big Ben patted his shoulder affectionately; in return Jack Rhyce gave him an affectionate punch on the chest—just two big boys roughhousing. There was no softness in Big Ben's midsection, as he had observed already at Wake. He was more of a wrestler than a boxer, but these were not the right thoughts for the moment,

166

when even a thought could be detected if it influenced attitude.

"Say," Big Ben said, and his voice had a wheedling note in it, "now you've got yourself lubricated up, how about a little harmonizing? Ted here can play almost anything on a squeeze box. How about a piece from *The Red Mill*? How about 'Every Day Is Ladies' Day with me'? Huh, Jack?"

"Oh, say," Jack Rhyce said, "why that old chestnut?"

"Aw, come on," Big Ben said. "It's got real melody. It's a swell song."

"Why is it you have this yen for *The Red Mill*," Jack Rhyce asked, "when it was written before you and I were born, Ben?"

Big Ben drew his hand across his eyes.

"I know," he said. "It don't sound reasonable, does it. Yet it's a kind of a theme song with me. Will you sing it with me if I tell you why?"

His invitation, which included the group around them again, had a professional tone. He was a born master of ceremonies, and in the relief he must have been feeling, he might have dropped his guard.

"Why, sure," Jack said, "if it's a good yarn."

"Aw, shucks," Big Ben said, "it isn't much of a one—just kid stuff. You know how it is when you're a kid, how things kind of happen so you don't forget." His voice was eager and appealing. "It was senior year in this Baptist college down South. . . . It's a kind of corny yarn, now I think of it. . . . There was this banker in town—the local rich guy, and he had this pretty daughter with golden hair. Well, my folks were poor, in the missionary business actually, and I was sort of shy back then. For two years I used to walk past her house most every night, without daring to knock on the door, and then comes Senior year. That autumn when I'd sort of built up my ego by playing football, why I walked up the front stoop and rang the bell, and there she was all alone, and she asked me to come inside. Well, I was shy, but she asked me if I liked hearing music on the phonograph. It was one of those kind you wind with a crank, and there were lots of records belonging to the old man that went a long ways back. Well, we played them for a while, and then she put on this *Red Mill* record, and held my hand, and then— well, we kinda got to loving each other with that old *Red Mill playing*. Then her old man came in, and he kicked me the hell out, and I never saw her again, but that's how I remember *The Red Mill*." Big Ben's voice grew softer. "And I haven't forgot that old aristocratic bastard, either."

He had completely held his audience, and there were sympathetic murmurs applauding his tale of young frustration. The pride and sensitiveness that had run all through the incident had revealed themselves only in the last sentence. Something had happened then, something more than was told, of course, but *The Red Mill* was its monument to a new beginning, and the music of early youth was always the best music.

Big Ben shrugged his shoulders. "Then after that, before the war, I was with a sort of musical caravan, and what should happen—there was *The Red Mill*. Anyway, it kind of stays with me."

"That's quite a story, Ben," Jack Rhyce said, and he meant it. He had learned a lot from the story.

"Well," Big Ben said, "let's make a quick switch. Stand up here, fella. Let's show 'em. Strike up the band. 'Every Day Is Ladies' Day with Me.' "

Bill Gibson was dead at Chrysanthemum Rest. Their arms were draped over each other's shoulders as they sang, and Jack knew the words better than Big Ben.

And my pleasure it is double if they come to me in trouble,
For I always find a way to make them smile, the little darlings!

Applause came from all over the bar when they had finished. Show business was written all over Big Ben when he took in the applause.

"Say, Jack," he said, "if we only had straw hats and canes, we could soft-shoe it, couldn't we?"

If you played the game you had to play it through.

"We don't need hats and canes," Jack Rhyce said.

"Why, we don't sure enough," Big Ben said. "Come on. Strike up the band."

It wasn't a bad show either. Jack Rhyce had to admit that they both had an unusual gift of comic interpolation. In fact there was one moment when he was almost tempted to join in the laughter of the crowd as he watched Big Ben slip deliberately and recover himself. Actually his impulse to laugh died when he saw Ruth Bogart's expression as she watched them. Then an instant later he picked out the face of Mr. Moto. Mr. Moto was standing near the street entrance of the bar. Jack Rhyce remembered being ashamed of Mr. Moto's seeing him making a deliberate fool of himself, but then there was no reason why Mr. Moto should not have been there since he had been given the evening off. After all, enough was enough. Jack Rhyce was never surer of the truth of that aphorism than when the dance was over. He looked once toward the spot where Mr. Moto had been standing, but the Japanese was gone and Jack Rhyce could hardly blame him.

"Well, folks," Jack Rhyce said, "it's been nice seeing you. Come on, Ruth. Let's say good night."

They had done what was necessary. They had showed up in the bar and the clock showed it was ten minutes to twelve. He could tell from the tight grip of her hand when they walked toward the Cozy Nook ell that her nervous resistance was wearing thin.

"Jack," she said, as they closed the door of their room. They had not spent much time there, but the edges of unfamiliarity had been rounded off already, and they were both through with cover for the moment.

"Just a minute before you say anything," he told her, removing his coat and tie. "Just let me wash the touch of that goon off me first. I'm sorry, Ruth."

"You needn't be sorry," she said. "Nobody could have done better than you did, Jack."

She was standing just where he had left her when he came back rubbing his face and shoulders with a bath towel.

"Darling," she said, "you've washed the lipstick off and now you won't have anything to remember me by. Please

169

unzip the back of my dress. I don't know why people always sell unzippable dresses."

"Maybe they do it to get girls into trouble," he said.

"Jack," she said, "don't you think it would look better if we turned out the lights?"

"How do you mean," she asked, "look better?"

"More conventional," she said, "more what's expected of us. We don't know who's watching or listening."

"Just get it into your head," he said, "no one's watching or listening. We're out of this as of now."

"But it won't be long," she said. "And it would be better if you did turn out the lights. I must look like hell."

"Oh, no, you don't at all," he said.

"Well, I feel like hell," she answered.

"All right," he told her, "I don't blame you. So do I. We haven't exactly been playing charades tonight."

He turned out the lights, except the one in the bathroom, but he could still see her standing there.

"We used to play charades at home," she said. "Did you ever play them?"

"If it's just the same with you," he said, "let's not get reminiscing. Why, yes, I used to play charades with the banker's daughter, dear, until the banker threw me out."

"Jack," she said, "wasn't it God-awful?"

"Yes," he said.

"Jack," she said, "I don't know anything about Bill Gibson's setup here, do you?"

"No," he answered, "and we won't now Bill's dead."

"Jack," she said, "what are we going to do?"

It was the question he had been asking himself for quite a while, because he was left with nothing, now that Bill Gibson was dead—no contacts, unless he communicated with home, and that was far too dangerous under the circumstances.

"I don't know," he said, "but maybe we'll think of something in the morning."

"Is that the best you can do?" she asked. "Come here. Come closer. I want to ask you something."

If only because they were in the same predicament, they were close enough already.

"I haven't got any bright answers," he said. "I couldn't win any giveaway show tonight."

170

"Why did they kill Bill?" she whispered.

"Because he knew something they didn't want passed on," he said. "You know that. That's always why we kill people in this racket."

"But what did he know?" she asked.

"He didn't tell us," he said, "but we've got to try to find out, come morning."

"Jack," she said, "wasn't it awful?"

He felt her arms steal around his neck, and she buried her face against his shoulder.

"Go ahead and cry if it does you any good," he said. "I don't blame you, Ruth."

"I'm not going to cry," she said, "but I'm glad you're here, Jack."

"I wish you weren't," he said.

"Oh, Jack," she said, "I don't think that's very polite, considering everything."

"I mean it's too damn dangerous here," he said. "Let's face it. I mean I love you, Ruth—and I'm not pretending."

"Well," she said. "I'd almost given up hoping that you'd ever say it."

"Well, I have," he told her. "But it's a damn fool thing for anyone like me to say."

He was right about that last statement. It was bad for business to fall in love, especially with anyone like her, but he had said it, and there they were, alone together with their secrets, miles away from any help except what they could give each other. Miles away from anything that made for common sense. . . .

Hindsight was always simpler than foresight. Later it was easy enough to tell himself that no one should rely on convictions that had no solid foundation of fact—except that his belief that they were in the clear did have its own foundation: he could always return to the indisputable point that Bill Gibson would not have been killed in the way he had if anyone had suspected who Jack Rhyce and Ruth Bogart were. As a matter of fact, time was to prove that Rhyce had been right in these assumptions. But still he should have allowed for the unexpected. He should have been more alert, after finding the Japanese in his room, and particularly after the incident of the footstep

171

on the temple path. The trouble was, there had been so much on his mind, that he had finally yielded to the temptation of blacking out the whole problem for a few hours that night, which had been inexcusable. You always paid for such a thing as that in some coin or other, but he never dreamed that he would pay so soon. In fact, he did not even bother to do anything about the lock on the bedroom door, because he was so sure that they would be undisturbed.

The hour when he was awakened must have been shortly after two. The two double whiskies he had drunk may have made him sleep more soundly than usual, but he doubted it. The truth was that the callers were such expert operators that even if he had propped a chair beneath the doorknob they could have handled it without waking him. He had often heard older men in the bureau, including the Chief, say that prewar Japanese agents were tops in the field. They loved intricacies, and if they knew what they wanted, their patience was inordinate.

Actually the first he knew of anything wrong was when they switched on the ceiling lights. It was the light rather than the click of the switch that had aroused him. In the instant his sight was adjusting to the light, he was on his feet. In fact, before he could see clearly, he heard someone speaking just in front of him.

"Please, Mr. Rhyce, no noise, please."

Then everything was cleared. Mr. Moto and two other stocky Japanese in blue serge suits were in the bedroom. Operator was written all over them.

Ruth Bogart, in her twin bed next the wall, reached for her handbag, but the man nearest to her knocked it from her hand.

"Quiet, please," Mr. Moto said. All the previous awkwardness had gone from his voice. His English had become impeccable, and his accent was highly educated. "Get dressed, please, Mr. Rhyce. The man here will hand you your clothes." Mr. Moto smiled politely. "He was a valet once for a member of your cabinet in Washington—before the war, of course."

The loquaciousness disturbed Jack Rhyce because it indicated Mr. Moto's belief that he held the cards. So far no

172

one had pulled a gun, which also meant that the situation was in hand. Jack Rhyce wished he was not barefoot in pajamas, and he also wished that he could keep down his rising anger.

"I'll give you and your chumps just ten seconds to clear out of here," he said, "or else by God I'll throw you out, right through that window."

The three Japanese were a crowd, but given luck, Jack Rhyce believed that he might do it.

Mr. Moto raised his hand in a placating gesture.

"Please," he said, "make no disturbance, Mr. Rhyce, or I shall be obliged to call for the police."

"How's that again," Jack Rhyce said, "you little yellow bastard?"

"Please do not be insulting," Mr. Moto said, "though I can understand how you feel at the moment, Mr. Rhyce. I mentioned the police."

"Oh," Jack Rhyce said, "so you're a cop, are you?"

Mr. Moto looked grave and shook his head. "Not what you call a cop" he said. "I am just what you are, Mr. Rhyce, and you and I do not want cops, do we? I only want a quiet talk with you. It would be a pity if I were to call the police."

"Go ahead and do it," Jack Rhyce said, "and I'll use the same word to you again. Go ahead and do it, you impertinent little yellow bastard. Call in your police."

He had made the Japanese angry, which was perhaps a useless luxury.

"I do not understand," Mr. Moto said. "You must be an intelligent man to have been sent here, Mr. Rhyce, and your work was very good last evening—but not the police, Mr. Rhyce. I should have to tell you and the lady here had murdered Mr. Gibson. I think you would help me rather than have me do that, Mr. Rhyce."

Then Jack Rhyce realized that he was in grave difficulty, and the expressions of the two assistants confirmed the fact.

"Well, well," he said, "so that's the picture, is it? All right, tell your goddam valet to hand me my pants and a clean white shirt. From the way he looks I'll bet he stole the plans for the wrong battleship, even if he could find his way around Washington." There was no change in the three foreign faces watching him. He grinned at Ruth Bogart. "Anyway," he said, "the house detectives haven't got us, Ruth."

While he pulled on his trousers over his pajamas, Mr. Moto rubbed his hands together softly.

"Now that is better," he said. "I understand how a sudden intrusion can be upsetting."

The first surprise was leaving Jack Rhyce. Although he still needed time, the directions were growing clearer. He pointed to his shoes and socks, and where they were handed to him he sat on the edge of his bed and stole another glance at Ruth Bogart. The whiteness of her face showed that they both were beginning to see where the Japanese were fitting in.

"Oh, yes," Mr. Moto said. "Please, may I repeat, you did it very well? So neat with the pills, so nice with the needle—so nice to be a big strong man, Mr. Rhyce. No reason to tell the police. Your chief and my chief would prefer it otherwise, don't you think?"

Jack Rhyce pulled a clean shirt over his head, tightened his belt carefully, took the tie that was handed him and knotted it deliberately. Mr. Moto had not moved his glance from him, nor would Jack have done so either, if he had been in Mr. Moto's place.

"Not the belt, please," Mr. Moto said, "Mr. Rhyce. I should rather hear Big Ben strike only over the BBC."

He heard Ruth Bogart draw in her breath, and her mind must have gone, as his had, to Fisherman's Wharf in San Francisco.

"So that's the way the ball bounces," Jack Rhyce said. "You've got me down for Big Ben?"

"Yes," Mr. Moto said. "Your coat, please, Mr. Rhyce."

Jack Rhyce snatched the coat from the blue-suited man.

"I'll put that on myself," he said.

He had a sudden unreasoning fear that if he were helped they might pinion his arms behind him.

"We will leave quietly," Mr. Moto said. "I never like to do more than is necessary. That is why Miss Bogart will stay here. She will understand that it will do no good to make trouble. I shall drive her back to Tokyo myself in the morning."

174

Ruth Bogart cleared her throat.

"You don't know what you're doing," she began.

It was not the time to break security; indeed it was still a question whether they would have been believed if they had attempted to explain.

Jack Rhyce smiled at her and shook his head.

"I don't really think there's much you can do, Ruth," he said, "the way the ball is bouncing."

"But, Jack," she said, "they're going to—"

"Let's not be mind readers," he said.

Mr. Moto rubbed his hands together again.

"It is so true," he said, "what you say about the ball bouncing. One day it is you. One day it is me. The young lady is not important, Mr. Rhyce. I can give you my assurance that I will see her off for home, myself, from the airport tomorrow." He picked up her handbag and tossed it to one of the men. "I shall give it back also tomorrow."

"Okay," Jack Rhyce said. "Do you mind if I ask you one question?"

"If it is short," Mr. Moto answered. "The sooner we leave the better, Mr. Rhyce."

Jack Rhyce nodded toward the curtained windows.

"What makes you think I killed that man down there?"

"Because he knew too much about something you know, too, Mr. Rhyce," Mr. Moto said. "We're going where we can have a quiet talk, and I think you will tell us what he knew before we are finished, Mr. Rhyce. Moscow does not know all the tricks."

"You ought to know I'm not a graduate from there," Jack Rhyce said. "Well, as long as I have your word about Miss Bogart—"

"I repeat," Mr. Moto said, "never do anything unnecessary. Why should she come to harm? Are you ready now, Mr. Rhyce?"

"Jack—" Ruth Bogart began. Her voice was dangerously loud.

It was not a time for handsome speeches, and besides, everything was strictly business.

"Don't, Ruth," he said—"but it's been nice to have known you. Come on, let's go."

He still was not recovered from surprise, but he began to see that there were several reasons why they should have mistaken him for Big Ben. Everything, he knew, was very dangerous.

They walked in a compact, softly stepping group down a flight of stairs and out into the night.

"By the way," Jack Rhyce said, "what time is it?"

Mr. Moto turned his head quickly.

"Why?" he asked. "Have you an appointment, Mr. Rhyce?"

Jack Rhyce did not answer. It was dark and very still. The hotel and the small town around it seemed sound asleep. The car that had brought them there was parked on the drive.

"You will sit in the front with me, please," Mr. Moto said. "The men will be in the back. One of them will have you covered. He is a good man with a pistol."

Jack got into the car without speaking. Mr. Moto took the wheel. The place where they went was not far from the hotel. It was a substantially built Japanese house surrounded by a high wall. The car stopped at the entrance door.

"You will step out quietly, please," Mr. Moto said.

Jack Rhyce gave way to a purely professional piece of exasperation.

"Tell that goon of yours to take his hands off me," he said. "I can still get out of a car."

A light burning above the doorway showed the raised platform where one sat to remove one's shoes, but there was no neat row of shoes such as one might have seen if the house had been occupied. Its dark windows and the unkempt condition of the shrubbery indicated that it had stood vacant for some time and had been opened only for this special occasion. Mr. Moto gave an order and one of the men opened the front door, at the same time switching on the lights in the entrance hall.

"The man will not touch you," Mr. Moto said. "Walk just behind me into the house, please. It belongs to a Baron. An American general had it as a resthouse during the Occupation. Many of its rooms are European."

Jack Rhyce was not interested in the ownership or the architecture of the house, nor did he have time to think of the incongruity of what had happened to him. The dark night, the strangeness, and the belief that time might be

176

running short were things that one thought of later. There was a distance of about six paces of gravel driveway between the car and the lighted hallway of the house. Mr. Moto walked a pace ahead of him, not bothering to look back, which showed that he trusted the man who was walking a pace behind, but the man behind was overanxious. He was too close, as Jack could tell from the sound of his steps, and if you held a gun at someone's back, one of the first principles was to keep a decent interval.

If one debated on whether or not to take a chance, one always ended with indecision. In the last analysis it was the contempt in Mr. Moto's tone that made Jack take the chance, in spite of the obvious risks involved. He whirled on the ball of his right foot, and he was correct that the man in the blue suit was too close. Jack Rhyce had his wrist in his left hand and the barrel of the pistol to the ground in the split second before he brought his fist across to the jaw with all the momentum of his body behind it. The pistol exploded at the same moment. Then the hand that held it relaxed, and Jack Rhyce had the weapon—from its size and weight, another one of those Berettas. Mr. Moto turned with the light of the door behind him. Jack Rhyce spoke before anything went further.

"Shall we leave it the way it is?" he said. "I told you I didn't want that man crowding me—and tell the other one to stop."

The other blue suit was back in the doorway, and Mr. Moto gave a curt order.

"I am so sorry he annoyed you," Mr. Moto said. "Yes, he was very clumsy."

"Not clumsy," Jack said, "just overanxious. Let's not you and me get overanxious. I'll get you anyway before you and the other one get me."

They stood completely motionless for seconds that seemed to Jack Rhyce to last for a long while.

"Yes," Mr. Moto said. "Yes, and what do you suggest?"

"You tell that friend of yours behind you," Jack Rhyce said, "to come over here and help his friend. He's coming to, now. I don't like being treated this way, Mr. Moto."

Mr. Moto was silhouetted by the light behind him so that it was impossible to see his face, and now one could gauge his reaction only from his voice.

"Yes," Mr. Moto said, "yes?"

The rising inflection of the last word turned it into a question.

"You tell your two people to keep out of the way," Jack Rhyce said, "and I'll go into that house with you. I want to talk to you as much as you want to talk to me. I'm not Big Ben, and I didn't kill Gibson. Frankly, he was my boss."

The light from the doorway was on his face, and he still could see only the shadow of Mr. Moto, but part of the tension was gone. The disarming of the guard had done it, and there was doubt in Mr. Moto's voice.

"You say you are not Big Ben?"

"You're damned well right I'm not," Jack answered. "I'm on the American team, the same as Gibson. He came up here to meet me. He was dead by the time we got there, and I want to know what he knew as much as you do. Maybe we can do some business if we go inside."

He heard Mr. Moto sigh softly. "You may put the pistol of the clumsy man in your pocket, Mr. Rhyce," Mr. Moto said. "If you gave it to him now he would kill himself for shame, but I am grateful to him for his clumsiness. You would of course have shot it out with me if you had been Big Ben."

"Yes," Jack Rhyce said, and he sighed, too, now that the tension was easing. "That's exactly the point I've been trying to make, and I had to move damn fast to make it. Here, take the gun, I don't need it any more. I never did like the balance of these Italian rods." He tossed the pistol on the driveway.

"Thank you," Mr. Moto said. "I am very mortified that I should be so mistaken. Excuse me, please."

"That's all right," Jack Rhyce said. "I've been sort of trying to explain you myself the last two days. It's too bad we didn't know sooner we were after the same boy."

"It was so very stupid of me," Mr. Moto said again. "I was so stupid, I think, because I have tried too hard, and thought too hard. So you were after Big Ben, too?"

"Yes," Jack Rhyce said, and everything was easy now, and relaxed. "That's why I was sent over from the States for. Gibson was worried and wanted help."

178

XV

Either tell the whole truth or none at all was an almost infallible business maxim. Under present circumstances, even though the position of the Japanese was still equivocal, the only solution was frankness. At least they were after the same thing. At least they were all in the business.

The man on the ground groaned and struggled to his hands and knees. Jack put his hands beneath his arms and pulled him to his feet. After all, there were times when one could afford to be cordial.

"Out like a light, weren't you, Mac?" Jack Rhyce said, and slapped him affectionately on the back. "Never mind. We're all pals now. Your gun's right over there."

Mr. Moto laughed in a completely genuine way.

"His English is not good. Tell him in Japanese."

"I apologize for your discomfort," Jack Rhyce said in Japanese. "So it was the tea and the coffee back there at the hotel that gave me away on the language, was it?"

Mr. Moto laughed again, and both the men in blue serge smiled. Everything could change very quickly in Japan.

"Oh, no," Mr. Moto said. "Earlier, Mr. Rhyce."

"Earlier?" Jack Rhyce repeated.

Mr. Moto nodded.

"In Burma, Mr. Rhyce," Mr. Moto said. "We had your name on file. Japanese linguist, born in Japan. I even had a glimpse of you once in Myitkyina." Mr. Moto laughed heartily. "I did not speak because I was moving the other way, but I remembered you when I saw you at the airport, Mr. Rhyce." Everyone laughed heartily. After all, the war was over.

"The word always was that you people had good Intelligence," Jack Rhyce said, "but I didn't know you were working so hard at it now."

"Oh, not so hard," Mr. Moto said, "with shortness of funds and the misfortunes. Poor Japan. We would not have made a mistake such as I have made tonight, before the war. The machinery was not bad before the war."

"Still, there was the German, Sorge," Jack Rhyce said.

"Oh, yes, Sorge," Mr. Moto said. "Such a nice man, Sorge. So intelligent; but don't forget, please, we caught Sorge. And did you Americans catch Dr. Fuchs? And the British who always boast so much about their Intelligence—did they stop Burgess or MacLean? So hard, so very difficult to manage everything."

It was a relief to talk naturally, without being under the necessity of cover. That Mr. Moto spoke so frankly indicated more than professional courtesy. It showed a colleague's respect.

"It's a touch life all right," Jack Rhyce said. "It's beginning to get me down these days."

"Get you down?" Mr. Moto said. "I wish so much I could visit your great country more often. I cannot keep up with the idiom now. Before everything was so unhappy, I was over once a year at least, New York, Washington, or Honolulu. Even when my duties were in Paris and London I endeavored to spend a week or two of observation in New York. Ha-ha. . . . In old New York the peach-crop's always fine, isn't it, Mr. Rhyce?"

"I wish I knew where you picked that one up," Jack Rhyce said.

"A song from *The Red Mill* was sung in the third floor corridor of the Mark Hopkins Hotel in San Francisco," Mr. Moto answered, "the evening before you left, Mr. Rhyce?"

"You haven't got such a bad setup, have you?" Jack Rhyce said. "So the Japanese schoolboy tailed me from Fisherman's Wharf, but you Japs get things twisted. I was up on that floor, all right, but I didn't sing the song."

Mr. Moto sighed.

"So sorry I have been so very stupid," he said. "He was so sure that you were Mr. Ben that when he gave the signal, I came myself to meet you at the airport instead of ending someone else. I mention it only so that you will give me some excuse. But why do we stand out here?"

"That's easy," Jack Rhyce answered. "Because you haven't asked me in."

Mr. Moto drew in his breath in a loud deprecating way.

"Oh!" he said. "The work has got me down, too, as you put it, so that I have lost my manners. This house is only loaned for a purpose for which I am so glad is now not necessary, by a very kind Japanese nobleman. So really little money now that individuals contribute. Poor Japan. He would be honored to know that you have been his guest. Come in, please, and my associates will warm us some saki. Do not be concerned about them. It is only they and me here, and unpleasantnesses are entirely over. Please to enter, Mr. Rhyce, and no need to take off shoes. This part of the Baron's residence is European."

The lights were on in the hall and also in a large room to the right. It was one of those newer houses. Jack Rhyce could see, that wealthier Japanese had built in the proposerous years that had preceded the war—a house half-European, half-Japanese, that had the schizophrenic quality of as much in present-day Japan. No Japanese, as far as Jack Rhyce knew, ever wishfully inhabited his Western rooms except for reasons of hospitality; and Jack Rhyce did not blame them, because the European section of such houses was usually as ugly and uncomfortable as its Japanese counterpart was beautiful. The house he entered now was no exception. The furnishings of the entrance hall gave forth a musty odor, from age and disuse; but they had been elaborate once, designed to impress, and perhaps please, the European guest, and also to display the owner's close acquaintance with Western living. The hall carpet was crimson, sprinkled with fleur-de-lis; the wallpaper artificial Cordovan leather; the mirror bad Victorian; and the chairs golden oak, upholstered with red plush.

Mr. Moto must have read the thoughts that ran through Jack's mind.

"We used to try so hard, Mr. Rhyce," he said. "Poor

181

Japan. The chairs are equally hideous in the parlor, bu
Americans like chairs."

Several table lamps that were lighted in the cluttered
over-decorated parlor revealed oil paintings of Englis!
cattle, encased in immense gold frames, two pieces of arti
ficial tapestry, tapestry-covered Jacobean chairs and uphol
stered easy chairs of a turn-of-the-century design. Ther
was also a European fireplace with a coal grate, in which
Jack Rhyce noticed a coal fire glowing in spite of the ho
night. The coffee table had been cleared of its cigarett
boxes and impedimenta; on it were knotted strings and
leather thongs and a pair of handcuffs.

"Well, well," Jack Rhyce said, "so you were fixing t
have a singing school."

Mr. Moto laughed boisterously.

"Ha-ha," he said, "so nice a way you have of saying
funny things, Mr. Rhyce." He called an order in angr
Japanese. "Take these away and bring the saki and ciga
rettes. Please sit down, Mr. Rhyce."

Jack Rhyce sat down in one of the easy chairs. Th
saki had come at almost the moment that Mr. Moto had
called, in a jar with a glaze that looked like celadon.

"Beautiful," Jack Rhyce said, nodding to the jar.

"You appreciate it?" Mr. Moto asked. "I am so
pleased. It has been in the Baron's family for many
hundred years. The Baron would be pleased to present i
to you, I think."

"What makes you think so?" Jack asked. "Maybe he's
anti-American."

"Oh, no," Mr. Moto said. "He is my cousin. You enjoy
the wine?"

He was grateful for the wine from the fragile thimble o
a cup that one of the men offered him.

"These two boys you have with you," Jack Rhyce said,
"look as though they had been in the Imperial Mar
ines—very tough, I mean."

"So nice of you to notice," Mr. Moto said. "I hope you
like the wine."

"I do," Jack Rhyce said. "It's nice and hot. I only wish
it were a Texas jigger."

"A Texas jigger?" Mr. Moto said, and he burst into ap
propriate laughter when Jack Rhyce explained the phrase

"Please tell the Marines in Japanese. They will appreciate about the jigger. One of them will stand beside you, ready to fill the cup."

Even into that European room there had crept an atmosphere of Oriental hospitality, politeness and good manners.

"To happy peace between the United States and poor Japan," Mr. Moto said. "Very foolish men made the war. Ha-ha. Nearly all of them are dead."

Jack Rhyce drank a second thimbleful of wine and held out his cup for more.

"Judging from my short stay here," he said, "it looks to me as though Japan is going to make out pretty well."

"You think?" Mr. Moto said. "There are so many dangers, but I am glad you think. It is very lovely to talk to an intelligent American agent who is engaged in my own line or work. Poor Japan. We had such a very lovely Intelligence system before the war."

"We heard you were starting work again," Jack Rhyce said. "Frankly, I didn't know it would be so good."

"Oh, thank you," Mr. Moto said, "but only in such a small way now. So little money. Let me see. There was once such nice men in your Intelligence in Washington. Do you remember Colonel Bryson? He was such a lovely man. I was so sorry he broke his neck in Vienna. Then there was Mr. Makepeace. They used to call him Tommy. What has become of him, I wonder?"

Obviously Mr. Moto was checking on Jack Rhyce's background, and Jack Rhyce was relieved that he could come up with an answer.

"He was in Prague six years ago," Jack Rhyce said, "but since then Mr. Makepeace has not been heard from."

"So too bad," Mr. Moto said. "Well, ha-ha, you cannot blame poor Japan for Mr. Makepeace. So too bad so many lovely people cannot live forever."

"That's quite a thought," Jack Rhyce said, "but we don't, you know."

The social amenities were nearly over. Mr. Moto waved to one of the attendants for a match and lighted a cigarette.

"And you?" he asked, pointing to the box.

"Thanks," Jack Rhyce said. "I don't use them."

"So right of you," Mr. Moto said. "So very, very right. I was taught that when I first entered the Intelligence. In the late twenties, it was. My Chief, dear old Mr. Naguna, never smoked cigarettes, for they left untidy traces. Dear old Mr. Naguna. Some more wine, Mr. Rhyce?"

"Thanks, I could do with a little more," Jack Rhyce said.

Mr. Moto gestured to one of the men.

"He is stupid," he said. "I told him to stay near you, Mr. Rhyce, but in his simple brain he was thinking that you must have had enough, just as in his simple brain he thought that you would not turn on him as you did outside, because he had a weapon directed at your back. Poor Japan. We never can understand how you Westerners can drink so much and not lose your wits. Confidentially, that is why the German Sorge puzzled our Mr. Naguna for several years. It did not seem possible that Mr. Sorge could be brilliant, with his drinking. He was like a figure in a Kabuki play."

"I told you I could do with a drink," Jack Rhyce said. "I didn't mean a teaspoonful at a time."

Mr. Moto laughed. The Japanese sooner or later laughed too much.

"Mr. Rhyce, I like you so very much," he said, "because you are so—doctrinaire, as the French say, about cigarettes and everything. That turn on the left foot, out of doors, was very beautiful. I could admire it even when I did not know what might follow. But I did know that the move was not Russian—at least not what the procedure was in Moscow before the war, Mr. Rhyce."

"Thanks," Jack Rhyce said. "They'll be pleased to know that, back home."

Mr. Moto drew in on his cigarette and passed his hand over his closely cropped, graying hair.

"When I see someone like you, so bright and young, in the profession, there is some excuse for my mistakes," he said. "I have never been familiar with Western features, but it would be my fallible opinion that you have a kind face, Mr. Rhyce. Please, I hope you will treat my error kindly. I did not have the benefit of records because our were destroyed in the bombing, and such as remained which we did not burn ourselves, were taken over by your General MacArthur. Such a very nice man—but poor Japan. Therefore, I can only rely on memory—but you were in Japan until the age of five. You were in Japanese language school in Colorado, because one of my own young men taught you and reported you as far above the average. Please do not make a mental note. Your Counterintelligence found him out. Then you were in combat Intelligence in Burma. Reports that came later said that your conduct with our people was most correct. Then there is an alert in my echelon, just as there must have been in yours. Elements in the Politburo were moving in. Poor Japan. So many people, so poor. So much discontent. The intellectuals so *après guerre*. Orders to look for a new personality. An American on file. The name on the intercept—Big Ben. Popular. Entertainment organizer, like someone on your stage, perhaps, or one of your motion picture entertainers who loved Russia. Look out for this American—Big Ben, with the singing voice and with the weakness for singing a song from that old entertainment called *Red Mill*. I heard it in New York when a very small boy, when my father was in the consulate in New York."

"That sure dates you," Jack Rhyce said. "That show opened in 1906 in old New York."

"Yes," Mr. Moto said. "But they still had the tune in 1912. Imagine my joy to hear of you from San Francisco. So pleased when I saw you at the airport. So pleased about the Friendship League which we have watched with interest. So pleased about your week-end excursion, just where Mr. Gibson was going. So pleased when you and the pretty Miss Bogart entered Chrysanthemum Rest—and then to find you are American Intelligence is difficult. My mind, I know, you too made up. I should have kept an open mind, but you will admit that everything did fit."

Mr. Moto paused. He had, after all, made his point.

"Don't blame yourself too much," Jack Rhyce said. "Anyway, you're not Russian. I've been worried about that from the first time you picked me up."

"Not Russian," Mr. Moto shook his head. "Nationalist Japan Party, Mr. Rhyce. Fascist, perhaps, but pro-Emperor, anti-Communist. So much trouble—poor Japan.

But when the typhoon ceases, back will spring the bamboo."

An earnestness in Mr. Moto's words made Jack Rhyce realize that he might be hearing a true explanation of the Japanese mood and the Japanese aspirations.

"Are Nationalists anti-American these days?" he asked.

Mr. Moto shook his head vigorously.

"Not now," he said. "Not enlightened ones. The United States is so very useful. Later perhaps, but not now. So silly to shoot Santa Claus, as your politicians used to say when I was in Washington. You see, I'm being very frank, Mr. Rhyce."

"I'd say you give every appearance of being," Jack Rhyce said. But from his experience, frankness in the Western sense of the word did not exist in the Orient. The difficulties among most people always lay in a misconception of each other's values. There was always an ultimate shift of meaning—even between Americans and Englishmen, who thought as nearly alike as any two nations.

"I am being frank," Mr. Moto said, "because I hope so much that we will be temporary partners, Mr. Rhyce. There are groups here on the Left, and on the Right, too, so anxious to arouse feeling against America. And the plain Japanese man can change so quickly."

Mr. Moto paused, and while Jack Rhyce waited for him to continue, he had a moment to speculate on Mr. Moto's background. He came from the old aristocracy. He must have been educated abroad, probably in an Eastern American university. There had been all sorts of strains and cleavages in his mental upbringing, but there could never have been any wavering in loyalty. He stood for Old Japan.

"The Left Wing has been growing very dangerously lately." Mr. Moto said. "That is the trouble with fanatics. One should always multiply their danger by ten or twenty, I believe. At the moment we are as anxious as you are to uphold American prestige, and I am willing to pool information if you are, Mr. Rhyce."

Jack appeared to hesitate, even though the man seated opposite must have known already that he had no choice. With Bill Gibson dead, he did not know the organization and things were closing in so rapidly that the only pos-

186

ible hope of achieving success was to rely on outside chance.

"I don't see why we shouldn't do business," he said lowly, "and maybe I know a few things you don't." He aused again. It was better to start slowly. "I have no riefing from Mr. Gibson, you understand. That was to ave occurred up here. He only told me that he was being ollowed, and intimated that he was in danger. He didn't vant us to be seen together."

"So right," Mr. Moto said. "Yes, so very right."

He did not blame Mr. Moto for looking discouraged. It vas time to hurry on and show that he had some value.

"Still Mr. Gibson sent us back a few facts," Jack Rhyce went on. "This man, Big Ben, has been meeting a Russian agent named Skirov at intervals. Do you know his Skirov?"

Mr. Moto's features sharpened.

"Not prewar," he said, "an *après guerre* Russian, very vell trained and very dangerous, Mr. Rhyce, I'm sorry we ave not seen him, but I believe he had been in Japan."

"We rate him above this Big Ben," Jack Rhyce said. "Skirov has a very high priority back in our office."

"He is very well trained," Mr. Moto said, "a man of reat potentials. We have tried very hard to find him."

"This Big Ben might lead him to us," Jack Rhyce said.

"Yes," Mr. Moto answered. "Why are you smiling, Mr. Rhyce?"

"About this Skirov," Jack Rhyce said. "I've never seen im, but we have a photograph and an accurate descrip-ion. It might amuse you to know that when I found you p there in our room I had a hunch for a few minutes hat you might be Skirov."

Mr. Moto smiled politely, but Jack Rhyce thought that e was startled.

"So funny how often people confuse things when they et fixed ideas," Mr. Moto said. "That was my difficulty vith you, Mr. Rhyce. I had such very fixed ideas. What ther information did Mr. Gibson send back home?"

"This meeting between Skirov and Big Ben," Jack Rhyce said, "Bill Gibson believed that there was one oming up, and there was something so important about it hat he was upset. He had learned something new, but he

187

did not have time to tell me in Tokyo, and he can't tell u[
now."

Mr. Moto lighted another cigarette. "I think I will hav[
another cup of wine," he said. "Perhaps I know some[
what more than you about what was troubling M[
Gibson. I am sorry, of course, that you do not know you[
apparatus here. It is a deep disappointment to me. I wa[
hoping we could have profitable exchange of facts."

"You mean you won't tell me any more because yo[
don't think I know anything worth while? Is that it?" Jac[
Rhyce asked.

"Yes," Mr. Moto said, "so sorry, Mr. Rhyce."

Jack Rhyce allowed a few moments to elapse before h[
spoke. It was clearer than ever to him that he coul[
achieve nothing unless he had co-operation. There wa[
still a risk, but it was a necessary one.

"Okay," he said. "Suppose I told you I've found Bi[
Ben. Suppose I could say that I could finger him for yo[
. . . then would you tell me what you think was on m[
boss's mind?" He had not anticipated the full effect c[
what he said. The Japanese gave a violent start before h[
could conceal his excitement.

"How very nice," Mr. Moto said. "You mean he's her[
in Japan now? I am so anxious for your answer, M[
Rhyce."

Jack paused again. Now that they each had somethin[
that the other wanted he was certain that they could d[
business.

"You tell me what Big Ben and this Skirov are going t[
do," he said, "and I'll tell you who this Big Ben is. Is it[
deal?"

"Oh, yes," Mr. Moto said, and there was no doubt tha[
they would do business. "This Russian Skirov, do yo[
know him?"

"I know all about him," Jack Rhyce said.

"Oh, yes," Mr. Moto said. "You were in Moscow i[
1946, and you speak Russian very nicely, do you not[
You made a remark to Mr. Molotov in 1946. You said a[
men are brothers."

Jack Rhyce winced at Mr. Moto's words. It wa[
growing clearer every minute why Mr. Moto should hav[
confused him with Big Ben.

188

"Just how the hell did you know that?" he asked.

Mr. Moto's hand fluttered to the lapel of his coat, and is fingers moved softly over the cloth.

"From a Chinese friend," he said. "We still have a few ontacts. We have to know what is happening, as best we an. Poor Japan."

Jack Rhyce still spoke deliberately. The value of time vas different in the East from what it was in the West, nd it was never wise to be overeager.

"I'm not so sorry for poor Japan as I was before I met ou," he said. "What is it that's so important about this kirov meeting?"

A slight shifting of Mr. Moto's glance showed that he lid not know all the answers either.

"We are still trying to discover," Mr. Moto said. "As ou know yourself, it is hard to break the Communist se-urity. The date is three days off. I'm so afraid that Mr. Jibson knew, or he would still be living. Our present in-ormation is that they are planning some coup that would ave serious political repercussions that would adversely ffect your country, I am afraid."

Jack Rhyce took his delicate porcelain wine cup from he table. He sipped the warm wine very slowly.

"You mean some sort of revolution?" he asked.

He knew that the question was not so preposterous as t sounded, because in the past there had been political pheavals in Japan, as sudden and violent as the island arthquakes.

"No," Mr. Moto said, "not Communist revolution. The icture is not yet set for that, but something that will ause popular disturbance, something that we think would e anti-American." He paused and laughed in the apolo-etic way of his countrymen when they were about to im-art bad news. "I think there will be political murder, Mr. Rhyce, and afterwards public demonstrations."

There was sense in everything that was said. Political ssassination, like public suicide, had often been an in-trument of Japanese policy. One only had to turn the lock back as far as 1936 to recall the killings by the rmy clique.

"Who's going to get murdered?" Jack Rhyce asked.

"We hope to find out," Mr. Moto said. "It would be a

murder, if I may venture to guess, that would be ascribe
to United States imperialism; one of a liberal politician
but we do not know whom. But we do think we know th
date—three days from now."

Bill Gibson must have known the date as well. Jac
Rhyce was trying to put together again the details of tha
hurried call on the day of their arrival, the battered Chev
rolet with the Beretta in the glove compartment, and t
connect them with his visit to the Asia Friendship League

"Do you know a man named Mr. Harry Pender," Jac
Rhyce said, "who is heading the Asia Friendship Leagu
now? He was transferred recently from Cambodia,
think."

Mr. Moto raised his eyebrows.

"I know," he said. "You spent the day with Mr. Pende
before you drove here, Mr. Rhyce."

"That's right," Jack Rhyce said. "Have you any in
formation on him?"

"He is a very naughty man," Mr. Moto said. "His alia
is Harry Wise. Hank is his cover name in the apparatu
Does that mean anything to you, Mr. Rhyce?"

Jack Rhyce nodded. The truth was that the nam
meant quite a lot.

"Washington must know him," Mr. Moto said, "if eve
our little Bureau knows him. What is it you say in th
United States? They have been moving their first teams i
here, in the last two weeks. But now I wish to hear fro
you. Where is Big Ben, Mr. Rhyce?"

"Haven't you guessed?" Jack Rhyce said. "You said
was singing that *Red Mill* song in the bar. He was rig
there with me, and you saw us do that dance together.

Mr. Moto was on his feet before Jack Rhyce had fi
ished.

"Back at the hotel?" he spoke almost in a whispe
"Describe him, please."

"Flight engineer on an American airline. You saw
dancing side by side," Jack Rhyce said. "Six feet fou
Weight about two-thirty, sandy hair, bushy eyebrows. E
pression affable. In theater business I think, and loves
sing. Favorite tune, *The Red Mill*."

"Mr. Moto slapped his hand against his forehead. "O
dear me," he said. "Oh, yes, I saw you."

"Well, that's the thumbnail sketch," Jack Rhyce said. "Does he ring any bell with you, Mr. Moto?"

"Oh, dear me," Mr. Moto said. "Excuse me, I'm so sorry, Mr. Rhyce. This is very serious. I've been so very stupid. We must leave here right away."

"Well," Jack Rhyce said, "I'm glad it rings a bell with you."

"Ha-ha," Mr. Moto said, "yes, it rings a bell. Yes, I shall recognize him. Mr. Rhyce, because he was the one who fingered you, as they say in the United States."

"How's that again?" Jack Rhyce asked, and he was also on his feet.

"Ha-ha!" Mr. Moto said. "It would be funny if I were not so ashamed. He said he was United States Intelligence, last night, after you sang the song, and he was so very, very nice. He told me you were Big Ben, Mr. Rhyce."

Momentarily Jack Rhyce must have looked as surprised as Mr. Moto had, but he regained his composure immediately.

"But when you saw us both together," he said, "and then he spoke to you afterwards, it must at least have crossed your mind, didn't it, that *he* could have been Big Ben? He answered the description too, didn't he?"

Mr. Moto eyes him solemnly and nodded in slow agreement.

"Yes," he said. "Oh, yes, it crossed my mind. I can make no good excuse for my very great carelessness, except that I was so sure of you already; but I might say one thing more—if you will excuse it, Mr. Rhyce."

"I'll excuse it; I'm still curious," Jack Rhyce said.

Mr. Moto hesitated as though he did not like what he was about to say.

"Excuse me, please," he said. "When in the bar I only felt the more sure I was right in selecting you. You were so much more intelligent, so much more of a trained agent, Mr. Rhyce, so much more dangerous—while he, if you will excuse me, was so immature, so harmless, so like so many of your government officials, Mr. Rhyce, I believed there was no doubt, but please believe I was astute enough to recognize my error when you took my man's

191

gun away. You would have begun shooting, not hav
waited to talk, if you had been Big Ben."

Jack Rhyce laughed shortly. There was no time to con
tinue with post-mortems.

"That shows he's smarter than I am," he said.

Never to underestimate the methods of an adversar
was a motto of the business. Never to think with pain c
what he had done to you, but to try immediately to figur
what you could do to him in return. The best way t
achieve this last result was to put yourself in his plac
and to think like him and not like yourself. Although ev
eryone was fallible, Jack Rhyce could not believe that h
had been wrong in his more basic ideas. Big Ben's mov
had been inordinately clever, but it was not the time t
dwell on the measure of his cleverness. It was time to pu
oneself inside Big Ben's mind to see why he had done i
and to estimate what he had won and lost.

Had he learned through some fluke who the couple i
Cozy Nook were, and had he taken that method to knoc
them out of the game? This was still unbelieveable i
Jack Rhyce's judgment. The nature of the murder dis
puted the possibility and so did all of Big Ben's subse
quent behavior. Life had made Jack Rhyce enough of
cynic so that he was positive that he could detect sincer
ity. Big Ben had shown no professional interest in then
while they had been in the bar, but something had oc
curred later to cause a change, and Jack Rhyce believe
he knew exactly what the circumstance had been. M
Moto must have entered the bar while they were singing
and Big Ben's glance must have picked out the face in th
crowd and instantly have identified it. Mr. Moto had bee
the one who spelled danger, and the improvisation tha
Big Ben had conceived, though brilliant, also had a touc
of desperation in it. It was the red herring across the trai
the smoke screen that permitted escape. The idea mu
have come to Big Ben while each was following the othe
in that ludicrous softshoe dance.

The truth was that the sight of Mr. Moto must hav
come to Big Ben as a stunning shock. He knew who M
Moto was. He also must have known that the Japanes
were on the lookout for him and had doubtless obtaine
some sort of description. In face, Big Ben's mind probabl

192

had moved further. He must have suspected that Mr. Moto had come to the hotel to make contact with Bill Gibson, the American agent. While they were still doing that soft-shoe dance Big Ben must have been fairly certain that Mr. Moto would visit Chrysanthemum Rest, if he had not done so already. Mr. Moto, as a secret agent, would know that it was murder. Already, in fact, Mr. Moto might be looking for the murderer. It was no wonder that Big Ben had been obliged to mope quickly.

"I think we'd better leave," Mr. Moto said. "You can continue thinking while we're moving, Mr. Rhyce."

"All right," Jack Rhyce said; "but let's get our lines straight first. You saw us go into that cottage. You were watching us all evening. Right?"

"Yes," Mr. Moto said, "watching carefully."

"Then you went into the cottage yourself," Jack Rhyce said. "Right?"

"Yes," Mr. Moto said, "so very right."

"When did you get to the bar?"

"When you and he were dancing," Mr. Moto said.

"And after I left, what happened?"

"He walked over to me," Mr. Moto said. "He asked me if I were looking for Big Ben."

"So he knew who you were," Jack Rhyce said. "He'll be halfway to Tokyo by now. He was frightened when he saw you or he wouldn't have thought so fast. Frightened people are the ones who think the fastest. Have you ever noticed that?"

"Yes," Mr. Moto said. "I am thinking you are unusually intelligent, Mr. Rhyce."

"Thanks," Jack Rhyce said, "but let's remember one thing more. He was startled when he saw you. That means he hadn't seen you earlier. Do you agree?"

A shadow of doubt crossed Mr. Moto's face, and he shook his head.

"I don't agree," he said. "It might also be he knew I was following you all the time. Both you and he are such very clever men."

It occurred to Jack that ironically enough both their lines of thinking were academically correct, even though one must be right and the other wrong.

"I think you presuppose too much," Jack Rhyce said.

193

"He's good, but everyone has failings. Don't forget, he had a lot on his mind last night. I don't believe he saw you until you were in the bar, because of one thing my thoughts keep coming back to."

"You are interesting," Mr. Moto said. "To what do your thoughts go back?"

"If he had known that Miss Bogart and I were up there to meet Bill Gibson, he wouldn't have killed him that way. Don't forget he knew who you were. If he had seen you tailing us he would have made some guesses as to who we were, too. He didn't know. He saw you the first time in the bar."

Mr. Moto nodded, and at least he looked half-convinced.

"He's going to be tougher to catch now, because he knows you're after him," Jack Rhyce said. "I suggest that we drive straight back in the morning, and I'll see Pender first thing Monday, just as though nothing had happened. The name is Ben Bushman. You can check on him at the hotel and you can find his airline, but you had better let me try Pender."

"Yes," Mr. Moto said. "And what is it that Mr. Gibson knew that makes him dead tonight? Fortunately we have people working. I hope in another day to have the full details."

"And you'll let me know?" Jack Rhyce said.

"Yes," Mr. Moto said, "with pleasure, Mr. Rhyce."

"I'll appreciate it," Jack Rhyce said. "I know you've got a lot to keep you busy, but maybe you wouldn't mind walking back with me until you can point out the hotel."

"Yes," Mr. Moto said, "we should be moving before it grows too light. There is only one thing more I have to say. If you'll excuse me, there may be much trouble."

"Yes," Jack Rhyce answered. "We'll have to be ready for it."

Mr. Moto hesitated. He seemed to be considering the happiest way of phrasing an embarrassing suggestion.

"Then it might be just as well," Mr. Moto said, and his words were measured, "if you did not tell Miss Bogart what we have been saying."

"I agree with you," Jack Rhyce said. "She won't be
194

useful here any longer. Suppose we send her home on Monday?"

Mr. Moto nodded.

"With so much pleasure," he said. "She is a very lovely lady. And now we should start back."

It was still dark outside when they passed through the gate to the road, but a refreshing coolness in the air told the hour almost as accurately as a watch. In half an hour the sky would begin to lighten and the stars would disappear.

XVI

"A very lovely dawn," Mr. Moto said. "In a few moments I shall let you proceed alone. A lovely time for a walk if one has difficulty with sleeping. That is what I should say to the hall-boy if you should see him. Say it in Japanese. He will be so interested to see you returning. He also is in what you call the business, Mr. Rhyce."

The hotel was dark, except for the lights in the corridors and along the drive. A path with steps to break the steepest portion of its ascent led, through a garden of ponds and tiny cascades bordered with dwarf pines and maple, to the upper terrace. He walked up the path carelessly, as though he had been out for a stroll because of inability to sleep. The terrace with its chairs and wicker tables was dark, except for a light shining over the ell marked Cozy Nook. He was halfway across the terrace when he saw Ruth Bogart, and he knew she had been standing in a shadow watching as he walked up the drive.

"Jack," she whispered, but he was only a hotel guest again.

"Why, sweetness," he said, "were you out looking for me? I only went out for a little stroll. I thought you were sound asleep."

She tapped her foot petulantly.

"I wish you'd told me, dear," she answered. "It did make me frightened to wake up all alone, and I couldn't find you. Are you all right?"

"Oh, yes, dear," Jack Rhyce said, "and I'm pretty sleepy now. It's only that I do wake up in the middle of the night sometimes, and I don't believe in these sleeping pills after what I've read about them. Instead, I go out for a walk."

196

"But where have you been?" she said. "I couldn't find you anywhere."

"Oh, just down the road a piece," he said. "It's lovely country here, and such a clear starlight night."

"You honestly should have told me," she said. "It was mean of you to make me frightened, dear."

"I'm sorry," he said. "But let's forget about it now, and sneak upstairs to old Cozy Nook, or else people will think we've had a quarrel or something."

"We really will have a quarrel," she said, "if you walk out on me again."

They had said enough to explain themselves to anyone who might have been listening, and now they walked carefully up the stairs of the Cozy Nook ell without another word until they were back inside their room. From the way she clung to him he knew she had been afraid for him. It all went to show how unwise it was for two people in the business to become emotionally involved. Instead of planning objectively, his concern for her threatened to throw other factors out of balance, but there was nothing he could do about it, except to feel more convinced than ever that she must be kept free from involvement. It was no place for her, and the Chief should never have sent her out. Although they were talking in whispers, they might as well have been speaking out loud.

"What's the matter, Jack?" she asked.

It was a woman's question. They always knew when something was the matter.

"It's all right," he answered. "There wasn't any trouble."

"You made them believe you?" she asked.

"Oh, yes," he answered.

"Did you have to tell them who we were?"

"Oh, I had to tell them this and that," he said.

"But exactly what did you tell them?"

"Oh, this and that," he answered.

"Jack," she said, "did you find out what Bill Gibson knew?"

"No," he answered, "not exactly."

"Jack," she whispered, "you're not being fair. Why aren't you telling me the truth?"

"You ought to know why," he answered: "Because from now on it's safer to keep you in the dark."

"I don't care whether it's safe or not," she said. "I want to stay in this with you."

It was bad soap opera, but although he was intellectually aware of it, he was moved by her wish. That was the trouble with being emotionally involved.

"Thanks," he answered, "but the thing's moved far enough so that you're not necessary on the job here any more. I want you to be back in Washington ready to meet me at the airport when I get there. It would be common sense even if I had not lost my head about you, Ruth."

Yet he could not be sure that he was right. If he had not cared about her, it was possible that he might have still thought of her as useful. Anyone as attractive as she and as good an operator, always did have uses.

"This shouldn't have happened with you and me," he said. "It was all a great mistake—professionally speaking, Ruth."

"I don't know," she said, "and I don't care. Anyway, I'm not going back. You're going to want me around when you know what I know."

"It's got to be awfully good," he said.

"It is," she answered. "I know how to get Big Ben, and it's got to be me, and nobody else. You were right. He's fallen for me, flat on his face. Now what do you think of that?"

In the realm of Intelligence the first rule was never to underestimate any individual, but as events developed, another rule crept in—never to overestimate him, either. Everyone had his weaknesses. *The Red Mill* was a weakness, and in Intelligence a woman always—or almost always—made her appearance eventually. That was the reason for the Mata Haris. They were always there for some useful, though seldom proper, purpose. They were the ones who finally caught the best ones out. At any time any man might become a fool about a woman.

"You mean you've seen our boy again?" he asked.

It was dark, and they were whispering, but still she was able to giggle in that annoying way that she used so well as cover.

"Am I going home on the first plane out?" she asked.

198

"Go ahead," he answered, "and tell me about our boy."

"My boy," she answered. "And he's pretty cute in some ways, too—wistful. You're not mad at me, are you? It was all done in a business way, and you've been pretty businesslike, yourself."

"I've had to be," he said. "I'm not able to move from one thing to another indefinitely."

She giggled noiselessly again.

"That's why you need a girl along," she said. "You must be awful in a man's world, Jack, thinking clearly and cutting down everybody by the numbers."

"Go ahead and tell me about our boy—I mean your boy," he said.

"Well, he was kind of sweet," she answered. "You see it was this way. After you left with those people I didn't know exactly what to do. I know you told me to stay right here, but I couldn't help being upset, considering. We shouldn't let our emotions get involved, should we?"

"No," he said, "we shouldn't."

"Anyway," she said, "I felt I had to do something, and so I went downstairs, and outdoors and out to the driveway, and who do you think I saw?"

"All right," he said. "You got out on the driveway and you saw Big Ben. What was he doing?"

"He had come out of the hotel with one of those big army Val-paks," she said. "He was putting it in the back of a car."

"It was a dark green Chevrolet coupé with a dented fender, wasn't it?" he asked.

"Yes," she said. "Naturally."

"They haven't got much of a car pool, have they?" he said. "But then, they didn't know that we'd spotted it. Was he in a hurry?"

"No, he was perfectly natural," she said. "That's one thing you can say about him. He's always natural. I didn't think we ought to let him go away like that, so I walked out into the driveway and said hello."

"Was he surprised? How did he act?" he asked.

"Natural," she said. "He didn't seem surprised at all. He said, 'Why, hi, there. Are you out looking for the boy friend?' And I said, 'Yes. A sort of funny thing

199

happened. A Japanese knocked on the door awhile ago and asked him to step out for a minute, and he hasn't come back, and I'm wondering where he is.' "

If he had planned it he couldn't have given her better lines. She had said all the right things, and she knew her business.

"He laughed," she went on. "He said, 'It was only a little joke I played, honey, and I'm hell on jokes. He'll be coming back all right. Why, I was just coming up to knock on your door myself, as soon as I'd stowed this bag.' "

Putting oneself inside Big Ben's mind, it was barely possible that he had been amused by the collegiate quality of the episode. Big men were more apt to be practical jokers than smaller ones. It was just as serious to overestimate as to underestimate.

"I asked him if he honestly meant that he had got you out of the way on purpose," she said, "and he said, 'It was just a kind of a gag. But I'm crazy about you, honey, and what you need is a real man, honey, and not one of these do-gooders who talks like a greeting-card salesman.' How do you like that one, darling?"

"I don't like it," he answered, "but it was the way I've tried to talk. What did you tell him then?"

"What did you expect?" she asked. "I said I was beginning to like him, too, and I said that you were always so prim and proper, and that I liked people with a real sense of humor. I said I wished he wasn't checking out and leaving so soon. I had to say something, didn't I, Jack? That's what I'm here for, isn't it?"

"Yes," he said, "I guess you're right about that one, Ruth."

"You see," she said, "he liked me. In fact, he liked me so much that he forgot one or two things. It was important to play up to him, wasn't it?"

"Yes," he said. "How did you play up?"

"Oh, not so very much," she said. "But never mind it, Jack. Only, when he held me in his arms I kept thinking of Bill Gibson, and wondering where you were. It was damned unpleasant, Jack. And if you want to know, I'm tired of sex tonight."

It helped him only a little to tell himself that of course

she had to do what she had done, and that he had to view the whole business as objectively useful.

"For just a second I thought he was going to take his bag out of that Chevrolet and stay," she said. "But he didn't."

"Not even when you asked him?" he asked her.

"Right," she said, "not even when I asked him. And if I may say so, I sounded awfully good. He honestly did want to stay, but there was something that made him know he had to go in a hurry. He kept saying, 'Gosh, I wish it wasn't fixed so that I had to leave here.'" She gave a perfect imitation of his accent.

"Yes," Jack Rhyce said, "but anyway, he went."

"But not immediately," she said. "He kept saying, 'Gee, I'm crazy about you, honey.' He seemed to be trying to make up his mind about something."

"All right," Jack Rhyce said. "And then he made up his mind?"

"Yes," she said, "he made it up. He said, 'Honey, this mustn't be good-by. Call me as soon as you get to the city.' Then he wrote down a telephone number and gave it to me. If he wasn't there I was to leave my name and he'd call me back."

After all, when you were in the business you had to give it everything you had.

"Good going," he said. "I can use that number."

"Oh, no, you can't," she said, "because I've torn it up already. Besides, he'll know my voice. When you want him, I'm the only one who can talk to him, Jack—and I guess you want him, don't you?"

"Yes," he said, "I'm going to want him all right."

"Then you've got to keep me around," she said, "and now let's stop being so businesslike, Jack. God, I wish we both were on the outside."

They were a long way from the outside, but the desire for escape and humdrum security formed a tantalizing vision that had an unattainable quality.

"I'm going to talk to you about being on the outside when we get home," he said.

"Let's talk about it now," she said. "We could have a cabin by a lake like the people in that book who took to the woods. I'm a pretty good cook, and you could fish or make snowshoes or whatever they do in the woods."

"Yes," he said, "but we'd better talk about it sometime later, not now."

"As a matter of fact, you wouldn't have to do much of anything," she said. "I have a pretty good income. You'd be surprised. We could travel and see the pyramids or the Taj, or we could go into the Mau Mau region."

"No," he said, "I'd rather buy a farm."

"A dairy farm," she said. "You could put on white overalls and a jumper every time you milked a cow."

"I can milk a cow, as a matter of fact," he said.

"I wish I could talk you into traveling," she said. "Only think what it would be like if you and I went to London, and if we didn't have to check in anywhere, and didn't have to be startled when we saw one of those damned familiar faces—if we could just be ourselves, having a quiet breakfast and reading the papers, without having to watch for anything, without a single damned compulsion."

"Without having to talk to anyone," he said. "Without having to find out anything, even the time of day."

"Without having to look over our shoulders once," she said.

"Without a switch-blade in your handbag, dear," he said; "without a pill, or anything."

"That reminds me, what happened to my handbag, Jack?"

Her question broke the illusion. They never should have indulged themselves with talk about the outside, or with the immature wishes that such talk engendered.

"Moto has it," he said. "He'll bring it in the morning. Look. It's getting light already. We're going to pull out of her first thing after breakfast."

"Going where?" she said.

"Back to Tokyo," he said.

"Doing what?"

"Doing just what we did before," he said. "The Friendship League. Mr. Harry Pender, all that sort of thing."

"Aren't you going to tell me anything?" she asked.

"No," he said. "What you don't know won't hurt you."

"You've found out something, haven't you?" she asked.

202

"Never mind," he said. "What you don't know won't hurt you, Ruth."

"Is it as tough as all that?"

"Never mind," he said.

"I don't," she said, "as long as it means you like me."

"That's the trouble," he said. "I like you."

"I won't be any trouble, Jack," she said. "I'll promise you I won't."

"I know you won't," he said.

"Then let's talk about the outside some more," she said. "There are all sorts of things I'd like to tell you—about when I was a girl at school, about parties, about all sorts of things. Jack, it's time we got to know each other in an outside way."

"I know," he said. "Later—there isn't time right now."

There was never time to think about yourself when you were in the business. Externals kept crowding in, each offering its own insistent problem. He wished to heaven he could keep her out of it, but it was too late now, after what she had told him. You had to move forward. You never could move back, and outside it was daylight, and the first birds were singing. Bill Gibson was dead in Chrysanthemum Rest—an overdose of sleeping pills—but still the show had to go on. He would have known better what to do if he had only known what Bill Gibson had been prepared to tell him. Yet even without the knowledge the picture was growing clearer. Time was all that was needed. He wished that he did not have the feeling that time was running out.

XVII

Jack Rhyce knew a great many stories about the business; and all of them, when one delved beneath their surfaces, had one thing in common—a universal element of simplicity. After all, the framework of an apparatus could not be complex, if only because too many links and convolutions threatened confusion, and Communist techniques ordinarily left their own dreary signatures. Consequently, later, whenever Jack Rhyce reviewed his procedures in Japan he was not surprised to find how little there was about them that was bizarre or even interesting. A series of coincidences had given him a lucky break, although the break had been complicated by the killing. There was also the mistake in identity that had arisen between himself and the Japanese element in the picture, which fortunately had been rectified. Aside from these complexities, the picture was like any one of dozens of others that kept repeating themselves in various parts of the world. Any trained agent, Jack Rhyce knew well, could have achieved the final results that he did. As soon as he had made contact with the Japanese, the lines all began to untangle. It was only the old story of infiltration and cover. As soon as he had spotted Mr. Pender and the Pen Pal room in the Asia Friendship office, most of the rest began to be routine. There was only one unknown element that made him apprehensive, and this lay in Mr. Moto's remarks about political assassination. The balance of everything in the Orient was precarious. It was his duty to learn more, especially if it would have anti-American repercussions. The Japanese had their own network of agents and, as Mr. Moto had said, they doubtless would turn up facts. However, there was every reason for him to do some thinking of his own.

After they returned to the Imperial Hotel on Sunday afternoon, he left Ruth Bogart in her room. The less she knew, the better off she was. He told her to sit quietly and to read a good book, but not to leave the room in case he telephoned. He and Mr. Moto left the hotel together in the Buick. He was the foreigner again who needed a guide, and if anyone was listening, they had only heard him ask to be taken to the Mei-ji Museum. They talked while Mr. Moto drove expertly through the traffic. Although the ride was a short one, they were able to say a good deal by the time they had parked the car in front of the conventional European building that housed the pictures illustrating the reign of Japan's greatest Emperor. The hour was late enough so that the place was closed, but under the circumstances, it was all the better.

"I know the guardians," Mr. Moto said. "They will put on the lights, and while I telephone you may enjoy the pictures. I think I can do everything from here very safely."

It was only a question of Moto's getting the latest news, which was the province of the Japanese, not that of Rhyce, and so Jack walked alone up the great marble staircase to the two great galleries. Granted that the pictures themselves had little individual artistic merit, together they made a panorama that illustrated one of the most dramatic life spans in history. The Emperor Mei-ji had been born and had spent his childhood and youth in a feudal Japan, insulated from the world. The Emperor had been a figurehead in those days, under the rule of the great Tokugawa lords. The early scenes of his birth and coronation showed the rituals of a country which had hardly changed since its cultural contacts with the Tang dynasty in China. It was the appearance of the American Navy in the early 1850's that had finally awakened the nation's latent instinct for survival. There were the pictures of the Emperor arriving in Tokyo to establish his rule in the Tokugawa fortress, scenes of war and incipient rebellion, and the strangely touching painting of the Emperor's mission departing on foreign ships to study the civilization and customs of the West. There was the Emperor drilling his troops in the European manner; there was the war with China, the war with Russia, the European costumes and uniforms, the Europeanized Japanese Navy, the annexation of Korea; and finally the crowd at the moat by the black wall of the Tokyo fortress lamenting the Emperor's death in 1912. If the current of time had run more swiftly since that year, nothing, not even the atom bomb at Hiroshima, had presented a greater succession of contrast; for in the Emperor's lifetime, a nation with smaller resources, more backward and seemingly less adaptable than China, had become a modern state and a world power, and its future was still implicit in the pictures. He must have examined these for more than half an hour before Mr. Moto joined him.

"You understand them, do you not?" Mr. Moto said. "They are our Bayeux tapestry. Poor Japan."

He had not thought of comparing the pictures with the tapestry of the Norman ships embarking their horses and their chain-mailed soldiers, with their steel helmets and nose protectors, for the battle of Britain, but it was not a bad comparison. Under the rule of the Emperor, Japan had gone through many crises as great as Hastings, and the story was not over yet.

"Skirov is believed to be here, but cannot be traced," Mr. Moto said. "There is much activity. Large quantities of banners have been made already saying 'Down with American Imperialism' and 'Avenge the People's Martyr.' Communists are always so well organized for demonstrations."

In view of what he had seen in other parts of the world, the news was normal and not surprising. The Rosenbergs not so long ago had been the people's martyrs.

"We will have more definite news by tomorrow, I hope," Mr. Moto said. "Some of our best people are working tonight. I shall be out myself. I should also tell you that they have found the lodging of your Mr. Ben, but he has not returned."

"Miss Bogart can get him if necessary," Jack Rhyce said.

Mr. Moto shook his head slowly. "It will not be necessary," he said, "if he is not hiding."

"You can reach me at the hotel tonight," Jack Rhyce

206

said, "and tomorrow at ten-thirty I will be there at the Friendship League, talking to Mr. Pender."

They did not speak as they walked down the marble staircase. After all, the business was routine, and the only question to be answered concerned the reason for the meeting of Skirov and Big Ben.

"I'll drive you to the hotel," Mr. Moto said. "It will look better."

They did not speak again until they were in the Buick, but both of them were thinking.

"Is it only your idea, or is it straight information," Jack Rhyce asked, "that there is going to be a killing?"

"There are the signs," Mr. Moto said. "Our people have seen them. 'Avenge the People's Martyrs.' They are meant to be out on the streets, Mr. Rhyce. They are not being made for nothing."

He had cultivated a deep respect for Communist agitation. Although the art was as old as revolution itself, Communist discipline had streamlined old processes until a mob could now be organized for any purpose as neatly as a billboard artist could paint a picture.

"Will it be a large demonstration?" he asked.

Mr. Moto nodded.

"Simultaneous outbreaks in different quarters. The street fighters are being given special training. It will be ugly, I am very much afraid, but not on the largest scale. It will be another step forward for Russia. Poor Japan."

"It's funny, isn't it," Jack Rhyce said, "to know that riots are being planned, without knowing what's going to set them off?"

"Yes," Mr. Moto said. "These people understand my country." He cleared his throat in a nervous way. "You do not, perhaps, remember the army officers' uprising in 1936 which cost the lives of so many very nice people in the government? A very unpleasant time. Ha-ha. So many of us were so busy. A great deal can be accomplished by assassination."

"Depending on whom you assassinate," Jack Rhyce said.

"Exactly," Mr. Moto said. "I am afraid they will pick out someone very good."

"From the slogans on the banners," Jack Rhyce said,

"it sounds as though they were going to take out a left-wing Liberal."

"Yes," Mr. Moto said; "yes, I think."

"Can you name some prospects?" Jack Rhyce asked.

"Oh, yes," Mr. Moto said, "there are several possibilities. Eight, perhaps ten I have considered. I wish so very much your Mr. Gibson were alive. Are you sure you only know him and no one else in his apparatus?"

"I told you once I didn't," Jack Rhyce said. "Don't you trust me?"

"Oh, please," Mr. Moto drew in his breath carefully. "Yes, as much as you trust me, I'm very much afraid."

"I'm working with you," Jack Rhyce said. "As long as we both want the same thing we can keep our cards face-up."

"I am not anti-American," Mr. Moto said. "I hope so very much that you are not anti-Japanese, Mr. Rhyce."

"Not at the minute," Jack Rhyce said. "I'm anti-Communist right now."

Mr. Moto drew in his breath again very carefully.

"Americans are so very nice, but sentimental sometimes. May I ask you what you intend to do about this Big Ben?"

"It depends on what he's up to," Jack Rhyce answered.

Mr. Moto cleared his throat and sucked in another breath.

"Would you object," Mr. Moto asked, "if any people were to question him?"

"Not if it's necessary," Jack Rhyce said, "but I'd rather have him followed. He can lead us to what we want just as easily that way as by our going to work on him."

"Ha-ha," Mr. Moto said. "Americans are always so very sentimental when they are not using flame-throwers and napalm. Ha-ha. Excuse me. If we cannot trace him tonight, I am very much afraid we should use Miss Bogart to find him."

"All right," Jack Rhyce said. "You can use your own judgment. Maybe we shouldn't leave him loose too long."

"Thank you," Mr. Moto said. "I am so very pleased that you trust me a little, Mr. Rhyce."

"Oh, I do," Jack Rhyce said, "maybe quite a little."

There was not much more to say.

"From now on," Mr. Moto said, "there will be a car and driver in your name, outside of your hotel. He will take you to me at any hour, I am so sorry that I am so busy."

"Are you sure you wouldn't like me to go out with you and help?" Jack Rhyce asked.

"So very sure," Mr. Moto answered quickly. "You would only be conspicuous, Mr. Rhyce. And please take care of Miss Bogart. She may be so very useful tomorrow. You understand?"

Jack Rhyce nodded. It was easy enough to understand when everything was lapsing into ordinary routine. Emotion had no value in the business. He and Mr. Moto and Big Ben were all expendable pieces on the squares of Intelligence. Jack Rhyce was glad to discover that his momentary desire for vengeance on Big Ben had almost evaporated. As matters had turned out, Big Ben was common property now, and after hearing Mr. Moto speak it was difficult to be under much illusion regarding Big Ben's future. The net was around him, and a European was too conspicuous in the Orient to hide for very long. The number of Big Ben was nearly up. Ben was paying the price of stupidity. That was the only way Jack could assess Ben's having given the telephone number to Ruth Bogart.

She was sitting quietly in her room when he returned, and the adjoining door was open.

"Is everything all right?" he asked.

"Yes," she answered. "Everything's very dull. Have they picked up Big Ben?"

"No, not yet," he told her.

She smiled at him.

"Isn't it lucky that I'm here?" she said. "Do you want me to try that number?"

"No," he said, "not yet."

"Then suppose I put on an evening dress and we go out for dinner," she said.

"Only in the hotel," he answered. "I don't want us to be buzzing around too much right now."

209

He arrived at the Asia Friendship League offices at half-past ten next morning to find that Mr. Harry Pender was already seated in his private office wearing a fresh Aloha shirt. The light from the window glinted cheerfully on his spectacles as he waved a welcoming hand.

"Come in, Jack," he said. "Come in. Are you ready to pick my brains?"

"I'm all set and raring to go, Harry," Jack Rhyce said, "if you honestly have time to give me some more fill-in on the League picture."

"Why, all the time in the world, Jack," Mr. Pender said. "Sit down. Have a cigarette?"

"No thanks. I never use them, Harry," Jack Rhyce said, and he seated himself in a comfortable modernistic chair.

He was embarrassed that he had not placed Harry Pender until Mr. Moto had explained him, but after all, he had only seen the face in a group photograph, and never in the flesh. Very little doubt remained with Jack Rhyce now. The man before him was certainly the individual who was known as Harry Wise and who had recently been placed on the doubtful list at the office, a former American college instructor who had been holding a Communist card since late 1930's, but with no definite record of activity. He looked older than his photograph as Jack recalled it, and since he had not been heard from, he must have been behind the Curtain for some time. Conceivably he had been one of the Americans in Chinese prison camps who had been mentioned by American war prisoners; conceivably he had been one of the Europeans who had been mentioned in connection with the germ warfare accusations. It was a pity to be so far away from source material.

"It sure is nice to see you safe back from that place," Harry Pender said. "I see in the Japan *Times* that one of our fellow countrymen took too many sleeping pills up there. I hope it didn't spoil your fun."

"Oh, there was a little mix-up with the Japanese authorities," Jack Rhyce said, "but it didn't amount to anything. You see, we left yesterday morning and drove around seeing the sights. I sort of wanted to get oriented a little—you know, get the feel of the country."

"That's a very wise thing to do," Harry Pender said. "A first impression has a lot of value. You know what people say—either spend ten days or ten years. By the way, where's our girl friend? Ruth Bogart, I mean."

"She's back at the hotel," Jack Rhyce answered. The question had indicated an unnecessary curiosity. "She wasn't feeling so well this morning, a little Japanese stomach, but nothing serious."

"To bad," Mr. Pender said. "I hope you've given her something for it. Do you want me to send one of my girls over?"

"Oh, no," Jack answered. "She's going to be all right. I just told her to take it easy. Well, let's get down to business. I hope I told you emphatically enough the other day, Harry, how impressed I was with your whole layout here, and all the fine things you're doing. I want to read up on all the social studies you're making every one of them."

Harry Pender took off his horn-rimmed spectacles and held them between his thumb and middle finger.

"Don't read too much, Jack," he said, "or you won't see the forest for the trees."

"I know exactly what you mean, Harry," Jack Rhyce said. "But gosh, I've got to begin somewhere. Everything can't be as smooth sailing as it looks around here, Harry. You must have some pretty big policy problems."

Mr. Pender allowed his glasses to swing like a pendulum between his fingers. He raised his eyebrows inquiringly.

"I mean, for instance," Jack Rhyce said, "problems of personnel. You were mentioning this on Friday, I think."

"Oh," Harry Pender said, "of course every office has its turnover. It takes time making selections, but on the whole, we have a fine team all the way down the line."

"Oh, I never meant to say you didn't," Jack said quickly. "I was just wondering, well, whether you had any trouble with Communists or anything like that." He had intended to bring out the subject with flat-footed innocence, and from the tolerant way Mr. Pender laughed, he was rather sure he had.

"Excuse me for laughing, Jack," Harry Pender said, "but that question of yours is completely characteristic of

211

the point of view that everyone brings here from the States. Rumors become grossly exaggerated. Why, there's hardly a Communist in Japan, in the sinister sense of the word—but you will find varieties of liberals. From my observation, democracy has a permanent foothold in Japan."

"Well, it's mighty nice to hear you say so, Harry," Jack Rhyce said. "It's the sort of reaction I hope to fit in my report. I'm glad, too, if there's a healthy liberal party here. I hope they're interested in putting social welfare on a sensible scientific basis."

He watched the horn-rimmed spectacles moving in a slow, thoughtful arc, and he was happy to notice that Mr. Pender was giving him his smiling, friendly approval.

"You'll find liberalism here in the best sense of the word," he said, "and the leaders are highly dedicated people. I want you to get to know some, Jack, I want you to get this Communism bias thoroughly washed out of your hair."

"It's curious," Jack Rhyce said, "how distance distorts facts. Back in the States we hardly hear about Japanese Progressives, let alone learning their names. Who are some of them, Harry?"

He hoped that his interest appeared fatuously genuine. Mr. Pender's thoughtful eyes were fixed on him, but he could not detect a glint of suspicion or any diminution in the current rapport between them.

"I think we can help you there," Mr. Pender said, "because the League is just doing a pamphlet on the subject, with thumbnail biographies of eight or ten of the top-flight liberal politicians. There's Hata, for instance, and there's Iwara, and Yamashita and Nichiwara. I'll be delighted to show you the copy we're preparing."

"Gosh, Harry," Jack Rhyce said, "I'd sure like to see it. Who's the best of them, would you say?"

"Oh," Harry Pender said, and as far as Jack Rhyce could see, he was taking the question casually, "every one of them has quite a following, but Hata is head and shoulders above the rest. Noshimura Hata. I'll see that you meet him sometime."

"Can you arrange it?" Jack Rhyce asked. "It would be a real pleasure if you could, provided he lives around here."

212

"He does, as a matter of fact," Harry Pender said, "in an attractive house with a beautiful garden. His collection of dwarf trees is very widely known."

"I didn't know liberal intellectuals had large homes and gardens," Jack said.

"Hata is an educated liberal," Harry Pender answered. The swing of the spectacles in his fingers accelerated slightly. "An Oxford graduate, a member of a wealthy family, and a philanthropist."

"Oh," Jack Rhyce said, "then he can speak English, can't he?"

Granted that he had picked up the information he had wanted, had the cost been to great? Perhaps he should not have pursued the subject so long after the name of Noshimura Hata had been mentioned, and yet there had been the danger of dropping the thing too suddenly.

His attention was now riveted on the swinging glasses in the right hand of Mr. Pender. There was no doubt that the motion had been accelerated, and there was always betrayal in unconscious gesture. Instinct was delivering its message to Jack Rhyce, telling him that a crucial stage had been reached, the outcome of which depended on the next few words. It was time to drop all show of interest, to move on to something else.

"All you say," Jack Rhyce said, "goes to prove that preconceived opinions are always off the beam, aren't they? I have no idea that the Japanese would be so enthusisatic about sports, for instance. Now, if you've got the time, I'd love to hear whether you're dovetailing a good sports program in with your other projects."

"Sports had a leading priority with us," Harry Pender answered. "Nothing pulls people together so much as meeting on a playing field. In fact, I should put sports ahead of any other cultural interchange when it comes to the promotion of good will . . ."

At least they were away from liberalism, and embarked on a sea of verbiage which, to keep the cover right, ought to demand most of the morning for a crossing. It was necessary to sit there for an hour or more mouthing idealistic platitudes, being, as the Chief would say, a do-gooder in every sense of the word. Talking with Harry Pender was both real and unreal. It was ironic to think that they

213

were each talking only for the other's benefit. Did Mr Pender believe he was impressing him? And did his own artificial guilelessness seem real to Mr. Pender? He only knew that they both were artists, each concealing any impatience or boredom he may have felt while they discussed the Asia Friendship League.

It was quarter of twelve when he ventured to push back his chair.

"Harry," he said, "it's been swell of you to give me so much of your time. I have as many ideas packed in my mind as I have reading matter in my briefcase now. I guess I'd better take the rest of the day just sitting in the hotel room boning up on the material."

"It's been a good morning for me, too, Jack," Mr. Pender answered. "How about a bite of lunch before you start reading reports? Not more than five minutes away from here is the best beef sukiyaki restaurant in the world."

Jack Rhyce picked up his briefcase and endeavored to straighten out the wrinkles in his seersucker coat.

"There's nothing I'd like better, Harry. And please give me a raincheck on that offer," he said. "But right now I'd honestly better go back to the hotel and see how Ruth is. How would lunch tomorrow be, instead? Because I'll be right back here tomorrow morning, making a nuisance of myself with another batch of questions."

She was in her room, reading Terry's *Japanese Empire*. She looked up inquiringly when he came in.

"Has anything happened here?" he asked.

"Yes," she said. "One thing, Big Ben telephoned."

He tried to forget about her as a person, when she told that news. Nothing must interfere with the business, and she must have felt the same way, from the excitement in her eyes.

"What did he want?" he asked.

"He wanted to make a date for five this afternoon," she said. "I told him I wasn't sure that I could get away. I said I'd call back at three."

"That's my girl," Jack Rhyce said. "I think the time has come to pick him up, Ruth. It's a good thing you're along, all right."

214

"Thank you, sir," she answered. "How did you get on with Pender?"

"I wish I knew," he said. "He worries me a little. He's in the business all right. I think I'd better see the Japs again, right off. I'll be back in about an hour."

"Aren't you going to cut me in on anything?" she asked.

"Only about Big Ben," he said. "Don't ask for any more."

"I won't," she told him; "but, Jack—be careful. Don't be too sure of yourself."

Frankly, he wished he felt more assured.

He had not been under the hotel porte-cochere for half a minute before the car and the driver that Mr. Moto had indicated the day before appeared. The meeting place was the back room of a curio shop. Mr. Moto, still in his blue suit, sat at a table with a telephone in front of him, drinking a cup of tea.

"No more news than yesterday," he said. "So sorry."

"I'm sorry, too," Jack answered.

"And how is Mr. Pender? Did you see him?" Mr. Moto asked.

Jack Rhyce nodded. "You were right about him," he said. "We have his photograph, but he looks ten years older. He knows a lot about liberal politicians. I've been doing some thinking this morning."

"I am so glad to hear it," Mr. Moto said, "and I hope so much that you will tell me the results."

"We don't seem to know what's going to happen, do we?" Jack Rhyce said. "You only know that they're making plans for an organized demonstration, and you guess that there's going to be a political killing. We had the same word in Washington. But it's only a guess, isn't it?"

"That is true," Mr. Moto said. "Our people are working, but they have come on nothing new."

"Then I think we'd better pick up Big Ben," Jack Rhyce said. I'm sorry, I hate to break up an apparatus."

"No one has seen him," he said. "He is hiding very carefully."

It was time to tell the news, and time to lay the lines.

"Not so carefully," he said. "I think maybe we're over-rating our boy. He called up Miss Bogart this morning.

215

He wants to make a date with her for this afternoon. She said she wasn't sure that she could do it. She'll call him back at three."

Mr. Moto stared at the teacup, and his forehead wrinkled and he shook his head.

"I do not like it," he said. "It does not sound correct."

"Meaning it doesn't sound like the first team?" Jack said.

Mr. Moto's gold teeth flashed when he answered.

"I am so glad you use the expression," he said. "I wish that Miss Bogart would give us the telephone number. We could have traced it by this time."

"I told you she wouldn't," Jack Rhyce said, "and I decided not to put further pressure on her. The fact is she may be highly useful in picking up Big Ben, and she was sent over here to be useful. She'll call him any time we want."

"She does not want to leave you," Mr. Moto said. "That is very proper, Mr. Rhyce, but I do not like it. I do not like it."

"I agree," Jack Rhyce said. "A lot of angles in this situation worry me. You can trace the number when she calls him. We may need it if anything goes wrong, but I don't believe much in tracing numbers."

"May I ask why?" Mr. Moto said.

"Because it's too obvious," Jack Rhyce said. "They always use a public telephone in some public place—a bar or a railroad station."

"If we knew the telephone," Mr. Moto said, "we could be watching and take him when he makes the call."

"Yes," Jack Rhyce said, "but I don't think our chances would be good. He's a professional—he would be on the lookout for strangers. We're safer to let Miss Bogart call him. It's better not to be too busy when we're closing in."

Mr. Moto was silent for a moment. Then he nodded slowly.

"I think I am inclined to agree with you, Mr. Rhyce," Mr. Moto said. "I realize that Miss Bogart is a very intelligent girl who has had training in handling these matters. I shall call on you at the hotel at a quarter before three."

"And I'll go along with you later," Jack Rhyce said.

216

"Trace the call, then, if you want, but let's catch him where he's waiting for Miss Bogart. It will be safer and surer that way. And I want to be along when you pick him up—just out of interest, Mr. Moto."

XVIII

Jack Rhyce had played a part in several similar actions in America and Europe, the details of which seldom varied. Find your man and keep him at a given spot. Get the group distributed. Have the car ready. Close in simultaneously from all sides. This was the one maneuver that required expert coordination and experience. If properly executed, there would hardly be a ripple of a struggle. Often pedestrians ten feet away did not notice the group around the victim, trussed and pinioned in the approved style, being half pushed, half carried to the waiting car. Even if things did not move quite as planned, a well-placed blow at the back of the skull could solve the difficulty. Big Ben was a big man, but he could be handled, given the proper group. Jack Rhyce was certain that there would be no trouble if he were in the party.

"Oh," Mr. Moto said, "you do not trust us, Mr. Rhyce? You will think differently, I am sure, when you see my people. Poor men. They are not well paid, but they are as neat as your FBI."

The obviousness of the operation was a sufficient explanation as to why Mr. Moto did not like it, since the use of a woman to lure a man was among the most shopworn in the sordid bag of tricks which everyone knew backwards in the business. Yet it was a trick that worked the most frequently of them all. Jack only had to remind himself that he too had fallen in love with Ruth Bogart freely to accept the motives of Big Ben. The repugnance that he felt at having to use her in this venerable trick only convinced him further of Big Ben's infatuation and besides, he had seen them on the dance floor.

By the time he and Mr. Moto reached the hotel, the preliminary preparations were all in hand: the equipment

218

immediately necessary was packed in Mr. Moto's briefcase. When Ruth Bogart saw the briefcase she smiled a thin, Mona Lisa smile, Jack had never seen her looking prettier. The excitement and the exacting demands which would be made of her in the next few minutes had added to the delicacy of her features and the luster of her hair. Even her voice had a new seductive quality.

"So you boys need me, do you?" she said. "All right, rig up the telephone."

When Mr. Moto took out of his briefcase and methodically arranged the instruments, Jack watched him with approval. There were right and wrong procedures in wire tapping, and Mr. Moto knew all the proper ones.

"I suggest that we both listen, Mr. Rhyce," he said as he handed Jack Rhyce a pair of earphones of Japanese manufacture. The Japanese were able to make anything.

"Are you sure this won't be too big a load?" Jack Rhyce asked.

"Don't be silly, Jack," Ruth Bogart said. "He knows his stuff." She smiled her brightest smile. "I couldn't have set this up better myself, and now it is three o'clock, I think. Perhaps—if you are ready—I'd better make the call?"

"No," Jack Rhyce said. "Let him wonder. Let him sweat it out for ten minutes."

He never forgot the interval of waiting, or how happy Ruth Bogart looked.

"Jack," she said, "you're glad I'm along now, aren't you?"

"Yes," he answered, "at the moment, Ruth."

"It's nice to know I'm useful, under the proper circumstances," she said. "Maybe that's all any woman wants."

They did not speak for another minute or two, and then Mr. Moto broke the silence.

"Excuse the question," Mr. Moto said. "Do you carry a blackjack with you, Mr. Rhyce?"

"Funny you should ask that," Jack Rhyce answered, "because I was thinking of it myself. No, I haven't one with me."

Mr. Moto reached inside his briefcase.

"If you will permit, it will be a pleasure to present you

with this one," he said. "It may be useful, and ha-ha, it will be easier for you to reach him, if needed."

Jack balanced the instrument expertly in his hand before he slipped it into his back pocket.

"Thanks," he said. "I'll do my best to be neat and clean if necessary."

"I'm sure," Mr. Moto said. "So very sure you will be. And now perhaps Miss Bogart should make the call. Let us not have the gentleman too discouraged."

They sat silent while Ruth Bogart gave the number, and there followed, of course, a moment of suspense until they heard the answering voice. The connection was very clear. There was no doubt in the world that it was Big Ben.

"Gosh, honey," he said, and his voice was plaintive, "I've been settin' here. I mighty near thought it was a brush-off."

"Oh, Ben," she said, "I'm sorry, but I couldn't call until I was alone."

"You mean he's back with you?" Big Ben asked. "Why honey, I kind of got the idea he might have left you for good back there in the mountains. When did he come back?"

"He said he wasn't able to sleep," Ruth Bogart answered. "He just said he went out with some Japanese friends and drank some saki."

"And he's hanging around you now, is he?"

"Ben, don't be that way," she said. "I told you I was tired of him, and he's gone now."

"Well, don't forget you're my girl now, honey. How about say around six tonight?"

She first glanced questioningly at Mr. Moto.

"Why that would be lovely, Ben," she then said. "Will you call for me at the hotel?"

There was a silence on the other end of the wire.

"Why, honey," he said. "I had some trouble there, last time I was in Tokyo, and the folks there maybe don't like me too much. How about going down to the Ginza and meeting me outside the Cimaroon beer hall? It's a GI place, honey, with good food and singing and everything. I'll be waiting by the front entrance, come six o'clock."

"But, Ben, dear, I don't know this town."

220

"I'm going to see personally that you're going to know and love it before you're through, honey," he said. "It's o trouble to get there. Just you tell the hotel doorman. ny taxi driver can take you to the Cimaroon."

"Well, then you be right outside," she said. "It's ooky alone in a place where you don't know the lan- uage or anything. Are you sure you'll be there, Ben ear?"

"Sure as hell isn't freezing. Just you don't worry. Take cab," he said.

"All right," she said, "but it makes me a little ightened, Ben."

"Aw, now," he said, "there's nothing to be scared of, oney. Wear something cute and fluffy. I only wish it was x already. Don't forget—the Cimaroon. You got it, oney?"

They all had it—the Cimaroon—and the conversation as over, and they each sat for a moment in a questioning rt of silence.

"How did I do?" she asked.

Jack had been analyzing every pause and change of ne in the speeches. A voice over the telephone without atures or personalities to support it was a disembodied ing. Although he had no doubt that the voice belonged Big Ben, there was a doubt as to whether it had been holly credulous. In the end, everyone speaking on the lephone always assumed a new and peculiar personality. ven Ruth Bogart's voice had exhibited strain, and the me had been true with Big Ben, but there had been so ttle deviation that he could safely attribute it to the edium of communication.

"You did fine, I think," he said. "Don't you think so, Ioto?"

Mr. Moto was dismantling the wire-tapping device.

"It is not for me to analyze the European mind, but on e whole he gave me the impression that he wanted so ery greatly to see Miss Bogart."

Mr. Moto snapped his briefcase shut.

"The Cimaroon is a beer hall and night club, frequent- l by American soldiers and sailors, a suitable place for im to select," he said. "It should not be difficult to take im quickly if he is waiting on the sidewalk. I must be leaving now to make arrangements. The car and drive will be waiting to take you there, Mr. Rhyce. May I as you to arrive in front of the Cimaroon at half-past five?"

"Let's make it 5:15, if it's all the same with you," Jac said. "Those Joes have second thoughts, and get caref and early sometimes. Once I had to do a snatch i Paris—one of the first I ever was mixed with—but nev mind it now."

"Thank you," Mr. Moto said. "I quite agree wit 5:15."

"And what about me?" Ruth Bogart asked. "Am I g ing with you, or not?"

"Certainly not," Jack Rhyce said quickly. "There won be any need, Ruth."

"If he doesn't see me, he may not show," she sai "I've known it to happen, Jack."

As things stood then it seemed safe to discount tha possibility. Jack was actually experiencing a feeling whic was almost one of peace. As far as he could see, the Japa assignment was drawing to a close. If the ending was n wholly satisfactory, it was effective, and with the wa things were going, they could not beat about the bush fo ever. His main mission had been Big Ben. He took th blackjack from his hip pocket, tossed it in the air an caught it, with the same carelessness he would hav caught a baseball on the outside. It was very nicely co structed. The Japanese were always good at detail.

"No, it won't be necessary, Ruth," he said. "You' only be in the way if there's any kind of hassle. He's a b boy, and he may muss things up."

"I think Mr. Rhyce is correct," Mr. Moto said. "I a most grateful to you, Miss Bogart, and it would be so ni if I could pay you my respects when this is over. Perha a Japanese supper tonight; but—ha-ha—not at the Cim roon, and just with me and Mr. Rhyce. But—ha-ha—n with Mr. Ben. At 5:15, then, Mr. Rhyce, and thank yo very much."

The feeling that everything was over still persisted aft Moto had gone. It resembled the easing of tensions l had experienced before when a job was almost finishe and everything was in the groove. But this time elatio was added to his relief, which he tried to check becau
222

always distrusted elation. Finally his conscience trou-
bled him with a nagging suspicion that he was ending
things too quickly, not following them as far as he might
an ultimate conclusion. It was true that he was hedging
his bets, but it was better to hedge than lose, and they
were winning enough. At least they were crippling the apparatus by taking out Big Ben.

"You know, I feel pretty good on the whole," he said
to her. "When we get him, we can move the hell out of
here and head for home."

Her expression had brightened, too.

"It can't be soon enough for me," she said. "And why
can't we start being ourselves when we get on that
plane?"

"I don't see why we can't from there on in," he answered.

"What do you mean?" she asked. "From there on in?"

"A lot of things," he said, "and we ought to be able to
start discussing them as soon as I get back here."

"Do you mean you still love me?" she asked.

"It's unprofessional, but I do," he said, "and a lot of
other things. Come to think of it, I wouldn't have missed
any of this."

"Even being unprofessional?" she asked.

"Yes," he said, "even being unprofessional."

"Jack," she said, "what's going to happen to him?"

"He's not our problem," he said. "The Japs will take
him over. But it's the best we could do under the circumstances, Ruth." He turned and strode across the room and
back. "We might have gone further into this if Bill Gibson
hadn't died, but I think it's time now to stop this show, I
really do."

"It's sticky, letting the Japs take him," she said. "I wish
you and I weren't in it."

"We're in it all right," he said.

"You're too nice for it," she said, "and maybe I am,
too."

"I wouldn't be surprised," he told her, "but let's put
our minds on pulling out of here tomorrow, Ruth."

The interval before his departure for the Cimaroon always remained in his memory as a domestic sort of scene.

"I don't suppose we'd better inquire about plane reser-

223

vations yet," he said. "No reason for anyone to know th
we're checking out, but if you want something to do whi
I'm out you might start packing your suitcases. The
might be space on something tomorrow."

"Jack," she said, "don't you think you ought to wea
something heavier and darker than that seersucker coat?"

"Oh, I don't think so," he answered. "This won't b
night work, and it's awfully hot outside."

"I wish you were carrying a gun," she said, "just :
case. Wouldn't you like to borrow my fountain pe
gadget? It doesn't look as though I'm going to need it."

"I can do fine with this jack," he said. He was feelir
almost jovial now that everything was set. "I'm real
pretty good at controlling one of these."

"I think you ought not to wear crepe-soled shoes," sh
said. "You might slip in them. I don't know whether yo
ever knew Bobby Burke, who used to work in Paris. F
slipped making a swing at Oscar Ertz—you know, th
Czech—just outside the Gare du Nord. He skidded on th
pavement and had a shiv in him before he could recover."

"These shoes are skid-proof," he told her. "No, I nev
did know Bob, but I've heard plenty about him. Ought
to be jealous?"

"Darling," she said, "I never knew about you, dea
and you never knew about me. You won't ever need to l
jealous. Now let me take a look at you. You look awful
handsome."

"So do you," he said. It was time to be going, but he d
not want to leave her.

"Jack," she said, "if you do hit him, follow through. L
him have it all. He's an awfully big man, you know. No
you'd better kiss me good-by. I don't want you to be late

"Don't forget Moto's coming to take us out to dinn
when we get back," he said. "I wish we were going alon
We haven't had much fun here, what with one thing ar
another."

"Oh," she said, "there'll be lots of other times. Tal
care, Jack, please take care."

He remembered those last words most distinctly. In fac
they echoed in his memory all the way out of the hote
He had a final glimpse of her before he closed the doo
224

She was standing smiling, very straight and neat, and looking very happy.

The taste of the American GI was responsible for most of the innovations along the Ginza, and it was worth remembering that they reflected the immaturities of youth—naturally enough, since the age average was low in the American armed forces. Thus it was not wholly fair to be overcritical of the garish beer halls and night clubs, as full of gay plastic color and light as the jukeboxes at home, for they filled very adequately an intense demand for release. In fact, Jack Rhyce thought the Cimaroon offered everything that he would have wanted when he was an undergraduate at Oberlin—air-conditioning, cold beer on draught, an enormous gaudy bar, a jazz orchestra, a Japanese torch singer, and dozens of tables with pretty, smiling Japanese hostesses. He half wished he were back in the army. It had been different in the paratroops in Burma.

Although it was only 5:15, the Cimaroon was already full. The brash notes of the orchestra, the high voice of the singer, and the chatter of the patrons over their drinks rose to such an intensity that his transient wish that he were a boy again vanished. Instead, it occurred to him that the noise would be an excellent background for a shot, and it could easily be minutes before anyone would know just what had happened. You had to consider seriously such contingencies in a place like the Cimaroon, as well as check the entrances and exits. These were limited, as far as he could observe, to a wide entrance on the street, and to two doors in back leading to service quarters. He stopped making these mental notes only when he reminded himself that he was not running the party and that instead he was in the guise of a foreign attaché.

Mr. Moto was waiting at a wall table, facing the door—a conventional position under the circumstances. He waved a welcome to Jack Rhyce in an exaggeratedly European manner.

"Beer, of course?" Mr. Moto said. "It is so cool and comfortable here."

It was cool but noisy, and Jack had a feeling that the Cimaroon did not belong in Japan or anywhere else. He

225

took only a sip or two of beer because he disapproved of drinking before any such event as the one they were approaching.

"Everyone is posted," Mr. Moto said. "Ha-ha, we will use the same Buick in which I drove you."

"Have you looked for him all through this building?" Jack asked.

"Oh, yes," Mr. Moto said. "No sign. Are you thinking of something, Mr. Rhyce?"

"I'm just wondering whether he will be hiding until he sees her," Jack Rhyce said. "Maybe we were wrong in not having her drive up."

Mr. Moto thought for a few moments.

"I very much approve your thoroughness, Mr. Rhyce," he said. "It is too late. We might call her, from the manager's office."

The office was a cubbyhole of a room, only a few paces from where they were sitting, and it was startlingly silent, once they had closed the door. She answered almost immediately.

"Ruth, we've got a second thought," he said. "Maybe you'd better take a taxi and come here at six o'clock. Get out and stand by the main entrance.

"Okay," she said. "It's nice that great minds think alike sometimes. I'll be there."

He felt a momentary qualm as they returned to the table, simply because he disliked revising a plan on such short notice. It showed once again that he was not sure of himself when it came to Ruth Bogart; and besides, any revision always presented a new set of factors. Yet he had not the slightest premonition that he had made an error until it was six o'clock. It was six and there was no sign of any American girl, let alone Ruth Bogart, outside the Cimaroon.

"There is traffic," Mr. Moto said. "She may have misjudged the time. Do not let it upset you for five more minutes, Mr. Rhyce."

He had not meant to show his feelings, nor had he thought he would, for he had believed that experience had made him immune to sudden reverses—but he had not felt a shock of helpless panic for years comparable to

226

what he experienced then. Everyone went wrong some-time, he said to himself, and this was it for him.

"I'd better telephone and see if she's left," he said.

When he reached the manager's office and gave the number he noticed that his hands shook. It did no good to tell himself that he must quiet down. He had never in his life wished for anything so vehemently as that he might hear her voice answer, but there was no answer. She had gone. Outside the office he was startled at the sight of his own face, reflected from one of the wall mirrors.

"I think they've double-crossed us," he said.

Mr. Moto looked very grave, and glanced at his wrist watch.

"If so, I share your feelings," he said. "But wait, We gain nothing by hurrying, Mr. Rhyce. Remember that you yourself made her wait ten minutes, only not to appear too prompt. She may be doing this, too—and please remember just one thing more."

"What's that?" Jack Rhyce answered.

"I am to blame as much as you are, Mr. Rhyce. And—what is it they say in America? The show must go on in any case, Mr. Rhyce?"

He did not like the appraising look in Mr. Moto's eyes. After all, he was representing the Intelligence of his country.

"Damn it," he said. "Don't you tell me how to behave."

"That is better," Mr. Moto said. "I know I would not need to remind you, Mr. Rhyce."

Jack Rhyce stood up.

"I'm going now," he said.

"Where, please?" Mr. Moto asked.

He restrained his impatience. After all, he represented the Service.

"Back to the hotel," he said. "It's the place to start from, isn't it?"

He still did not like the inquisitive, measuring look in Mr. Moto's eyes. The Japanese was waiting to see how he would behave.

"Yes, that will be the proper procedure," Mr. Moto said. "I shall go with you. They have won this game. He was brighter than we thought him."

227

It was accepted practice on any battlefield to draw opponents to one spot, and then to strike in another. There were four of them in the car, two Japanese in front and he and Mr. Moto behind. They sat in rigid silence until they were slowed by the traffic at the Shinbashi station.

"I'm so very sorry," Mr. Moto said.

The remark jangled against the raw edges of Jack's nerves. The Japanese were always expressing sorrow which they did not mean.

"To hell with it," he said.

"I did not mean so sorry for you," Mr. Moto said, "as much as so sorry we both were mistaken. I am not being personal, Mr. Rhyce."

"Do you think they got her in the room or outside?" Mr. Rhyce asked.

"It would be the room, I think," Mr. Moto answered. "It would have been worked carefully."

He was relieved by that opinion because, if true, his asking her to join them was not responsible for what had happened. The car turned in the drive of the Imperial Hotel, and the lotus pool and the low building looked as ugly as his thoughts.

"Let us not appear too worried," Mr. Moto said. "I shall ask a question of two and join you in your room. I think we had better set up the telephone again."

"Why the telephone?" Jack Rhyce asked.

Mr. Moto gave him another inquiring look.

"Because they will be making contact with you," he said, "allowing only time for your return from the Cimaroon. Why else would they have caught her, Mr. Rhyce?"

What had come over him, he wondered, not to have thought of it before? He should at least have conceived of the possibility and have taken suitable precautions. Instead, he had been drawn off as easily as though he had been the third team. What had happened that had made them able to outguess him? At some point something had occurred to give away the show. It might have been something that night in the place called the Main Bar, or it might have been something that morning in the office of Mr. Harry Pender. Some detail had gone wrong somewhere, and now it was futile to guess what it might have

228

been. Play as safe as possible all across the board was another maxim of the business, and he had disobeyed it by not having her room guarded.

He had certainly acted like the third team. Neither his mind nor hers had been on their work. They had been thinking about the outside.

He never forgot the appearance of her room. What engraved it so vividly on his memory was that everything was exactly as he had anticipated. The lock of the door had been forced by someone who had examined the lock before, with an instrument that had made it give immediately. The only sign of struggle was an overturned suitcase that had fallen from the bed to the floor. Her handbag was gone from the table. They must have taken it with them when they left, but they had not bothered with any further search. Even with her gone, her personality was left. There was the faint scent of the Guerlain perfume she used, and the bottle was still on her dressing table beside her gold-backed comb and brush. He picked up the brush and gazed at the initials on the back, R. B. She had started packing, just as he had suggested, and her dresses and her lingerie that had fallen from the overturned suitcase still showed signs of careful folding. Mr. Moto came in while he was holding one of her dresses. Jack Rhyce laid it down gently.

"They were not seen to leave," Mr. Moto said; "but then, no one was watching. We should have thought of this and taken measures, but the conversation on the telephone sounded so very true. I am so sorry. I am also very much ashamed."

"You and me both," Jack Rhyce said. "Sorry and ashamed. What are you doing now?"

Mr. Moto, having adjusted the broken lock so that the door would close, had opened his briefcase.

"The telephone," he said. "We must both listen, I think."

"I don't see why you're so damn sure they'll call," Jack said.

"Please, it is inevitable," Mr. Moto answered. "They would not have taken her otherwise. They will call quickly before you go elsewhere. I have already taken steps to have the call traced, but I fear it will not help.

229

They are so very clever. Excuse. They know you are in love with her, Mr. Rhyce."

The words came out brutally in the ravaged room, and Jack felt his face grow brick-red, but he knew he had no right to be angry. His rights to be particular about anything had gone because of his stupidity.

"It was a mistake," he said. "We both knew we were damn fools—not that it does any good."

"Please, I am not criticizing," Mr. Moto said. "It may be a mistake, but sometimes one cannot help them, Mr. Rhyce."

"Unless it is necessary," Jack Rhyce said, "I'd just as soon not bring this subject up again."

It was infuriating to have something which should have belonged only to him and her tossed out in the open to be used as a point in a game. Mr. Moto's manner was considerate; his voice silkily smooth when he answered.

"I do not wish to offend," he said. "I only speak because I think you should be ready. I think they will be prepared to make you an interesting proposal, Mr. Rhyce."

Jack gave a start. He had been staring at the overturned suitcase, and his thoughts had wandered from what Mr. Moto was saying.

"What sort?" he asked.

"I do not know," Mr. Moto said. "So much of our work is always in the dark, but I think you have come close to finding something that worries them, Mr. Rhyce."

It was true about working in the dark. Even when a hand was half-played you never could be wholly sure where the other cards lay, but already Mr. Moto's words had aroused a suspicion in Jack Rhyce that gripped him with icy fingers. Bill Gibson's cynical statement about safety in sex flashed across his memory. He cleared his throat.

"Do you think they're going to propose a swap?" he asked.

When Mr. Moto answered, his voice was soft and measured.

"Yes, Mr. Rhyce," he said. "I believe they will offer to bring Miss Bogart safely back if you will agree to leave

230

here. You see, I think they are afraid you know too much."

Jack Rhyce felt a spasm in the pit of his stomach and his heart was beating faster, but still he could notice that Mr. Moto was watching him very carefully. He was even able to resent the detached critical manner and the air of academic curiosity. Mr. Moto was weighing him in an Oriental, not a European, balance.

"You will have to make a decision as to whether to leave or whether to stay," he said; "and I am so very much afraid I cannot help you, Mr. Rhyce."

Of course he had to make up his mind, and he had the training to do it.

"Damn you"—he said, and the sound of his voice warned him that he must compose himself—"you don't have to help me."

Mr. Moto was still watching him very carefully.

"So sorry for you, Mr. Rhyce," he said. "Will you have a cigarette?"

"No, thanks," Jack Rhyce said. "I told you I didn't smoke."

"Oh, I remember. Excuse, please," Mr. Moto said. "When I was a younger man I, too, was abstemious, in that and in other regards—"

Jack felt his face redden again. He took a quick stride across the room.

"That's about all I'm going to take from you," he said.

Mr. Moto watched him without moving a muscle.

"You do not allow me to finish," he said. "I was about to add that, even so, one cannot give up everything."

Just then the telephone rang. The small bell had a laughing, mocking sound, and he was not prepared for the sound because he had not been wholly convinced that they would call. Mr. Moto slipped the earphones over his head.

"Answer quickly, please," he whispered. "Seem to be anxious, please."

When Jack picked up the telephone he was steadier. He even felt a spasm of annoyance that Mr. Moto should tell him how to act. He had had it bad before—as bad as the small man who was listening had ever had.

"Hello," he said. His voice was even and agreeable. He

231

had learned long ago to give nothing away by voice. He was playing the old game of wits, and the fact that the telephone had rung at all confirmed Mr. Moto's assertion that he had something they wanted.

"Hello." He recognized the voice on the other end of the line immediately. "That's you, isn't it, Jack?"

"Indeed it is," he said.

His response was affable and easy. He had control of himself again.

"This is Harry Pender, Jack. You recognize my voice, don't you?"

"Well, well, Harry," Jack Rhyce said. "It's nice of you to give me a ring. I sure do recognize your voice. I'd know it anywhere."

"Okay, Jack," Harry Pender said, "then let's cut out the monkey business. You and I won't have to do our clowning from now on in."

"Thanks," Jack Rhyce said. "That's a big relief. Okay. What's on your mind?"

"We've got Ruth Bogart here. I thought you'd like to know."

Though he had anticipated it, he found it hard to control himself, and the instant while he struggled for calmness could not have been lost on Mr. Pender.

"Thanks for letting me know," he said. "I was beginning to be worried about her."

There was a good-natured laugh on the other end of the wire.

"We thought you might be. Well, take it easy, Jack. She's right here, and we wish you were, too. And she's happy and comfortable as of now, Jack. I'll let you speak to her in a minute."

"Why, thanks," Jack Rhyce said, "thanks a lot."

He heard Harry Pender laugh again.

"You know who I am, don't you, Jack? I mean you've got me taped by now?"

"Yes," Jack Rhyce said, "I've got a pretty good working idea, but I'm quite a ways away from the files."

Harry Pender's laugh had a corroding effect. He was too brisk and too excited, obviously on edge.

"I may as well admit," he said, "that I was pretty dumb regarding you. All of us were. In fact, we never got wise to you until just before lunchtime today. Nice going and congratulations, Jack."

At least it bolstered his ego to know that he had seen right in believing that he had been in the clear over the week end.

"Thanks for the compliment," he said. "Anybody in our line of work appreciates a kind word, Harry."

"No reason why we shouldn't all be friends in this thing, Jack," Harry Pender said, "even if we are on different sides of the fence. That's the thought I want you to hold for the next minute or two if you can manage, Jack. As I was saying, we have been sort of dumb around here, but you haven't operated in the East much, have you?"

"Why, no, Harry," Jack Rhyce answered. "This is my first time out here on a job, in case the fact is useful."

"Well, that's what threw me, Jack," Harry Pender said. "And you did look damn good for what you were, and the boys had cleared you in 'Frisco. When we heard you'd been looking at the bookshops, I admit, I should have taken the news more seriously, instead of discounting it. Maybe you'd still be fooling me, if it hadn't been for a very nice guy who just blew in here, by the name of Skirov. Remember him, Jack?"

"The name's familiar," Jack Rhyce said, "but I can't say that I remember him exactly. I don't think I ever saw him, but I'm sure I'd recognize him."

"Well, he remembers you, boy," Harry Pender said. "He saw you in Moscow back in '46. He was a waiter at one of those big parties, and passed you caviar. Just as soon as I described you he clicked. You were talking to Molotov back in '46. You were saying all men are brothers."

Jack exchanged a glance with Mr. Moto. The Chief had said it was a damn fool thing to say, and the Chief had been, as usual, correct. Never try to be conspicuous, the Chief had said.

"Now we're on the subject," Jack Rhyce said, "I was kind of slow in locating you myself, although I had you down for a phony the first time you came in. It's nice to know that Skirov's safe in town, and thank you for the information, because we're interested in Skirov."

A pause followed and Jack Rhyce, who had never lis-

233

tened harder, was conscious of faint sounds of others listening on the far end of the line.

"You've been real busy during your stay here, haven't you, Jack?" Harry Pender said.

"Yes," Jack Rhyce said, "busy as a bird dog.

"And dogs have their day. Ever hear that one, Jack?"

He fought down the frustration that was growing on him, and spoke with patience.

"Let's cut out the hamming, Harry," he said, "and get down to the point."

"All right, Jack," Harry Pender spoke soothingly. "We're busy here, too, as you may have gathered—busy enough so we didn't want Bill Gibson around, and we don't want you, either, Jack. Do you get my drift?"

"I get some vague idea," Jack said. "Is it a threat or a promise, Harry?"

There was another silence on the line, longer than the one that proceeded it.

"It's neither, Jack," he heard Harry Pender answer. "It's a firm offer that we're making."

His eyes encountered Mr. Moto's half-inquisitive, half-blank stare. He felt as though a cord were being drawn open mind."

"Well," he said, "go ahead and make it. I've got an told what was coming.

He had been standing all that time. Now he would have reached for a chair and sat down if the Japanese had not been watching.

"I thought you'd have an open mind, Jack." Harry Pender said, and his voice was placatingly gentle. "That's why I'm going to such trouble to have this little chat—because now that we've pooled our notes here, we know you've a real reputation. Skirov, for instance, knows about that job you pulled at Istanbul, and that other one in Athens. We know you're a pro, Jack, and not someone off an analytic couch."

"Go ahead," Jack said. "It could be, if I'm a pro, that I'm tracing this call, Harry."

"It could be," Harry Pender said, "but it takes time, and we're moving out of here when I hang up."

"Then let's cut out the hamming," Jack Rhyce said. "I'm waiting for that offer, Harry."

It came in mild, insinuating tones.

"You're fond of Ruth, here, aren't you, Jack? You wouldn't want to have her taken to the mainland, for instance, or go through any kind of drill? She wouldn't be much fun to see afterwards, would she? And you know, they do keep alive—surprisingly often—don't you, Jack?"

Jack Rhyce tried to laugh. It would have been shameful if he had betrayed his pain. Anybody in the business could have tight about his head.

"I understand your build-up. Why don't you get to the point?" he said.

"Don't get mad," Harry Pender said. "The point is, we're busy here, and we don't want you monkeying around. We want you the hell out of here. How does that one sound, Jack?"

He felt his heart beat faster. Mr. Moto had been right. They thought he might know something that was dangerous.

"If you want it straight, Harry," he said, "I don't like this town much, or the folks in it, including you."

"Now you're talking," Harry Pender said. "I had an idea we could get together, Jack. You'd like to have Ruth Bogart back at the hotel tonight, safe and sound, wouldn't you, and you know what I mean by safe and sound, don't you? If not, there's a pal of yours named Big Ben here who might explain it. Would you like to talk with Ben, Jack?"

He could hear Big Ben singing at the other end of the wire. He was singing "Every Day Is Ladies' Day with Me." Jack Rhyce put his hand to his forehead. His face had grown damp, but he kept his voice steady.

"Let's cut out the technique," he said. "Consider you've scared hell out of me. Yes, I'd like Ruth back safe and sound. So what's the proposition?"

"It's easy." Harry Pender's voice was as warm and as enthusiastic as a radio announcer's advertising a commercial. "Half an hour from now Ruth here will be knocking at your door. There's a night flight leaving for Honolulu at eleven, and we have two tickets for you free. Merely pack your bags, and shut up and go to the airport. How do you like that, Jack?"

235

"It sounds wonderful," he said, and he noticed that there was genuine relief in Harry Pender's voice. He was thankful that, under the circumstances, he could still put two and two together.

"I thought you'd get the point, Jack," Harry Pender said. "There's nothing like being reasonable."

"That's right," Jack answered carefully. "And how do I know we'll ever get to the airport, Harry?"

"You've got to trust us for that, Jack," Harry Pender said, "just the way we're going to trust you. Give me your word—you communicate with no one from the minute you set down that telephone, and Ruth here will be back with you in half an hour, with a nice boy from our office to expedite your passage. And you have my word, you'll get that plane, Jack. How does it sound to you? Would you like to speak to Ruth?"

"Yes, I'd like to speak to her," he said. There was a pause, and he was glad that it was not a long one. He was trying to think of some palliation—some way out. Then he heard her voice, and it was excruciating agony to hear it. Her voice was faint and level.

"Hello, Jack."

"Ruth," he asked, "are you all right?"

"I'm all right, Jack," she said, "but don't do it. Don't—" Her voice was choked off in a stifled gasp that ended in a scream.

Mr. Moto was watching him, and Mr. Moto's expression had changed when their glances met. Jack could not tell whether the expression was one of sympathy or surprise. He only knew that his own expression had revealed his pain. It was over in an instant because Harry Pender's voice was back on the wire.

"Sorry for the interruption," he said. "Will you take the proposition, or won't you?"

"Suppose I don't?" Jack Rhyce said.

"We'll handle you anyway," Harry Pender said. "Give us twenty minutes and Ruth will tell us what you know. Won't you, Ruth?"

Jack Rhyce felt a new wave of nausea sweep over him, and he set down the telephone. There was one thing certain—she did not know enough. He sank down in a chair,

236

drew out a handkerchief and mopped his forehead. Then the telephone rang again.

"Let it ring," he said. "To hell with it. Let it ring." For a moment he felt as though he were going to be sick to his stomach. For a moment he could not speak.

"Take those goddam earphones off," he said. "Excuse me. I'll be all right in a minute." He felt his shoulders move convulsively and he hid his face in his hands for a second.

"Excuse me," he said.

"That is quite all right," Mr. Moto said. "Would you like a little whisky, Mr. Rhyce?"

Jack Rhyce shook his head.

"You didn't think I'd do it, did you?" Jack Rhyce said.

"No, I did not," Mr. Moto said. "You are a very nice man. But please be easier in your mind, for you did what you should have, Mr. Rhyce."

"How in hell can I be easy in my mind," he said, "when we should have put a guard here?"

Mr. Moto raised his hand and let it fall abruptly to his side.

"It is something that we'll regret always—you more than I, I am so very much afraid," he said. "But in life we cannot relive regrets."

"That's right," Jack said. "Excuse me again, I'm all right now."

He was far from all right. He knew that he would never be the man he had been an hour or so before. There was certain things that could haunt one always—things that time itself could never solve. But he had to go on with it. He had to keep moving straight ahead, and all he could do was to try to make what was happening to Ruth Bogart to some extent worth while.

His training had not left him. He had learned long ago not to forget words or pauses on a telephone.

"Pender said a boy from the office, didn't he?" Jack Rhyce said. "That was a slip, I think."

"I'm not quite sure that I follow you," Mr. Moto answered.

Jack Rhyce was not impatient. He actually did not care whether Mr. Moto followed him. His mind was moving forward to another fact.

"We know right from the horse's mouth that Skirov is in town," he said. It was Skirov who would be calling the plays, now that he was in town. It was necessary to give thought to this other personality. "That's another mistake of Pender's. Maybe we can connect with him now. Anyway, there's no use hanging around here any longer."

"No," Mr. Moto answered. "We must go to where the call came from. They will have gone, but there may be traces."

"I wouldn't do that," Jack said. At least his mind was moving forward again out of the nightmare of self-incrimination that had entangled it. Mr. Moto's statement was still true, that they would not have attempted what they had if they had not been afraid that he knew something, and Harry Pender had said himself that they had not guessed his identity until just before lunch. He remembered the accelerated swing of the glasses in Mr. Pender's hand that morning when he had pursued the subject of liberal politicians, and he recalled the exact point in their conversation when the swing had changed.

All that Intelligence finally consisted of was finding facts, evaluating them and fitting them together until they formed a larger fact. A lot of it was choice and chance. You often could not tell whether you were right until the very end, and there were many times when you had to leave the path of painfully accumulated evidence to play a hunch. All he had left was a hunch—not a good one, but one which at least could fit the circumstances as he knew them. He was prepared to play it because it was all that was left, and it was better to move than to do nothing.

"I wouldn't go chasing down that call," he said again, "and if you do, I won't go with you. Did you ever hear of a man named Noshimura Hata?"

"Oh, yes," Mr. Moto said. "I know Mr. Hata."

"He's a very important liberal, isn't he?" Jack Rhyce asked.

"Yes," Mr. Moto said. "Where did you hear of him, please?"

"In Mr. Pender's office, this morning," Jack Rhyce said. "Pender said he was head and shoulders above any other politician in the liberal party, and afterwards I think he was sorry that he had said it."

Mr. Moto's gold teeth gleamed, but he was not smiling.

"So—" Mr. Moto said, "so—"

"It's only a guess," Jack Rhyce said, "but maybe it's worth a gamble. I can only tell you what I think."

"Yes," Mr. Moto said. "Thank you, and tell me what you think."

"I think they were going to kill this Mr. Hata tomorrow—but now I think they will do it tonight, now that I didn't take their offer. I'd get him out of his house, if I were you. I'd be delighted to wait there for whoever is coming to do the job, and I'll bet it will be Big Ben."

Mr. Moto was on his feet.

"I think that is a very nice suggestion, Mr. Rhyce," he said, "and I think you are a very nice man. Let me have the telephone. We must arrange to move at once."

"It's only a guess, you know," Jack Rhyce said.

"Yes, but one must always guess," Mr. Moto answered. "I shall be there with you, Mr. Rhyce, to wait for whoever may be coming."

Jack Rhyce had a friendlier feeling for Mr. Moto than any he had previously experienced.

"I don't know whether you are a very nice man or not," he said, "but anyway, you're willing to take a chance."

"Thank you so very much," Mr. Moto said. "And now if you will move, please, I shall use the telephone, Mr. Rhyce."

Mr. Moto spoke in Japanese. His voice was not strident like that of most men in authority; instead it was gentle, musical and melodious. Jack Rhyce stood for a moment listening. It was a matter of logistics, men, motors and distance. As he listened, his own anguish, which had been dulled for the last few minutes, returned to him again. He could control it now, but he knew that it would be with him always. He walked to the overturned suitcase and replaced the tumbled-out clothing very carefully in an order of which he hoped she would have approved. He walked to the dressing table, picked up the comb and brush and perfume bottle, and put all three in the suitcase. He touched his lips to the back of the brush, and he did not care in the least whether Mr. Moto saw him or not. He closed the suitcase and snapped the lock, and, as he did so, he knew in his heart that he was doing all he ever could for Ruth Bogart.

XIX

He must have been on fifty similar cases since he had been connected with the business, although in this one the setting was more interesting than in many. Again it was the old matter of waiting. Again, it was the trap or ambush or whatever technical name you might choose to give it. But this time, from the very beginning, there had been a feeling of promise in the air. Since so much of Intelligence consisted of moving tentatively into the unknown and never knowing exactly when you would finally collide with a stone wall or step upon the deadfall, it was never wise to leave premonition out of any calculation. Again and again in his professional career Jack Rhyce had experienced the gambler's conviction that the right numbers were coming up, and if you had it, it was surprisingly apt to be correct. You could call it nonsense, or fourth dimension, but it was there—whatever name you gave it. He knew as sure as fate that things were going to work that night. If you sacrificed enough, he sometimes thought, you were bound to get something in return, and the only thing that we wanted just then was to see the job through, and meet Big Ben in the process. He had paid down enough for the privilege. For the rest of his natural life he had given up peace of mind. Even though she had told him to go ahead—and her voice and her scream would echo in his memory always—he would wonder whether duty had been worth it. Ever afterwards his ingenuity would work on belated plans that might have saved her and still have achieved what they were there for. Undoubtedly, given time, he would figure out a way.

The actual plan for assassination was conventional and safe. As it turned out later, the prognosis was correct that it would look like an American job. A stolen American army car was in the picture, and the only thing that gave Jack Rhyce a shock was that wallet subsequently discovered on the premises—purported to be his, with excellently forged identity papers considering the short space of time allowed for their preparation. They had said that they would handle him, and they had meant it either way.

The house and grounds stood in one of Tokyo's most comfortable and desirable districts on land not far from the palace grounds themselves. In the old days the great Tokugawa fortress had been surrounded by concentric ramparts. Beyond these had been a further ring of houses occupied by the Shoguns' most trusted retainers. Further back the houses of the minor officials had stood, including the land of the Hata family which had been subdivided toward the end of the last century. The house of Mr. Noshimura Hata still occupied part of it. Actually, as it happened, Jack Rhyce never set eyes on the liberal politician, because Mr. Hata had been carried to a safer spot before Mr. Moto and he made their appearance. So also had the servants, who had been replaced by operators. The operation had run with a smoothness that had impressed Jack Rhyce professionally.

The lights were on by the gate in the small front garden, and the larger garden with the lawn in back was also lighted by stone lanterns.

"It is fortunate," Mr. Moto said, "that Mr. Hata likes to leave many of his ground lights on at night. He is afraid of burglars, which is amusing I think, when he is such a very liberal man."

After what had happened earlier, rigorous precautions were taken in case the house was watched; a schedule had been made of the household routine. This had all taken time, but it was worth it. It was half-past eight o'clock once they were inside the house, and Mr. Hata's retiring hour was ten.

"First he walks through the garden," Mr. Moto said, "Having put on the kimono and recited Buddhist prayers. I shall be Mr. Hata, and you may watch me from the house. We must all be very careful, but I do not think the killing will be in the garden."

The austere charm of that house formed a violent contrast to Jack Rhyce's thoughts. The sparseness of its fur-

242

nishings, the bare space of its walls, gave a balanced beauty to its interior that was a rebuke to the overcluttered houses back at home. Space had a more eloquent appeal in an overcrowded country like Japan. It was prized more than material possessions, and Jack Rhyce had never been more conscious of its beauty than he had been when he stood on the resilient floor matting in the sleeping room of Mr. Hata's house. It was a room intended solely for rest. Aside from the bedding prepared for the night and a black lacquer head rest, there were no other furnishings except a low table and a scroll painting of flowers in a niche sunk into the inside wall with an arrangement of flowers beneath it. The outer wall was formed entirely of sliding glass panels that opened on Mr. Hata's garden, and on that warm evening the panels had been pushed back so that the garden with its stone laterns was a projection of the room itself. Although his thoughts were still in turmoil, Jack Rhyce was not immune to the garden's beauty. He was vaguely aware of a way of life different from his own, more serene and more peaceful, and one deriving pleasure from a few small things rather than from ostentatious masses of larger ones. The garden from the standpoint of area was a very small affair, but assiduous art gave the illusion of its being a Japanese countryside. The lawn was a plain, the carefully twisted and trained pines and the small deciduous trees that bordered it became in imagination wind-swept forests. The eccentrically eroded stones that had been placed in relationship to each other only after hours of study were mountains and wild country. The miniature chain of ponds magnified themselves to lakes. While watching this miniature achievement, one could think with sorrow how fast the world was changing, and how a little time might be left, tomorrow, even in Japan, for a garden like Mr. Hata's. The garden spelled peace, but it did not give him peace of mind that night.

Nevertheless, he had not been outwardly restless. The business had taught him long ago the patience of a fisherman or a hunter, who could be alerted at any second— but there was more to it than that. Patience in the business demanded an endurance that raised the watcher beyond self, to a realm where personal consideration meant nothing. It resembled an artist's dedication, although it could hardly be said that the business was an art. He had not been restless, because of training; but his thoughts were beyond control. He was back again looking at the suitcase that had tumbled on the floor. He tortured himself again with what might have been if she had not been left alone, with how she had looked on that long drive to the mountains, with what she had said when they were alone at Wake, and finally with the knowledge that everything was ended and all contact had been cut forever. He could not think what was happening to her now, or speculate on whether she was alive or dead. It was best to know that it was absolutely ended.

He was waiting in a corner of the sleeping room when Mr. Moto stepped through the paneled windows from the garden.

"Is it time to turn off the garden lights?" Jack Rhyce asked.

"Yes," Mr. Moto said, "as soon as I have seen arrangements are understood, the house will go to sleep. We may still be a long while waiting."

It was impossible to know how long they would wait, but by then they both must have believed they would not draw a blank. There was a feeling in the air, a telepathic sense of something already moving.

"When the garden lights go out," Mr. Moto said, "I shall ask you to step outside," Mr. Rhyce, and stand by the corner of the house. I shall rest on the bed. The windows will be open. I think he will approach through the garden and attempt to enter by the windows. When he is near enough you may move on him, Mr. Rhyce, but please let us be patient and wait until he is near, for we do not wish shooting. There are so many questions in a neighborhood whenever shots are fired."

It was Mr. Moto's party and not his.

"Don't worry. I haven't got a gun," Jack Rhyce said, "only the jack you gave me."

"It is so much better," Mr. Moto said. "There are others here who will take the further steps if necessary. If he enters this garden or this house, I do not think he will get away from us."

"That's fine with me," Jack Rhyce said. "I want him out as much as you do."

Both his tone and his wish showed him that he had traveled a long way in the last few hours. He had never waited avidly wanting to kill before. The desire was neither practical nor professional in a field where personal wishes should never have intruded.

"So glad you agree," Mr. Moto said. "He will plan to use a knife, I think. Perhaps you would like one also, Mr. Rhyce?"

"It is not necessary," Jack Rhyce said. He had a tingling feeling of anticipation which was premature when there might still be a long period of waiting. "He won't cut me. There's only one thing I want."

"Yes?" Mr. Moto said. "What is that, Mr. Rhyce?"

"I want you to let me handle him. I want him to know I'm here."

"It will be a pleasure," Mr. Moto said, "if he comes through the garden and not through the house, when he will be my responsibility, Mr. Rhyce."

"Even so," Jack Rhyce said, "I'd like him to know I'm here."

"I can understand your viewpoint, Mr. Rhyce," Mr. Moto said. "I hope so very much that he will know we both are here, but there can be no chances."

"We won't miss any," Jack Rhyce said.

He had learned how to take cover as skillfully as any jungle fighter in Japan. When the lights were out he blended into the shadows by the angle of the house so completely that he was a part of the shrubbery. The night was warm as a Burmese rain forest, but drier, and the glow of the city's lights was reflected in the sky. The grounds and the house were peacefully silent in spite of the monotones of the great city that rose all around them. The noises of the Orient were more eccentric and more staccato than those of the West, shriller voices, shriller music, shriller laughter. Still, it was possible to attune the ear to closer sounds. A stirring of the bushes near the driveway revealed the presence of one of the guards and Jack Rhyce could hear a whisper of breeze in the pine trees.

The approach was made with such care and deliberation that Jack Rhyce had heard the first sound fully ten minutes before Big Ben slipped through the bushes at the far end of the garden and began his walk across the lawn toward the bedroom ell. He moved unhurriedly with a noiseless, deliberate confidence which showed he was wholly familiar with the house and grounds. Once he was on the lawn the background of the trees and shrubbery combined with the lights reflected in the sky made him stand out clearly. He wore a seersucker suit, almost identical with the one Jack Rhyce had worn earlier in the evening. He paused to listen as he drew near the house. He would have been an easy target for a pistol with a silencer, Jack Rhyce was thinking, and he was glad that the idea had not crossed Mr. Moto's mind. He wanted Big Ben to know that he was there. Ben was drawing nearer, lazily, gracefully. When he was a few yards from the house he reached in his side pocket, drew out a knife and switched open the blade carelessly. Jack Rhyce coughed gently, but loudly enough to hold the other momentarily motionless. Then before Big Ben could move, he was on top of him, and his blackjack had struck the knife out of the hand holding it. Big Ben took a step backward; he must have known in that second that he could not get away. Jack Rhyce spoke softly, as though there were actually sleepers in the house.

"It's me, Ben. It's Jack." He could not see the expression on Big Ben's face, but the laugh was all that was necessary.

"Hello, you gum-shoe bastard," he said. "That girl of yours was pretty good, but she didn't last for long."

The words, and not the time or place, robbed Jack Rhyce of his judgment. He had told himself long ago that it would be unsafe to close with Big Ben, yet that was what he did; and before he could get a wrestling hold, Ben had him by the throat. The feel of the hands was what cleared Jack Rhyce's head even before the thought flashed through him that his neck would be broken in seconds. He was in luck to be close enough to bring up his knee before Big Ben moved clear, but he had to strike again before the hold relaxed. There was a vicious moment when they rolled together on the ground. Before

246

Jack was able to get a full swing to the jaw, he could feel Ben's thumbs groping for his eyes. He rolled free and was on his feet while Big Ben was still on hands and knees. He delivered a kick with all his force to the side of the bleeding head, and Big Ben rolled over on his face.

Ruth Bogart had been right about the crepe-soled shoes. Hard leather, lumberman's boots, would have been better. Then he felt arms, holding him, and he heard Mr. Moto speak.

"That is enough, Mr. Rhyce," he said. "You can leave him to the others now, I think. It would be so much nicer, as you Americans say, if you were not killing, Mr. Rhyce. Perhaps you would feel unhappy about it later. Americans are such sentimental people."

He felt his breach coming in gasps that made it hard for him to be able to speak.

"He's not half dead," he said.

"No," Mr. Moto answered, "but I do not think we need worry about the ultimate result. My men are very conscientious, and I am afraid you will have to wash and rearrange your clothing. You did very well indeed, but I was glad I had a knife with which to strike him in the back. He was so very strong. Let us go. We are not required here any longer, Mr. Rhyce."

Jack Rhyce's first impression was one of shame, that he had not been capable of finishing Big Ben without Mr. Moto's intervention; but as far as he was concerned, the thing was over. It was something that never would be repeated, and now he had to move on to something else. Again there was nothing but a hunch to work on, but again he had the gambler's instinct. Besides, there was always some return if you paid a price.

"All right," he said. "That's one down. Now let's go and get this Skirov, or I'll go myself if you're not interested."

It was too dark to observe facial expression, but he heard the sharp intake of Mr. Moto's breath.

"I shall be very pleased to accompany you," he said. "But where is Skirov?"

Although it was only a hunch, it was still based on a line of reasoning. Skirov, who always kept in the background, would be in a quiet place where he would not be

247

likely to be under surveillance. He would not be at any headquarters. He would be in communication, but removed from the center of trouble.

"It's only a guess," Jack Rhyce said, "but it's an educated one. I believe he's in Mr. Pender's office in the Asia Friendship League. Anyway, it may be worth trying."

"And what makes you think that?" Mr. Moto asked.

"Do you remember Pender on the telephone?" Jack Rhyce answered. "He was too damned elated on that telephone. He was talking about a boy from the office seeing us off for the airport. I think he made a slip when he used the word 'office.' "

He heard Mr. Moto laugh. He was beginning to understand the various meanings of Japanese laughter.

"It would be a pleasure to try," Mr. Moto said. "I think, Mr. Rhyce, that you are a very clever man."

XX

So he fell out the window?" the Chief asked.

"Yes, sir," Jack Rhyce answered. "Eight stories, from Mr. Pender's office in the Asia Friendship League."

"You're sure he was Skirov?" the Chief asked.

"Yes, sir," Jack Rhyce said. "There was time to take photographs and fingerprints before he fell out the window. This Japanese—this Mr. Moto—checked them with his records. I have them with me, sir."

"Moto," the Chief said. "That's not a name. It is a suffix."

"Yes," Jack Rhyce answered. "That's what Bill Gibson told me."

He was having difficulty adjusting himself to the results of plane travel. Less than forty-eight hours previously he had been in Tokyo, and now he still had the feeling experienced by other air passengers, that some part of him had been left behind, and this illusion was sharper than it had ever been before. Certainly, after other trips, the Chief's office had seemed like home, or if not home, a threshold to rest and safety; but now it extended no such welcome.

"Oh, yes, Gibson," the Chief said. "That's a tough one. It's no fun sitting here on this job, hearing that people you've raised and been fond of are gone. It's no fun because you can't do anything except send out more. Maybe you'll face it yourself sometime. I'm not going to hold down this desk forever, Buster."

He was still such a long way from home that it had almost skipped his mind that the Chief sometimes called him Buster. At another time, the open hint that the Chief had given him that he might be in the line would have wakened a thrill of pleasure, and his conscience told him that it should right now.

"I don't think Bill had a hard time, sir," he said. "I'm afraid it was different for Miss Bogart."

The Chief picked up a pencil and tapped its eraser en softly on his desk.

"I've often wished this business were not coeduca tional," he said, "but then the score more than makes th trip pay off. We can scratch Skirov and this Big Ben cha acter, but what's your evidence on Pender?"

"The word of this Mr. Moto," Jack Rhyce said; "an there was a piece in the paper before I left that Mr. Pen der was struck and run over by a truck in Tokyo."

"It's a queer thing," the Chief said. "I used to be som thing of a specialist on the prewar Orient, but I nev heard of this Moto. Of course, they're devious ov there."

"You might have missed him because he was abroa sir," Jack Rhyce said. "If you want my suggestion, would inquire from State. From what he said, he wou have been some sort of embassy attaché. And I have a other line on him. He said his cousin is a Baron wl owns a semi-European house in Miyanoshita—that is, he was being straight. I can fill out the description and g it in the works."

"Yes," the Chief said. "We ought to get a line on hi It's hard to understand why Bill Gibson didn't kno him."

"I have a hunch that maybe this Moto is like you, si Jack Rhyce said, "from one or two things he let go."

"If it's all the same with you," the Chief said, "I rather not be like a Jap. I don't forget the war."

"I didn't mean it that way, sir," Jack Rhyce said. "B now you've brought the matter up, I'd rather be like M Moto than most of them. I only intended to suggest th he's behind the scenes like you in some dummy office. don't believe he steps out front often. He's getting on, y know, for the rough stuff, Chief."

"That's right," the Chief said. "I'm getting on, myse As I said, I won't be warming this chair indefinitely. It only a question of whom I pull out from the rough stu as you call it, to occupy it. But let's stay with one thing a time. I'd like to get a little more of the feel of this Mo

ck. I'd almost like to hop a plane and go over and take
look at him."

"I think you'd find it hard to come up with him, sir,"
ack Rhyce said. "I don't think he'd have appeared at all
he hadn't set me down for this Big Ben. One thing else
out him—he's as slick as a whistle with a shiv, and I
ight to know."

He felt no enthusiasm for what he was saying, still, he
as no longer being two things at once, as he sat there in
le Chief's office. He was not a do-gooder any more, en-
nored of an enthusiastic American girl, whose profile he
uld not forget, whose hands were both strong and deli-
ate, whose loyalty and humor were both impeccable. He
as out from cover, and far from safety in sex.

"He sounds like a right guy," the Chief said.

"If I were guessing, I'd say he's from the nobility, sir,"
ack Rhyce said, "or in the very high officer class. He
ight have been something in the Imperial household,
ducated in America, the East coast, I should say. But I'll
et it all down on my report and put it in the works."

"Quick with a shiv," the Chief said. "It always amuses
ie, this talk about stabbing someone in the back. It's ten
 one you hit a rib, and when someone's moving around
natomy doesn't count."

"As a matter of fact, sir," Jack Rhyce said, "the knife
as one of those small samurai blades. I think it was
artly in a rib because it was still in the back at the time I
ft."

"Well," the Chief said, "that's enough for a quick run-
ver. Are there any other loose ends that we ought to tie
p?"

"That's all, sir," Jack Rhyce said, "except for disposing
f Miss Bogart's personal effects. I brought them with my
iggage, and they're outside now."

"I'll attend to them," the Chief said. "That's one of the
ugh things about where I sit, Jack."

"By the way, sir," Jack Rhyce said, "I suppose Ruth
ogart is a cover name?"

"The Ruth's real, the Bogart isn't," the Chief said. "If I
ere you, I'd only be inquisitive when you're asked to be,
uster."

251

He appreciated the Chief's reproof, but also he resente
it.

"When you've been in the business ten years, sir," h
said, "and trained on the Farm, and have all your persor
ality knocked out of you on the road, even so sometime
you can't help being personally interested if you have t
throw in with someone for a while. Occasionally, in spit
of finishing school, you can't help being human, sir."

The Chief picked up his pencil again, but he did n
tap it on the desk. From where he sat, he had frequentl
had to deal with temperament. He understood better tha
most phychiatrists the inevitable results of long repression

"I forgot to remark, you're looking tired, Jack. I kno
you've had it rough," he said, "but I know you, and it
nothing that a couple of weeks off and some sleep won
fix."

His diagnosis could have been correct some weeks ag
but it was not right intrinsically any longer. Somethin
had happened that was new and different from the mo
ment Jack Rhyce had seen the empty room in the Im
perial Hotel in Tokyo, yet he had not known exactl
what had happened until the Chief rebuked his inquis
tiveness.

"Even if I rest up," he said, "I'm afraid I'll still sta
human, Chief. I won't be the old smooth-running machir
again."

The Chief smiled at him tolerantly.

"Listen, Buster," he said, "you're in no shape to ar
alyze yourself right now. What you need is a shot in th
arm and sleep. The Doc's in from the Farm today. He'
take you home and sit with you until you cork off. Neve
mind putting anything in the works until tomorrow afte
noon. I know enough to get the framework started."

"Very well, sir," Jack Rhyce said, and he pushed bac
his chair.

"That's better," the Chief said. "That's my boy. Any
thing else on your mind before you go?"

"Only one thing else, sir," Jack Rhyce said. "If I can
know her name, I'd appreciate it if you could see your wa
clear to give me a photograph.

The Chief raised his eyebrows rebukingly and let h

encil drop to the desk, and the minute disorderly sound
t made was an adequate measure of his surprise.

"So that's the way it was?" he said. "I wouldn't have
hought it of you, Jack. I'm sorry for you, son."

Jack Rhyce was glad that the thing was in the open for
once, and it would only be for once.

"That's the way it was," he said. "We fell in love like a
ouple of kids. We both knew it was a damn fool thing to
o, but it didn't spoil the operation, Chief."

"She wouldn't have wanted it to," the Chief said. "She
vas a very good girl, Jack."

"She wanted me to go ahead," he said. "She told me
o, over the telephone. Anyway, we couldn't have found
ier in time."

"You didn't tell me she spoke to you," the Chief said.

"I left it out," Jack answered. "Maybe I should have
his time. It's something that belongs to her and me. As I
vas saying, sometimes you can't help being human,
^hief."

He was talking too much, and he despised self-pity. He
vanted the interview to finish.

"I'll tell you all about her someday," the Chief said,
"but I don't believe now is quite the time."

"Thanks," Jack Rhyce answered, "if it's just the same
o you, I'd rather not know any more about her, except
vhat belonged to us. I admit it wasn't very much."

He stood up. He had not intended to speak his full
nind, at that particular interview, but that brief talk
.bout her had crystallized his thoughts.

"As I say, it wasn't much," he said. "We both knew we
vere being foolish, and we didn't have many opportunities
o talk, but we both decided that we'd go back to the out-
ide when we came home. She isn't here, but I'm going,
.nyway, sir."

"Now, wait a minute—" the Chief began—"this is all
in the spur of the moment. Is it anything I said that made
ou come up with this?"

"No, sir," Jack Rhyce answered, "nothing you said, but
'm going to hand in my resignation, sir."

"Now, Jack," the Chief said, "you can't do that. You're
he best man in the office. You're in line to follow me

253

here. I as good as told you, didn't I? You'd be like a fish out of water, on the outside. You can't do this, Jack."

He was aware that what the Chief said was true. He had intended to talk it over and think it over, but instead it was done already.

"I've got reasons, sir," he said.

"All right," the Chief said. "Just name the reasons."

Jack Rhyce squared his shoulders and pulled his thoughts together.

"Things happen sometimes," he said, "that you can't put into words, sir. After what happened over there, even if I stayed on the job, I could never be the man I used to be. I felt it coming over me in Tokyo. Being with her made me too human, Chief, and when you get too human you get fallible, and when you get to thinking about the outside you get forgetful—part of you is on one side and part of you is on the other. Part of me's back there. I've lost something, and I'll never get it back."

The Chief was also on his feet. "You're talking off the top of your head," he said, "and everything you say is specious, Jack."

"You may be right, sir," Jack Rhyce said. "It isn't so much what I say as what I feel. And besides, she wanted me on the outside. She asked me to promise."

"Jack," the Chief said, "give yourself a chance before you start crossing Rubicons. You're going through what everyone in the outfit goes through periodically. I've seen it and heard it all. Sure, something chips off you every time you go through anything, but you're the kind it only makes sharper, Jack. I'm willing to make you a bet: in a week or so you'll want to stay in the business on account of her, and not leave it because of her. You've got too much Moxie to take a step like that. Now don't interrupt me."

Jack Rhyce had cleared his throat but he had no intention of interrupting.

"I just want two promises from you," the Chief said. "Don't say anything to anyone about this talk, and promise me you won't make a decision until you've had that shot in the arm and two weeks away somewhere."

"All right," Jack said, "if that's the way you want it."

At any rate, he had said exactly what was on his mind.

nd he believed that he was right in everything he had tated, and he felt closer to her, now that he had spoken, nan he had since he had gone. He knew as sure as fate hat he was not coming back.

All Time Bestsellers

- ☐ THE AELIAN FRAGMENT—
  George Bartram   08587-8   1.95
- ☐ THE BERLIN CONNECTION—
  Johannes Mario Simmel   08607-6   1.95
- ☐ THE BEST PEOPLE—Helen Van Slyke   08456-1   1.75
- ☐ A BRIDGE TOO FAR—Cornelius Ryan   08373-5   1.95
- ☐ THE CAESAR CODE—
  Johannes M. Simmel   08413-8   1.95
- ☐ THE CAIN CONSPIRACY—
  Johannes Mario Simmel   08535-5   1.95
- ☐ DO BLACK PATENT LEATHER SHOES
  REALLY REFLECT UP?—John R. Powers   08490-1   1.75
- ☐ THE HAB THEORY—Allen W. Eckerty   08597-5   2.50
- ☐ THE HEART LISTENS—Helen Van Slyke   08520-7   1.95
- ☐ TO KILL A MOCKINGBIRD—Harper Lee   08376-X   1.50
- ☐ THE LAST BATTLE—Cornelius Ryan   08381-6   1.95
- ☐ THE LAST CATHOLIC IN AMERICA—
  J. R. Powers   08528-2   1.50
- ☐ THE LONGEST DAY—Cornelius Ryan   08380-8   1.75
- ☐ THE MIXED BLESSING—Helen Van Slyke   08491-X   1.95
- ☐ THE MONTE CRISTO COVER UP
  Johannes Mario Simmel   08563-0   1.95
- ☐ MORWENNA—Anne Goring   08604-1   1.95
- ☐ THE RICH AND THE RIGHTEOUS
  Helen Van Slyke   08585-1   1.95
- ☐ WEBSTER'S NEW WORLD
  DICTIONARY OF THE AMERICAN
  LANGUAGE   08500-2   1.75
- ☐ WEBSTER'S NEW WORLD THESAURUS   08385-9   1.50
- ☐ THE WORLD BOOK OF HOUSE
  PLANTS—E. McDonald   03152-2   1.50

Buy them at your local bookstores or use this handy coupon for ordering:

B-5

Popular Library, P.O. Box 5755, Terre Haute, Indiana 47805

Please send me the books I have checked above. Orders for less than 5 books must include 60c for the first book and 25c for each additional book to cover mailing and handling. Orders of 5 or more books postage is Free. I enclose $_____ in check or money order.

Name_____

Address_____

City_____ State/Zip_____

Please allow 4 to 5 weeks for delivery. This offer expires 6/78.